MORNING BY MORNING

MURPHY BROTHER STORIES, BOOK 8

JENNIFER RODEWALD

ROOTED PUBLISHING

CONTENTS

PROLOGUE

(in which there is a time to mourn)

TWO YEARS.

A cool wind curled off the hills, sweeping across the rolling landscape and pressing against Connor's face. Leaves, still wearing their fresh spring green, danced in the trees overhead, adding their gentle rustle to the cheerful morning birdsongs and the breeze whispering through the pines. Part of Connor's heart—the part that still clung to ache—resented the loveliness of that morning.

All of him had resented it two years ago. The bright sunshine, the loveliness of such a late-spring day. It had seemed a mockery of all that he and Reid had endured, all that they were then required to let go. A mom. A wife. The unexpected love of his life.

Gone with the final breath of Sadie Murphy.

Though they had been given warning, none of them had been ready. Who could be? Who could ever be ready to surrender such a woman to heaven when they loved her so much here on earth?

Connor hadn't been ready.

Weeks before that awful day, he had unwillingly submitted to the hospice nurse's advice to say what needed said before the end came, but he hadn't been ready to say goodbye. He had not *wanted* to say goodbye, and he'd fought it.

But he'd done it, because Sadie had insisted.

"Don't let's wait until I can't respond, until the crossing is too much for me to say goodbye to you. I want you to hear that I love you now, while I can speak with a clear mind. I want you to know my deep gratitude to you."

"No gratitude, Sadie. That's not what I want from you," he whispered through a tight throat. *"And I'm not ready to do this—"*

Sadie squeezed his hand, then pressed his knuckles to her cheek as she sat up in the bed. "We'll never be ready. I'm dying, Connor. There's no changing that. But I can choose what I leave you with, right now. And I want you to know that there hasn't been a day that's gone by in the past seven years that I haven't thanked God for you. Not one day."

"Sadie—" Tears choked anything more he could have said.

She kissed his hand. "I'll not risk it being unsaid. Aside from Christ Himself, you and Reid are heaven's best gift to me. You've been the husband I didn't deserve and are the daddy Reid needs, even though you didn't have to be." Sliding her hand over his wet face, she cupped his neck and anchored him against her. *"I love you, Connor. Forever."*

As Connor remembered that conversation, and the heartbreaking weeks that followed it, his shoulders quaked with emotion. Kneeling, he reached for the chilly granite bearing her name.

Sadie Allen Murphy. Beloved.

God, I miss her.

"I love you, Sadie. Forever."

It had been two years, and the ache had receded enough for him to breathe without a constant sting. For him to not wish every moment of every day that God had changed His mind and let Connor keep his wife. Enough for him to find reasons to smile again.

I'll be with Jesus, and I won't hurt anymore. I want you to live. Live, Connor. Promise me you will let me go, and live.

The echo of those words she'd mustered before she'd slipped into the last medicine-induced unconsciousness caused his lungs to squeeze. She'd loved him so well.

He was trying to honor that final request. Truly, he was. Man, though, he still missed her. As did Reid. They would always miss her.

"You gave me a fine son," Connor murmured as his thoughts landed on the twelve-year-old boy who now bore the Murphy name. "I told you that, right? I can't remember. He's a good boy, Sadie. He has your quiet determination. And he's excelling in math. He said that this year Coach said he could try centerfield. His arm is a lot stronger. I told him it was from all the chopping wood this past winter." He chuckled. "He rolled his eyes, but he was smiling. He doesn't fight me on stuff like that, you know. But . . . but I don't know, Sadie. He's twelve, and starting to pull—"

"Dad!"

Connor's fingers slipped off the smooth stone as he turned to look over his shoulder. Reid charged toward him, long legs pushing out easy strides. The sunshine caught the remaining bits of honey in his darkening hair. Connor would miss those flecks when they were gone—the golden hue had been from Sadie. Reid looked less and less like her these days. More and more like a young man. Possibly like his biological father. But his expressions still reflected Sadie—reserved, deep thinking, and kind.

Let him always be so, Connor prayed, not for the first time, as his son neared.

Reid slowed to a walk as he approached the grave, reverence stealing his youthful expression. He dropped to his knees beside Connor and reached out to touch the stone. "Hi, Mom."

Gripping his shoulder, Connor gave him a squeeze. "You want a minute?"

As Connor had expected, Reid gave that a moment's thought. Reid was like that—unusually reflective for a boy gliding way too fast toward thirteen. Reid rarely spat out an impulsive answer, rarely acted without careful reflection.

"No, not this time." Reid leaned into Connor's side. "But thanks."

Connor held him near for a moment, and then Reid eased away.

"Grandma said to tell you that Uncle Brayden and Aunt Audrey are getting ready to go. No rush or anything, but they wanted you to know they'll be taking off soon."

Nodding, Connor pushed up to stand, and Reid followed suit. "We'd better get back down that way, then. It'll be a while before we get to see little Isaac again." Glancing down, he caught the flash of sadness in Reid's eyes, and knew why.

Reid adored two-year-old Isaac. He'd loved all his younger cousins over the years, but there had been something special between Reid and Isaac. Connor wasn't sure what it was—perhaps the fact that Brayden and Audrey had visited Connor and Reid more than the rest of the family over the past couple of years. Whatever it was, having them move so far away was rough for them all.

"Why did Uncle Brayden pick Nashville, Dad? Couldn't he do his residency somewhere closer?"

"Yeah, he could." Connor anchored a hand on Reid's shoulder again and sighed. "I'm not sure why, buddy. To be honest, I wish they weren't going so far away too."

But he'd known Brayden had prayed hard over this decision, this move. His youngest brother felt God's leading in it, and Connor would be the last one to try to talk him out of that.

A beat of silence passed, and Connor was fairly sure he heard Reid swallow hard. "Does life just always change?"

Man.

Drawing a deep breath, Connor wrestled to regrip his emotions. He didn't remember life being as challenging for him when he was a kid as Reid's twelve years had been. Didn't seem fair. Tugging his son close, Connor squeezed his eyes shut. "Seems so, son."

He thought about the changes he'd faced as a kid and then as a young man. Some were hard. Ish. Mostly, though, he remembered looking forward to the next chapter of life, whatever that might be. Reid's life though

. . .

What Connor wouldn't give to have taken away some of the hard things Reid had already walked through. "I'm sorry, buddy."

Reid blew out a controlled breath. "Maybe a few minutes with Mom would be good." He looked up. "Is that okay?"

"Absolutely." Connor moved his palm to the back of Reid's head. "Take all the time you need. I'll meet you down at the park."

Reid nodded, and Connor walked away, mulling over change.

Please, can we have a break from it, Lord? There's been so much. Much more and my son might break.

That would be devastating.

No more for a while, Father? I beg You . . . no more.

CHAPTER ONE

(in which the world seems upside down)

DEAR SEVENTEEN-YEAR-OLD JADE,

Listen to your mother. He isn't the prince charming you hope for. And he won't change.

Jade Beck reread those brief lines she'd just penned, tears blurring her eyes. It'd been a long time since she'd journaled. Longer since she'd been that seventeen-year-old girl—young, hopeful, and stupidly in love. Over fifteen years since.

Over fifteen years spent devoting herself to a man who never did change. Loving him even when the romance had long since snuffed out. Remaining faithful even when he'd obviously lost interest. Fixing his meals, cleaning up his messes, accommodating his schedule. Bearing and raising his children.

Their children. The hard bitterness that had lodged in her chest eased as she rested her thoughts on them. Lily and Kellen were her treasures in this mess. She would never regret them.

But Peter. . .

"Jade, these things happen."

Jade lifted her gaze from her fisted hands and glared at Peter. "No, Peter. These things do not just happen. We make choices. You and I made choices. Promises. To keep or to break."

He jammed a fist into his hair and sighed. "I know. I know, hon. Just . . . just give me a little time."

"Time? Time for what?"

"To adjust. To . . . to let her go."

"What?" Jade spat out the word like it was poison. Whatever was burning in her chest certainly must be poison. "To let her go? What does that mean?"

Peter looked at her with an imploring expression. Could she be understanding him right?

"You want me to give you time, as in share you with another woman?"

"It's . . . it's complicated. I can't just—" His face flushed.

"You can't what? Just go and break her heart?" Jade stood, flinging a pillow at him as she did. "Of course you can't. Me, on the other hand . . . I'm just your wife. The one you promised your fidelity to."

"I didn't want to hurt you!"

"So noble, Peter. That's why you've been lying to me. Because you were protecting me, right?" Crossing her arms, she dared him to respond. To add a fresh layer of his well-rehearsed manipulation. Surprisingly, he didn't. "Let's not lie anymore. I know that will be hard, since you've spent who knows how long doing exactly that, but right now let's be brutally honest for a change. You've been done with me for years."

"Jade, that's—" He wouldn't look at her.

Man, the truth was a fiery arrow. Except, Jade felt the piercing, even thought she'd been the one to take the shot. All at once the pain took her breath away, and she collapsed back onto the bed in an uncontrolled sob. Peter lowered onto the edge of the mattress. He didn't touch her, didn't speak. Just . . . sat.

Hugging herself, Jade fought to regain herself enough to speak. Finally, she shook her head. "I can't do it, Peter. I can't."

"What do you want me to do?"

"Figure out what you want. If you need time, then fine. Take it. But you can't have us both—you can't take the time here."

"You want me to leave?"

"Yes." Through the blur of tears, she watched him finally meet her gaze. He nodded. "It's . . . it's not . . . I just need to sort things out."

Jade clenched her jaw and didn't answer. So much of her hoped he was telling the truth. This would be a break. A bit of time for them to miss each other. For Peter to realize he still loved her and that he wanted the family she'd always wished they'd been. For him to finally, finally be the man she'd imagined.

Deep down, though, she knew. He didn't love her. He didn't want her. And he wasn't that man.

They were done.

It'd taken a year for it to play out, but time had proven that gut-deep knowledge true. Peter didn't want her anymore. And the double edge to that blade? The other woman?

She'd been a friend of Jade's from work. A fact that didn't surface until near the end of that year. Humiliation heaped on top of devastation.

As her heart clenched, Jade reread those words she'd penned in the light of her phone flashlight a few moments before. If time travel were a thing and she could hand deliver this note to her younger self, would that starry-eyed and stubborn young woman listen?

Likely not. She hadn't listened to her mother, who had spoken such warnings out of more than pure frustration. They'd been delivered with love and deep concern. Jade knew that better now than ever, having a beautiful daughter of her own.

But it's love, Mom. Strange, how clearly she could hear herself speak those words. Solemn and heartfelt, she'd really, truly believed that love would conquer all. And she had loved Peter. Likely, that attachment was still struggling for life in her heart. Even if, as she'd realized more and more over the past year, that love had put her in a one-sided and toxic relationship. It would explain why the pain was so complete—so deep and nearly unmanageable, producing toxic bitterness within its dredges.

How could so many years mean so little to Peter?

How could he betray her like this?

And Macey?

Wow. Jade knew how to pick 'em. Husbands. Friends.

Lying on her stomach on that hotel bed, Jade let her face fall in between her arms, pressing into the pillow as grief and resentment crashed over her yet again. Quiet tears seeped from her eyes, running cool against the skin of her less-than-toned biceps.

Maybe if I'd kept myself up better. Joined CrossFit like Macey . . .

Bitterness seethed against that. It wasn't as if she'd let herself become a marshmallow. Twenty pounds more than her graduation weight wasn't that much, was it? After all, she'd carried two babies, worked full time, and kept the house clean and full of food. Who really had time or energy to get up at four thirty in the morning and contort their body into hyperventilating pretzels every day?

Macey.

Yeah, well, Macey didn't have kids. And she was still in her twenties. Barely, but still.

Jade sniffed as the hot tears continued to stream.

"Mom?" A gentle hand touched Jade's shoulder as Lily's soft whisper drifted into the quiet room. "You okay?"

Jade tensed, one hand fisting her hair. "I'm fine, honey." Her lips trembled as she squeezed her eyes tight, trying to dispel her tears. "I thought you were asleep."

"Not yet." Lily rubbed Jade's shoulder, offering a small measure of comfort. "Kellen is though."

Jade nodded, her face still buried in her arms. "That's good. Go to sleep, sweetheart. I might need you to drive some tomorrow."

"Okay." But Lily didn't lay back, nor did the warmth of her touch evaporate. "Mom?"

"Yeah."

"We're with you, okay?"

At the loyal compassion in Lily's voice, Jade crumbled. A sob shook her shoulders, and she moved her hand to cover her daughter's. "Thank you, Lil."

Lily pressed her back with a fierce hug. "It's going to be okay, Mommy."

God, help.

She should be the one saying it was going to be okay. Assuring her sixteen-year-old daughter that they'd be all right. Not the other way around. But she couldn't right then.

Because she wasn't sure it was true. Her world was upside down, her heart mangled. She couldn't imagine what *all right* would look like from there. After so many years of believing it would all work out in the end, Jade Beck now knew one of life's devastating truths: no matter what you do, right or wrong, life didn't always go the way it was supposed to.

"I've found someone for you."

Connor froze, his hand gripping a hammer in midswing. Resentment coiled every muscle in his body tight, and he had to fight to control his rising temper before he turned to look at Mr. Appleton, who had spoken those obnoxious words.

He lowered the tool to his side. "Excuse me?"

"She's a single mom. Two kids. They're driving here from Kansas. Should arrive before dinner."

A fierce scowl squeezed Connor's brow as he glared at the man who owned Lake Shore Resort. Technically, Mr. Appleton was his boss. But for the past several years, he'd left the running of the lodge to Connor. Well, to Connor and Sadie, but Sadie had been gone for two years, so . . .

None of that seemed relevant. What on earth had provoked Mr. Appleton to do this? He'd *found* someone for Connor?

Aw, heck no!

Connor worked his clenched jaw. "Mr. Appleton, I'm not sure why you decided I needed you to find someone for me, but—"

"Lauren asked me to. Over six months ago."

"What?" Lauren! What right did his sister-in-law have to interfere with Connor's life? Man, when he got ahold of Matt, there'd be a reckoning.

How long had his family been scheming? Not a single one of them truly understood what it was like for Connor to lose his wife. Had they honestly expected him to just . . . just move on?

No. No way. Didn't matter that two years had gone by. Connor wasn't in the market for *someone*, and he certainly didn't want Mr. Appleton, of all people, fetching him a new woman.

A single mom from Kansas? And she was going to be there, with her children, *that* night? Man, did they all think he was the rescuer of fatherless children? Shove a mom who needed a dad for her kids in front of him, and Connor the Constant, the one who always did the right thing, would just take them in, along with their mother, and all would be rosy?

Didn't they know he had enough on his plate? He was a single dad to a boy who was edging toward manhood, a boy who silently grieved for his mom and was pulling away with every passing day, and Connor had no idea how to navigate any of it.

What would he do if Reid broke, if he lost it and rebelled? How was Connor supposed to handle it when Reid asked about his biological father—as Connor felt certain he would—and Connor had only bare-bones information to give him—the worst of that being *he knew about you, Reid. But he didn't want anything to do with you or your mother.*

Had his family, or Mr. Appleton, considered that Connor's life was complicated enough?

"Connor?"

Pulse throbbing with anger, Connor flashed his gaze back to Mr. Appleton. Fearing he'd unleash the storm brewing in his heart, he kept his lips sealed tight.

"You hoping to leave your fingerprints on that handle?" Appleton nodded toward the hammer Connor was squeezing for all he was worth.

"What?"

"Son, if you could set a fire with your eyes, this forest would be in trouble. What's got you riled?"

Was he serious? Connor swallowed, desperately fighting to grip some sort of respectful civility. "I didn't ask anyone to find *somebody* for me."

"I know that." Appleton spoke casual as you please. "Like I said, Lauren did. She just can't keep juggling the three kids, the bookwork and marketing she needs to do for the tree farm, and the same for the lodge—especially from over an hour away. She asked me to find someone to fill that spot."

The . . . the bookwork?

Hot breath seeped from Connor's lungs as understanding crept in. Appleton had found someone to replace Sadie . . . at the lodge. Not someone to replace her as his wife.

"Lauren didn't mention this to you?"

Posture sagging, Connor stared at Mr. Appleton while his world shifted back to right. "No," he mumbled. Had she? Maybe she had at the family gathering they'd had two months before, to say goodbye to Bray and Audrey. Connor ran his fingers through his hair, a mess that was long overdue a cut.

"Huh." Appleton glanced away, his expression briefly morphing into confusion. Then he shrugged. "Well, that's that. Jade Beck grew up in the area. Her parents live about an hour north of here. She'd like to have her children closer to them since she's now raising them on her own."

"Where's their dad?"

He shrugged again. "I wasn't sure that was an acceptable question to ask in a job interview these days. So I didn't."

Rubbing his bearded jaw, Connor nodded. "How long ago did you interview her?"

"A week. Over the phone."

Connor blinked. "Why'd you wait until now to mention it?"

Sighing, Appleton shoved his hands into his jeans pockets. "I wasn't sure how this was going to sit with you. Judging by your reaction, I'd say not so well."

Connor could do nothing more than look at his boots.

Appleton placed a meaty hand on Connor's shoulder. "I get it, Connor. Honest I do. And if I could have held off hiring someone until you were ready, I would have. But I can't. I can't keep expecting Lauren to keep that side of the business running, and since she did so much to get this place back on its feet, I can't abide letting it slide back to where it was when she and Matt first got here. That wouldn't be honorable."

"No, it wouldn't." Connor swallowed. "I'm sorry that you've been in an awkward spot the past few years. And that Lauren had to take up so much of the slack. I didn't realize . . ." He should have though. Sadie had done the bookwork and marketing for the six years that they'd lived together at the lodge. They'd been a team on this job—just like Matt and Lauren had been. Connor should have known that Sadie's death impacted more than just him and Reid.

But he just hadn't seen it.

He would need to apologize to Lauren. Poor woman. Why hadn't Matt said anything?

Connor sighed. "I'm sorry I reacted that way. I . . . I misunderstood."

Nodding, Appleton squeezed his arm. "I've been there, Connor. Grief is a hard thing to navigate, and no one can tell you how to do it."

Suddenly, questions bubbled up inside, wanting set free. *How long will the darkness last? I see flickers of light, but there's still so much gray. How do I live like Sadie wanted me to, when I feel like I've lost part of my heart?*

Connor buttoned the inquiries in and scrubbed a hand over his thick beard. "I'll finish fixing the corral and then go get the staff rooms ready. How many?"

"I'm thinking they'll be more comfortable in the cabin next to yours."

For some reason, Connor pressed against that. "That cabin is the most consistent rental we have."

Appleton squinted, and his hand went back into his pocket. "Would you want your family living in dorm-style rooms in the lodge?"

No. No, he would not. Heat crawled up his neck. "Right. I'll see that the cabin is ready for them, then."

"Thank you." Appleton turned to limp back toward the lodge. "You and Reid will be there for dinner tonight, right?"

Seemed like a loaded question, though Connor couldn't say why. If it was new summer staff coming for the busy season, he and Reid would be there. After all, Connor was Appleton's appointed manager.

Even so, resentment sent up a fresh new sprout. Connor had to turn back to the fence near the barn so that Appleton wouldn't glimpse it. "Of course we will."

Appleton continued on his way, and Connor returned to pounding rusted nails.

Lord, I asked for no more change. Whack, whack, whack. *This feels like ... like something I don't want to deal with.* Whack, whack, whack. *And what's Reid going to think?* Gripping the lowest rail, Connor held himself against the sudden urge to crumble.

He didn't know for sure what Reid would think, and he suspected that Reid wouldn't tell him. Gone were the days when they would spread out a million Legos and build stuff, and Reid's heart would slowly slip out as their construction came together. Reid was a teenager now, a quiet one who kept to himself more than ever before. Connor didn't know how to reach him anymore.

I feel like I'm losing him too.

The thought sent a searing pain through his chest. It was ripping his heart up all over again.

CHAPTER TWO

(in which two worlds collide)

"Reid?" Pausing with a pair of fresh-out-of-the-dryer jeans in his hands, Connor called for his son after he heard the front door slap shut. "Hey, buddy, can you come here for a minute?"

The sound of heavy footfalls grew louder as Reid strode down the hall. Size nines at the end of a lanky pair of legs sure could make some noise on the hardwood. Reid rounded the corner and poked his head into the office/laundry room. "Yeah, Dad?"

Connor tossed the pants he'd just folded onto the desk and pulled in a breath. Reid's dark hair glistened with sweat and stood on end, a hat ring evident above his ears. He'd been out for a hike, something Reid did often. These days, usually by himself. For a moment, a flashback streaked through Connor's mind, that moment years ago when Reid—age four at the time—slipped his hand into Connor's at Connor's suggestion that they go on a little "adventure." He'd known in that moment his life had changed forever. In a matter of months, he'd become father to that little boy, and the fierce love that had ignited that day had only grown. Every day since, Connor wanted only good for him.

He hated that he couldn't give Reid that. Only the good. Hated that life kept throwing punches.

"What's up?" Reid stepped into the room, his arms hanging casually at his side as he leaned against the wall.

Connor grabbed a T-shirt to fold. "I hope you were planning to have supper at the lodge tonight."

Reid shrugged. "I usually do."

"Yeah. I just wanted you to know"—Connor lowered onto the edge of the desk—"there are going to be some others tonight. And likely for the rest of the summer."

And well past summer, if this new woman worked out.

Confusion wrinkled Reid's brow. "It's August. Summer's over, Dad. Extra staff went home."

"Right." Something sour wrung out in Connor's gut. Like he didn't want this new woman to work out. He had no reason to feel that way. "This . . . they aren't extra staff."

"They?"

"Uh, well." Connor rubbed his neck. "Mr. Appleton hired someone to do the books and the marketing. To work the front desk full time. You know . . ."

"To do what Mom did." Connor looked to the floor.

"Yeah."

A beat went by, then Reid shrugged. "Okay."

"Okay?"

"Sure."

Reid still didn't look Connor in the eye. Sighing, Connor plunged forward with the rest. "The thing is, this new employee, she's a single mom. Has a couple of kids. They'll be moving into the cabin next to us."

Expression still stoic, Reid stayed still. There was a flash of emotion in his eyes though. Connor was pretty sure he recognized it: resentment.

Or maybe that was Connor projecting. He pushed off the desk and took a step toward Reid. "You okay, son?"

Another shrug. No eye contact. "Yeah, sure. Lots of people have neighbors."

True. But not a lot of people had to meet the woman who was going to take their mom's job and basically live with them in this family-style employment situation.

"Reid . . ."

"Come to think of it . . ." Reid finally looked up, his face still passive. "Trevor talked about doing pizza tonight. I might go if that's okay."

No, it wasn't okay. Mr. Appleton would prefer that Connor and Reid were both there to meet the Becks. But Connor really didn't want to say so. Would it be wrong for Connor to make Reid's excuses for the night? Maybe that would just prolong the inevitable.

Man, this was hard. Likely harder than it should be. Connor was making this a big deal, and probably he shouldn't. But . . .

I don't want any of this.

"Dad?"

Connor met his son's questioning gaze. "Reid, I really wish that—"

"So that's a no, right?" Reid's shoulders sagged.

Sighing, Connor reached to pull Reid into a hug. "Not tonight, buddy. I'm sorry."

Reid held himself stiff and then eased back. "I gotta shower."

"Yeah. Okay."

The boy, who had grown two inches over the summer and now suffered from the occasional voice crack, rolled into a pivot and walked out of the room.

Connor squeezed his empty hand, wishing with all his heart to feel those small fingers in his palm once again. Wishing he wasn't feeling his little boy, who had owned his heart from that first day, slip further and further away.

It's normal, son. Boys at his age start to pull away. It's just part of growing up. Connor's dad had offered his wisdom and encouragement when Connor had confided in him during their visit at the beginning of summer. *It doesn't make it easy though. Trust me, I do know this one. We went through it with all seven of you boys, and every time nicked our hearts. But it's not a cause for real alarm, that's all I'm saying.*

Though he clung to his dad's words, for the next half hour Connor battled a mix of melancholy at the slipping away of his son and a strong dose of resentment that he had to go forward with this gathering tonight.

The bottom line was that he flat out didn't want to meet the woman who was to take his wife's job.

As he waited for Reid to come downstairs from his bedroom and join him for the short walk over to the lodge, Connor sat on the edge of the couch, forehead pressed to his fisted hands. *God, help me to think, feel, and do right.*

This woman, this single mom, would need this job. And it'd be a good job for a young mom. Appleton was more like a kind grandfather to his employees than anything else, and working at the lodge had been a blessing to Connor and Sadie. It would be a blessing to a young woman in need of a shelter—likely a new life. If Connor could just get the right angle on this, he could maybe be a blessing to her and her kids. And Reid might really enjoy having some kids around to entertain—he'd really taken to Isaac, after all. It might be good for all of them, and Connor could certainly treat this young mom like he did his younger sisters-in-law.

With Your help, maybe I can. He swallowed, his eyes squeezed shut as he prayed. *Please fill me with Your Spirit, with Your help, so I can do right.*

A measure of ease settled his heart. He could be a kind older brother. He'd been so before . . . he could do so now. And as for this woman taking Sadie's job . . .

Sadie didn't need it anymore. Sadie was whole and healed and rejoicing with Jesus.

Tears rimmed Connor's eyelids as he forced his mind to that truth and asked God, not for the first time, for the heart to be joyful for his wife. He remembered how much pain she'd endured—and there'd been so much. Both when he'd first married her and they'd walked the first battle with her cancer, and then years later when it had come back with a vengeance. Particularly after the cancer had moved to her bones. Man, that had been awful. Honestly, Connor didn't wish for Sadie to keep struggling with that. It had been flat out torture to see her wince and writhe, to witness her tremble and the silent tears she'd tried so hard to hold back as the nurses struggled to get the pain managed.

He didn't want her back to endure that.

She's free now. No more pain. No more cancer. Thank You for that.

And she'd left him and Reid with her love and the blessing to *live*. Gifts she'd wanted with all her beautiful heart for them to hold on to with freedom and joy.

"Dad?"

Connor lifted his face, finding Reid at the bottom of the staircase, hair wet and body clothed in a pair of clean jeans and a freshly laundered Lake Shore Trail Blazers baseball T-shirt. Forcing a tight smile, Connor stood. "Ready?"

"Yeah." Reid looked hesitant. "You okay?"

There was his tenderhearted kid. The one that was so much like his mother. Connor held that gaze, that moment. "Honestly, I'm struggling with this, bud. You?"

Reid shrugged. "I bet it was hard for Aunt Lauren to do the tree farm and the lodge, so . . ."

"Yeah, that's what Mr. Appleton said." Connor rubbed his neck. "I didn't even think about it. I guess I've been too wrapped up with myself. Trying to find my way out of the darkness, you know?"

Looking to the floor, Reid nodded. "Calvin says that it takes as long as it takes, and that's okay. But to look for ways to be kind, and to be thankful, because that lets the light back in."

"Wise words from a good man." Connor squeezed Reid's shoulders. "I'm glad you have him."

There were truly things to be thankful for. Calvin, who was Reid's Child Life Specialist the hospice had provided, being a big one. True to his word, though Connor had doubted it when it was given, Calvin kept in touch with Reid on a regular basis. Though it stung a little bit to think that maybe Reid opened up to Calvin and not always to Connor, it was a blessing to know his son had people hanging on tight to him.

Calvin had been a gift in the deepest, darkest point of their pain. As had been the hospice where Sadie had died.

And there was this moment here, where Reid didn't almost immediately pull away, but rather pressed into Connor's shoulder.

Help me to hang on to the good . . .

And to give opportunity for the light to come in. In this evening's case, by being kind.

"You have so much of your mom's goodness in you, Reid. I really love that." Connor squeezed him into his chest and then let him go. "Thanks for reminding me to see others."

Side by side Connor and Reid left their cabin and made their way to supper. Connor felt a new confidence in facing this next chapter, his emotions buoyed by that moment of connection with Reid. He'd be kind. Seek to be a blessing to this young woman and her small children.

That peaceful resolve lasted until the moment he stepped into the large lodge kitchen and turned toward that long family table kept at the far end for staff meals. At that point, everything crashed.

As told, there was a woman. And two kids. But not what Connor had imagined. Where he'd imaged a young mom about the same age as his sister-in-law, Audrey, with a toddler and a preschooler, there was instead a woman likely in her thirties, and her kids—a girl and a boy—were midteens and somewhere about Reid's age, maybe a bit younger, respectively.

Not what he'd had in mind. Not what he'd made peace with. Especially the woman.

Timid brown eyes, tired and yet somehow quietly determined met his. They were large, soft, and . . . and lovely. And instant connection snapped, without one word between them. One of knowing life's battles, of being worn by them, and of seeking shelter.

Connor immediately resented that connection. As he did the fact that he couldn't possibly think of this woman as a younger sister. Not when his first thought after involuntarily taking in her pretty face and soft curves was *What man in his right mind would let her go?*

He punched down the instant attraction—something he hadn't had to do in forever—and hardened his heart against the dumb thoughts. Who said her husband did the leaving? Connor had no idea why she was divorced. After all, there were two sides to every story.

"Connor. Reid." Appleton smiled and hobbled his way toward the Murphy pair, motioning for the woman to follow. "Meet Jade Beck and her children. Lily, who is sixteen, and Kellen, the very tall nine-year-old you see here. Jade, this is Connor and his son, Reid."

Jade Beck held a quiet look on Connor, and that connection stubbornly remained. She slipped her right hand forward. "It's nice to meet you, Connor."

He didn't want to grip the offered handshake, but manners demanded he do so. Her fingers were rough, her grip strong. Working hands. And her voice soft but confident. Maybe not confident. Brave? Connor couldn't help but search her expression.

Battle worn. But determined still. Any other man in Connor's shoes would be filled with admiration at the quiet but clear strength Jade Beck exuded.

Nonsense. He wanted to shake his head at his own assumptions. On what basis did he have to imagine that she was strong and brave and resilient? He didn't know their story. Didn't particularly care to either, no matter what Jade Beck looked or sounded like.

Why on earth had Appleton brought this on them? *I found someone for you.* Connor didn't want this pretty face in his world. And he didn't want these other kids intruding on Reid's world.

I didn't ask for this!

A sharp poke of conviction pierced through Connor's internal fit, reminding him that he'd *asked* to think right, to feel right, to do right. Even so, he felt the hardening of resentment, and preferred it.

I don't want this.

He should have begged off supper. Maybe he should find a new job.

Or maybe he should stop having a spiritual tantrum and act like the thirty-three-year-old man he was. The one who Sadie had loved.

ele

"Where's your mom?" Kellen's inquiry came off in his newfound trade-mark tone: snarky and disrespectful. Which was fantastic.

Jade froze. *Thanks, son.* She held her breath as she held a bowl of green beans midair, intending to pass it to Connor Murphy, who sat across the table. The man possessed a scowl that could intimidate a bear, making Jade want to hunker down and hide. Or run away.

Where on earth would she go? She had nowhere.

No, she had *here.* She had this job—one that came with a home for her and her children—promised by Mr. Appleton. Jade stiffened her posture and met Connor's glower head on. If she could survive the harsh sting of rejection, the humiliation of being cheated on, the shattering of a divorce, and the terrifying reality of starting over with her two kids, then she could face a man with a bad attitude. Even if he would be her supervisor.

I need this job.

Jade sent that petition heavenward, though she wasn't sure it was as much a plea for help as it was a reminder: *Lord, I'm still here! Please take notice of me!*

The long, frigid silence was finally broken by Reid, Connor's rather good-looking and much-less-intimidating son. "My mom died."

The stiffness in Jade's spine softened as her breath eased from her lungs. "Oh. I'm so sorry." She directed her sympathy toward Reid. The boy—who was likely in between her two kids in age—gave a slight nod, keeping his emotions shuttered, and then looked at his plate.

Jade looked to Connor, though she wished she hadn't. She swallowed against the anxiety his stern brow provoked. "I'm sorry," she repeated, this time in a whisper.

Connor took the bowl of beans from her and said nothing.

Why was this man's gaze so hard? It was like he immediately disliked her. That wasn't her imagination—it couldn't have been. She'd seen his expression when he'd first come into the large kitchen, before he had seen her. His bearded jaw had been relaxed, his profile had looked kind, which had added to his handsomeness. He'd said something quietly to his son, and the bond the pair shared had been apparent. So much so, that Jade had felt a pang of jealousy on behalf of her own children. Why was their father not that way with them?

And then Connor Murphy had looked at her. A gaze that could have been attractive, all deep green and warm, morphed to ice and stone. Jade had no idea why. She'd done nothing, had said nothing.

Had Mr. Appleton not told him she would be there? Perhaps not even informed him that he would have a new coworker?

"Where's your dad?" Once again, Reid was the one to break the awkward silence. His question lacked the iconic Kellen snark.

"Reid." Connor Murphy's tone came out low and sharp.

"He asked me first," Reid said quietly. "Seems fair."

"It's fine," Lily said. "Our dad is back in Kansas. He and Mom are divorced." Lily glanced between Jade and Connor, her look daring them to speak. Or begging them?

Likely that. They were the adults here, not Lily. Poor girl was always trying to make things okay. Trying to ease tension and build bridges and paint sunshine into dark corners. Jade slipped a hand over Lily's and squeezed, offering her quiet encouragement.

"My parents live nearby—only about forty-five minutes from here," Jade explained, wishing without good reason that Connor's stiff frown would ease. Why should he dislike her so much when he didn't know a single thing about her? "After Peter and I divorced, I needed to start over. Seemed like a good thing to have my family close. And the kids have always enjoyed their summer trips out here, so . . ."

Why was she explaining herself to this man? She had no obligation to him. He might be her supervisor, as the lodge's manager, but ultimately Mr. Appleton was in charge. Speaking of, why was the older gentleman just sitting there during this wildly uncomfortable exchange?

This had all been a dreadful mistake. Another horrible life choice. *God, I prayed so hard about this! I need this job. This home. The kids need something stable.*

Jade wanted to bury her face in her hands and cry. But not at the dinner table. Not in front of her kids. Especially not in front of this bear named Connor Murphy.

"How long has your mom been gone?" Lily asked, all softness and compassion in her voice.

Heaven, make it stop! Please just make this misery stop.

Reid looked at Lily, no offense evident. It was almost as if he appreciated someone just asking, like it mattered. Like they cared. And Lily would care, with all of her tender, way-too-grown-up heart.

"It's been a little over two years now. She had cancer."

"Wow, Reid." Lily kept a sincere gaze on the boy across the table from her. "That must be so hard. I'm really sorry."

Again he nodded, but this time it seemed like he was less walled. Less offended. Ah, Lily. She had a gift with people.

"I'm sorry about your . . ." Reid glanced at Jade, his cheeks filling with heat.

"It's okay, Reid," Jade said. "It's a long, ugly story. But now we're starting a new chapter. Hoping for good things." Mustering a smile, she kept his gaze. "I'm glad to know that Kellen will have you here. I didn't know he'd have a buddy on site. That's a happy surprise."

"I didn't ask for a buddy," Kellen grumbled. "And let's just get this straight right now. You're not going to be like a big brother to me. I don't want one."

"Noted," Reid said, the shield reemerging in his expression.

Jade sighed. And there was her sour son, still present and now, once again, accounted for. As tenderhearted and generous as Lily was, Kellen was equally hard and difficult. But Jade knew why. Not every boy had a devoted father who paid attention and said encouraging things to them like apparently Reid had.

Well, based on that one moment Jade had glimpsed before Connor had taken one look at her and decided he hated her.

It went against Lily's need for everything to be okay to simply allow a tense silence to continue, no matter how many failures at conversation had proceeded it. "Did your mom work here too, before she got sick?"

"Yeah," Reid said.

"What did she do?"

Jade felt the burn of Connor's gaze on her even before she looked up.

"Your job." His dark reply was like a warning. Or . . . or Jade didn't know what. It wasn't good, that was all she knew. Connor's response was deep, heavy, and brimming with resentment.

And now Jade understood. Connor's clear anger didn't have anything to do with her, other than the fact that she was there. Taking his wife's place.

CHAPTER THREE

(in which Connor knows what is right)

THIS WAS A DISASTER.

Lost in the residual misery that had been their first supper at the lodge, Jade wandered onto the long dock that would allow her to walk on the evening waters of this massive emerald lake. Such a beautiful evening. Such a beautiful place. And yet her story continued with the theme of her life: strife.

Why was everything in her life a catastrophe? Every decision she made seemed to turn inside out and wrong. Was she cursed?

Her marriage failure she sort of got. Sort of. She'd recklessly dived into a relationship with an older guy who had already earned himself quite a reputation. Not the good sort. Mother had told her that boys like that become men who cheat.

Young Jade had caught Peter's attention with her pretty face and model-type body. She'd kept him with a steady stream of admiration and willingness to do whatever Peter wanted—go as far as Peter wanted her to. Which had gotten her pregnant at age eighteen. Married at nineteen. And suspecting her husband had a wandering eye—and more—by the time she'd turned twenty-five.

But she'd *tried*. She had tried so hard to keep Peter's attention. His heart. She had set out to be the perfect wife. Keep his house. Raise the kids. Do all the things. And work a job that she hoped would make him proud. After all, she'd climbed her way from a front-desk clerk to the lead marketing strategist, all with the hope that when someone asked Peter, "What does your wife do?" he would do something more than shrug and say, "She's just a housewife."

Candlelit dinners, special little nighties, a willingness to do *whatever* he wanted . . .

All to end up here. Tossed aside, unloved, unwanted. Replaced by a fit little minx in a size 2 dress and arms that didn't jiggle when she wrote.

Come to think of it, no, Jade didn't get it. *God, I did everything I could think of. I honored him. I submitted. I loved.*

She'd loved. Alone. With stubborn determination. Hadn't mattered.

Peter had cheated. Then he'd left her. Then . . . divorce.

"Divorced." Jade let that cursed word pass her lips in a whisper set on the sweet evening breeze. "I swore that wouldn't ever happen. I wouldn't ever be divorced." Raising her face to the sky, she felt the cool swirl of air chill the wetness of her lashes. "This wasn't how this story was supposed to go, God. Why did you let it happen?"

God could have changed Peter's heart. Heaven knew she'd prayed hard that He would. She shook away the poke of resentment that summoned. Goodness, she'd already been through this with God before. She didn't need to rehash it all over again. God hadn't changed Peter, hadn't saved her marriage, and hadn't given her a why.

Even so, she sensed His presence. That was hard to explain, especially to her young, angry son who was mad at his dad. Mad at her. And mad at God. But the Spirit was with her—she knew it beyond doubt. He left His fingerprints on the provisions—this job being one of them.

Jade lowered her chin, opened her eyes, and took in the grand beauty that stretched before her. The lake was stunning, all wide and full of secrets with the mountains edging its shores. She'd loved it as a girl and as a Kansas resident, had missed both the mountains and Tahoe's unique glory.

You again with that, right?

A home right on the lake, not far from her parents. That was nothing short of a love gift. Jade clung to it with all the worn-out strength she had left.

And that sunset . . . all streaking pinks and glorious golds. Something lovely, something hopeful, even after what had turned out to be an awful first impression.

Wrapping her arms around herself, Jade sorted through the evening once again—this time not with the intent to fume and complain, but to seek understanding. Reid was a nice kid. Quiet and respectful, though walled off. Which was understandable, considering he'd lost his mom. How sad for the boy.

How sad for a man to lose his wife. Assuming his marriage was better than Jade's had been. No, it was sad either way. And Jade was willing to bet that the wound hadn't healed yet. Not with the way Connor immediately disliked Jade. The only rational reason she could figure was that Jade's presence made the loss of his wife fresh all over again. That was sweet, in a way. Not for Jade, but sweet that Connor must have loved his wife so deeply.

Or she was inventing a story for him, to excuse his excessively rude behavior.

She blew out a breath, willing the spinning thoughts to stop. Instead, she shifted that anxious energy to prayer.

What would you have me do here? How should I treat Mr. Murphy, who doesn't want me here?

With respect. With kindness.

The offended bits of her recoiled at that. In truth, she wanted to tell the man off. To say, *Look, mister, I don't know your story, and you certainly don't know mine. But your attempt to scare me off is shameful, and you should know right now that I'm the stubborn type. I endured an unhappy marriage to a man who was never satisfied with me or with anything I did. I can certainly take on your less-than-gracious attitude, and if you intend to make this a contest of wills, you should know that I don't back down.*

She chuckled. That would certainly be satisfying. She indulged in imagining how Connor Murphy would react to such a bold speech. In her mind, his eyes grew wide, and shame tinted the skin above his beard deep crimson.

He hung his head in shame, nodded, and then said, "I'm sorry I acted like a little boy throwing a tantrum." And then he offered her a handshake and sheepishly asked for a do-over.

Wouldn't that be lovely? Neat and tidy, and then they could move on to being happy coworkers. Jade could settle into her small cabin and start the next story. *Jade Beck, Volume Two: Life after Everything Unraveled.* It'd be a tale of overcoming. Of happiness after heartbreak. Of her kids being okay despite everything. And of Jade finding satisfaction in the single life, not once pining for a romance that would last or wondering what it would be like to be truly, deeply, forever loved.

Scratch that last part. She needn't wonder it—she was that already. It was just hard to remember sometimes.

Satisfy me with Your faithful love, that I may be glad all my days.

Jade closed her eyes and let that prayer sink into the marrow of her soul. It was a modified version of Psalm 90 and something she'd clung to the past year. Her memory summoned a line she'd read recently on a blog: *Man's great failures cannot override the faithful goodness of God. He will bring light into the darkness, laughter to tears. Hope to the hopeless. Sometimes He simply asks us to wait.*

So, she would wait. And believe.

And in the meantime, there was this beauty around her. This job in front of her. And a man and his son who evidently needed grace and kindness.

Jade let her gaze trail over the hills that hemmed her and this vast lake in. Nodding, she turned her attention back toward the lodge and the pair of cabins she knew rested behind that great log building. To her new home.

God had given her tasks to do in the waiting. Two beautiful kids she couldn't be more grateful for, a new job and cute little home. And neighbors.

Jade had work to do.

"Is it okay if I watch *Battlebots*?" Reid turned to look at Connor, his hand on the screen door to their cabin.

Connor nodded.

"You gonna watch too?"

Shoving his hands into his pockets, Connor studied the wide planks of the front deck and then sighed. It'd be easier to simply default to distractions. Easier, but not right. He'd already done *not right* enough for the night.

"I think I need some quiet time, buddy." He peeked at his son. "Okay?"

Reid's brows puckered, and his gaze held questions. Connor could almost hear them. *What happened back there, Dad? You're not normally a jerk. I'd be in trouble if I acted that way.*

Yeah. Connor swallowed and rubbed the back of his neck while he forced himself to face the silent reprimand of his kid. "I didn't handle that so well. Thanks for being better than me with the Becks. Hopefully you salvaged the Murphy name with them."

Shifting his jaw, Reid let a quiet span between them before he nodded. "They don't seem so bad." He shrugged. "At least not Lily. And Mrs. Beck. Kellen . . ."

Connor snorted a soft laugh. "Right. Kellen and I were a pair, weren't we?"

A hint of smile poked up one side of Reid's mouth, and he shrugged again. Connor reached to muss his dark hair, struck by the fact that he had to lift his hand up quite a way. Another two inches and Reid would be eye to eye with him.

Too soon, too fast. Connor was reminded of the terrifying reality that Reid would be grown and gone way before Connor was ready, and it was up to him to teach him how to be a man. A good, godly, productive man.

Hadn't done that so well at that at supper.

Reid gave Connor a light slug on the shoulder and then turned to go into the house. Off to watch *Battlebots*, leaving Connor to his quiet time.

A reminiscent feeling of utter failure settled in Connor's heart before he made it through the front door. It was cold and slimy and something he remembered feeling that long-ago afternoon after he'd first kissed Sadie in high school—his motivation back then certainly not love, but rather to make another girl jealous. A selfish act that had led to a whole lot of regret. This same yucky feeling had fallen on him at other scattered times over the years. Fights with his wife when he hadn't listened well or had demanded his own way. Times when he'd disappointed Sadie. Worse, caused tears to fill her eyes.

She would be so disappointed in him that night. He'd been hard and cold, and the few jagged words he'd uttered to Mrs. Jade Beck had been uncalled for. By the diverting of her eyes and the contortions of her expression, she'd been intimidated and had felt anything but welcome.

Which, to his shame, had been his exact intent.

So much for practicing kindness. For doing what was right and being a blessing. What had caused him to become so caustic to a complete stranger?

Deep down, Connor knew what, but he didn't want to admit it.

Striding through the living space of their home, Connor climbed the stairs and walked toward his room. Shutting the door behind him, he paused in between the dresser and bed and took inventory of the silent space.

In the two years since Sadie had died, he'd not changed one thing about their room. From the sea-green-and-chocolate comforter on the bed to the framed pictures that sat on top of the dresser, everything remained as Sadie had left them.

Even so, Connor felt her absence keenly. Her scent no longer lingered in the closet they'd shared. There wasn't a collection of ChapSticks and hand lotions littering the top of the dresser. And the Bible centered on the table on her side of the bed . . .

Untouched.

Connor's chest constricted, and he moved to pick up the black leather-bound book. It was cool and heavy in his hands, and he rubbed his thumb over the gold embossed letters of her name. *Sadie Murphy.*

Lowering to the bed, Connor let the volume fall open. The pages separated in Lamentations 3, the parting made ready by a notecard kept in between the leafs. Fingers trembling, Connor pulled it free. Sadie's script handwriting swept in faded black ink across the lines, front and back, the words from a hymn his wife had held precious.

And then one day
I'll cross the river
And I'll fight life's final war with pain
And then As death gives way to victory
I'll see the lights of glory
And I'll know He reigns
Because He lives
I can face tomorrow
Because He lives
All fear is gone
Because I know
He holds the future
And life is worth the living
Just because He lives

Emotions rattled through Connor's body. Reading that sweet, profound hymn summoned the clear memory of her soft voice as she sang it. It was like a breaking all over again, but this time, not destructive.

Cleansing.

Because He lives, Connor could face tomorrow. Because Jesus lives, he had a future. A hope. Because Jesus lives, life was worth living.

And it was worth living well.

Through a stinging blur, Connor moved his eyes to the passage in the Bible that stared up at him, highlighted in pink. Lamentations 3:19–24. In the middle of that passage, these words gripped him hard: "Yet this I call to mind and therefore I have hope: Because of the Lord's great love we are not consumed, for his compassions never fail. They are new every morning; great is your faithfulness."

For a long time, Connor simply sat there, letting the words of the Word and those of Sadie's favorite hymn wash over him. He was overdue for a good soaking.

By the time his phone rang, the tide of emotions had subdued, and Connor answered his younger brother's call with a better internal grip.

"Hi, Brayden, how's Tennessee?"

"It's really beautiful. But we miss you and Reid."

"Back at you, from both Reid and me. Are Audrey and Isaac okay?"

"We're all good."

"And the residency?"

"Intense, but that was expected."

Connor imagined Brayden scurrying through a hospital filled with kids battling cancer. Four years ago it would have been a tough image to conjure up. Though there'd never been any doubt that Brayden was smart enough to be a doctor, there had been the question of if he'd have the heart to do it well. Arrogance had robbed the youngest Murphy brother of compassion, and it had seemed like Brayden had been on track for a train wreck.

And he had been. With Audrey Smith. But somehow they'd found a real, solid love somewhere in the wreckage, and Brayden had taken on a strength in humility to go with it.

Not somehow—only by grace.

"Connor, you doing okay?" Brayden must have read something into Connor's extended silence.

"I—" Connor cleared his throat. He was almost a decade older than Brayden, and sometimes it was hard to open up to someone you once thought of as an annoying, spoiled kid. But over the past two years, Brayden had come to Connor in trust as he sought help in being a better man. He'd also become a lifeline, sharing Connor's burdens and opening up about his own. They'd grown close, which was also a gift of grace.

"I messed up tonight."

"With Reid?"

"No. I mean, yeah, but not specifically toward him. He witnessed it though. Mr. Appleton hired someone for Sadie's job, and she came today. She and her two kids."

"Okay . . ."

"I didn't even know Appleton was looking to hire someone, that he was going to bring them here. I guess I thought Lauren would just keep filling that job forever."

"That's not really practical."

"No, I know that. I just didn't think—" He'd just not wanted any more change in his world. And he couldn't stand to imagine someone sitting in Sadie's chair at the front desk. Doing Sadie's job. He sighed. "Long story short, the woman arrived this evening in time for supper, and I wasn't real, uh, pleasant."

"Define *wasn't real pleasant*."

Connor would rather not. Heat crawled up his neck as he remained silent.

"Hmm. I'm guessing it involved the dark, disapproving Murphy scowl."

Exactly that, along with a few cutting words. "Worse than Dad's, I'm pretty sure. I'm also fairly certain that Reid was embarrassed by me."

Brayden chuckled.

It wasn't really funny, but having his younger brother laugh at him helped to uncoil Connor's edgy nerves.

"There's always room for an apology, as Mom would say," Brayden said. "Unless, of course, you scared this poor woman off and she's never coming back."

"No, she's still here." Connor strode to the window that offered a peek-a-boo view of the lake around the corner of the big lodge. "She and her kids are moving into the cabin next to ours."

As if on cue, Jade Beck turned from the far end of the dock and made her way back to shore. Before she stepped from dock to land, Jade paused and tilted her face skyward. Connor shifted his attention to the colors splashed overhead. Fading yellow, vivid pink, rich orange. God sure could put on a show. And by Jade's uplifted face, she appreciated His handiwork.

She's a lovely woman.

Exactly the sort of thought that had put Connor on edge and caused all the trouble in the first place. Why would he think it again?

"This woman . . ." Brayden paused, letting the rest of his question be a mystery for a moment. "She and her kids are moving in?"

"Right."

"Not her husband?"

"She's divorced."

Another pause. Then, "I see."

Connor wasn't sure what that meant. But whatever it was, it made him edgy all over again. He pushed against it, not wanting to feel more remorse of another conversation badly done.

"Connor, you're one of the best men I know, and I mean that. I have no doubt that you'll do what is right."

Brayden's compliment and confidence in him turned gratitude and conviction together. As he watched Jade Beck make her way toward the cabin next to his, Connor knew what was right. He just needed the courage and resolve to do it.

CHAPTER FOUR

(in which a do-over might be a good idea)

JADE TUGGED ON ANOTHER box in the trunk of her Explorer, the muscles in her back protesting the strain and her shoulders declaring weakness. Maybe joining a gym would have been a good idea. The thought soured her mood. She had grown extraordinarily tired of feeling less-than, unworthy, and comparatively pathetic to others. Specifically, compared to Macey, whose image always invaded her mind at such thoughts.

Ugh. Hadn't she just resolved to face this new chapter in her life with dignity and strength? Hadn't she intentionally soaked in the beauty of this place and thanked God for new beginnings? Why couldn't she keep her mind and heart steady?

Determination struggling for a comeback, Jade lifted the box that had been marked *Kellen's bedding* with a black Sharpie.

Huh. What had he packed in this thing that would make it so heavy? Along with the question, a fresh conviction flashed through her mind: Kellen had two arms and two legs, and her son was old enough to use his muscles.

Resting her arms on top of the box, she called up to the house. "Kellen."

Her boy took his time appearing in the doorway, his face intent on his phone.

Of course he was on a screen. Why would he simply think, *Hey, Mom and Lily are getting the boxes out of the car to make beds for the night. Maybe I should help.*

Goodness, she was failing with this boy.

"Kellen, get off your phone and come get this box."

"What box?" Kellen asked without interest, his eyes still trained on whatever game he was playing.

"Kellen. Get off your phone." Jade pushed upright and anchored her hands on her hips. "Now."

"Okay. Geez." Kellen lowered the device but kept it in his hand. "What?"

"Come get this box."

"Why?"

Anger simmered in her belly. "Because if you don't, you'll be sleeping on a bare mattress tonight."

Flinging his shoulders around in a little fit, Kellen stomped down the stairs and toward the back of the car. "What's Lily doing?"

"Making her bed, which is what you'll be doing as soon as you get this in your room."

"What?!"

"I beg your pardon?"

"I have to make my bed?"

"Yes. And you're also going to give me that stupid phone."

"No way. Dad gave it to me."

Jade held her palm out, her silent glare daring him to argue with her.

Kellen met her glare with angry defiance etched in his stance. Where had her sweet little boy gone? The one who would stumble out of his room every morning and come straight to her, lean his head on her shoulder, and just stay that way for several minutes? Who was this miniature delinquent defying her simple instructions? Where had he picked up this crappy attitude he'd been tossing around for the last six months?

She knew exactly where. And why. *Thanks, Peter.*

"That phone better be in my hand in three seconds, or I'll be keeping it for a week rather than a day. Back talk me anymore, and I'll cancel the plan that powers this little device of Satan."

"You can't do—"

She arched a brow. "Want to try me? Do it. Let's see how that works out for you."

The heat in Kellen's brown eyes communicated something close to hate, which pierced her heart like a hot javelin. With disrespectful force, he slapped the phone into Jade's hand. "Dad pays for it."

"I don't care." She closed her fingers over the phone and shoved it into her jacket pocket. "It's gone now."

"What!?" Kellen kicked the tire, sending dirt scattering along the drive with his shoe. "Come on, man! That's so dumb."

"You were warned. Now"—she nodded toward the box waiting in the car—"take that into your room and make your bed. Neatly."

"I don't see why I couldn't stay with Dad. This new life sucks."

The blade sank deeper, and Jade fought against a wince. Also against spouting off *you couldn't stay with him because your father didn't want you to.* The kids had no knowledge of that recent conversation. The one in which Peter said, *I deeply care about my children, Jade. You know I do. But the truth is, Macey and I need some space. Some time to get established.*

Crossing her arms over the throbbing pain in her heart, Jade stuck with the issue at hand, choosing not to drag her ex-husband into it. "You can make this life as bad or as good as you want to, Kellen. I have too much on my plate figuring out all of this to take responsibility for your happiness. Own it."

There. How was that for tough love? No more soft mama from this girl. It apparently hadn't done her son any good, and she was sick of being run over by the males in her world.

With an exaggerated sigh and then a grunt, Kellen wrapped his arms around the box and hefted it toward the cabin. When he got up the stairs, he paused to shoot Jade a scowl and then flung the front door open to storm through it.

Awesome.

Divorce log entry #57:

Day one in new life at the resort: Arrived to discover my supervisor is a bitter bear, that evening dinners are bound to be something like sitting through a lecture, and my son is a spoiled juvenile delinquent. God, is it ever going to get better?

Jade stood for an extended minute, mentally scribing that entry in the divorce diaries she kept only in her head, something she'd done on and off over the past year, starting with *Divorce Log entry #1. Peter says he cares deeply about me, but he's not ready to let her go. After a year of this—likely much longer on his part—I'm done. I filed.*

That day had been filled with an odd concoction of anger, grief, and—the strange part—relief. Like . . . like letting go of a loved one who had been suffering with a long-held debilitating disease. Only that loved one wasn't a person. It was her marriage.

Jade wasn't sure she should feel that way. Even a year later, she wasn't sure that was right.

But it was true.

With a sigh that came up from the deep, and emotions still playing pinball, Jade stepped away from the car, closed the trunk, and took in the cabin they were going to call home. Two story, built of rustic timber, and blending with the evergreen trees and mountain surrounding, It was adorable. *Thank You for the provision in this.* They had shelter—cute shelter. Food. Family nearby.

God did still see her.

If only Kellen would see things with a positive bent.

On that, frustration took the lead role again. Jade whipped out her cell phone, tapped to open Peter in her contacts, and pecked a text.

Kellen has lost his phone privileges. He can call you on my phone or on Lily's. Don't try to call him on his, as he no longer has it in his possession.

She paced toward the house, but before she reached the steps, the phone in her hand buzzed.

Peter: I bought that phone so I could reach Kellen. I want him to have it.

Jade: Sorry, but no. He's oblivious to the world around him, and disrespectful. I took it away for a reason, and he's not getting it back. You have other options.

Peter: Jade, you're being too hard on the boy. He's only nine. Give him back the phone. I'll tell him to be more responsible.

Like that was going to happen—or help.

Jade: As the parent on site and the one currently responsible, I am telling you no. This isn't negotiable. I only told you so you would know he's not ignoring you. This topic is closed.

Her hands shook as she zipped off that last text. Had she ever been this resolute? Had she ever really stood up to Peter at all?

Up until she'd told him she wouldn't share him with another woman, the answer to that had been no.

Taking a trembling breath, Jade pivoted from the steps and walked instead to a path that wound around to the back of the cabin. She stuffed her hands into her jacket pockets as she wandered, ignoring the text that vibrated her phone. Peter would argue until he got his way. And if she continued to debate him, she'd give in.

Better to let it lie. Better to breathe in the cool pine and warm earth. Better to keep moving, to find something good and lovely to focus on until her heart rate settled and her thoughts stopped fuming.

The narrow trail led to a firepit with six roughhewn chairs circled around. The sight teased a tiny smile from Jade's mouth. It was like a secret shelter tucked behind the cabins—something she felt certain had been put there intentionally for the people who lived at the resort full time. It'd be the perfect spot for morning coffee or evening s'mores with the kids. Even Kellen would appreciate that.

She hoped.

Visions of pleasant evenings with her children materialized in her mind as she drew closer. With a deep cleansing breath, Jade stepped in front of a chair facing the pit and lowered onto it.

But she stopped when a flash of gray caught her periphery. With a gasp, she looked at the chair right beside her—one also facing the pit and away from the cabins—and found *him* sitting there. Dressed in jeans and a steel-gray jacket and holding an open Bible against his leg, Connor Murphy almost looked . . . attractive—which was very different than a man simply being handsome. And also irritating.

He held her with that distant green gaze, the beard covering his face making the rest of his expression unreadable. But Jade could guess what it would tell her. *Annoyed.* She'd stumbled onto *his* secret sanctuary, and he'd be bothered by the intrusion.

Though embarrassment filled her cheeks with heat, an unreasonable surge of resentment flooded her chest. Yet another man in her world making her feel out of place. She rolled her fists in her pockets and tried to talk herself down from irritation. "I'm sorry," she said, though her tone sounded flat and insincere even to herself. "I didn't know you were back here."

He just looked at her with those intense eyes. Finally, he glanced back toward the cabins. "I was going to stop at your place when I was done."

Jade furrowed her brows in confusion. Why would he stop at their cabin? To tell her this charming firepit area was off limits? To give her a lights-out timetable?

She wasn't gonna have it. "Well, it appears I've saved you the trouble."

Slowly, Mr. Murphy closed his Bible, and then he visibly swallowed. "I was going to, uh, to offer to help with the trailer, Mrs. Beck. If you needed help."

Mrs. Beck. Jade's spine rammed straight. She didn't like that title. At all. "Help with the trailer?"

"Yeah, unloading. Whatever you need. Reid and I could help you."

"I wouldn't want you to go to any trouble." Though she knew it was juvenile, she couldn't put any trace of genuineness in her voice. It was all sharp snark.

To her astonishment, the skin above his beard bled crimson. Mr. Murphy rubbed the back of his neck as he focused on the empty firepit. At last he blew out a long breath. "Look, I'm sorry for supper. I was out of line."

"You—" Had this man she'd summed up as a bear just apologized to her? Did he mean it? "You're sorry?"

He looked at her, uncertainty shadowing his eyes. "Yes. I'm very sorry, Jade, for being so rude to you and your children. I'm not—I try not to be a jerk on a regular basis."

"O—oh." Utterly stunned, Jade couldn't form a thought. She simply stood there, lips parted, wondering when this man would stand, brush his hands together, and tell her to scurry on back to the cabin now so he could enjoy his solitude.

Mr. Murphy did stand, tucking his Bible under one arm. But the shocking humility in his face—in his whole stance—didn't diminish. Instead, he peeked at her with a look that she could only define as repentant. "Maybe we could have a do-over?"

Jade blinked. And gaped. Then she pulled her bottom lip under her teeth before she nodded. Slowly. "A do-over might be a good idea."

Or maybe it wouldn't. The past fifteen years had shown her that she was far too gullible, far too trusting.

"Thank you." He held out his right hand and cleared his throat. "I'm Connor Murphy."

She eyed the offered hand before she hesitantly took it. "Jade."

"Good to meet you, Mrs. Beck."

She cringed. "Just Jade."

A look as if he felt trapped creased the corners of his eyes, and Jade wondered why. She didn't want to be called by Peter's name. Truthfully, if it weren't for the kids, she'd go back to Tifton, her maiden name.

Connor nodded. "Okay. Jade." He cleared his throat. "Can my son and I help you unload your trailer?"

"That would be . . . nice." It felt so stiff and unreal, this unaccounted-for politeness. "But I wasn't going to tackle the trailer until the morning."

Another uncertain nod. Another rub of his neck. "The morning, then." With a move of his chin, he forced himself to meet her gaze and then dipped one more nod. "We'll be there. In the morning." Then he stepped around her.

"Mr. Murphy."

He paused, glancing over his shoulder.

"I didn't mean to interrupt you." Warmth unfurled in Jade's middle at the scarcest hint of the man's smile. A reaction she didn't understand and certainly wasn't going to trust. She gestured toward the chair he'd occupied. "Please don't leave on my account. I should go make sure my son is doing what I asked, anyway."

To her amazement and confounded delight, that ghost of a smile grew on Connor's mouth. He lifted his Bible. "I finished. Just needed to get some things ironed out in here." He tapped his chest.

"Oh."

"Good night, Jade Beck."

Jade stared after him as Mr. Murphy strode down the path and around the cabins, turning toward the one he lived in. She wondered if she could trust what had just happened. If she could truly believe that a man would not only admit his mistake but want to make it right with her.

It seemed almost too farfetched to be real.

CHAPTER FIVE

(in which Connor is that guy)

JADE BECK REMAINED LODGED in his mind for way too long.

Connor stared into the darkness, sleep elusive as his thoughts twisted and rolled about his new neighbor. Why couldn't he stop thinking about her? She was just a new neighbor. A new coworker. He shouldn't care that she seemed an intriguing concoction of strength and timidity. Shouldn't name that mix *resilience* and feel a well of admiration deepening by it. And he certainly shouldn't care that Jade, with her soft round face, large brown eyes, and dark hair, was a lovely woman.

He'd known plenty of lovely women. All his sisters-in-law, in fact, were pretty. Didn't keep him up at night.

It's loneliness.

Was he lonely? Yes. But that was a specific thing: he was lonely for Sadie. He missed his wife. That was all. Wasn't it?

Yes. No. Maybe?

Good to meet you, Mrs. Beck.

The look on her face—pain and anger, followed by something very like determination all passed over her expression before she insisted that it was *just Jade*. She didn't want to be called Mrs. Beck, which was very inconvenient, because *Mrs. Beck* was Connor's way of drawing a line. *Mrs. Beck* was a lovely, unavailable woman. A coworker who would remain distant by that title. He could see her every morning and say, *Good morning, Mrs. Beck*, and then carry on as usual, never wondering how she was that morning and if she'd slept well the night before. Never worrying that maybe her needs weren't met and her heart might be hurting.

At supper every night, he could say, *Please pass the green beans, Mrs. Beck*, and all boundaries would remain intact. He'd never be curious about what her favorite foods might be and if the meal was satisfying to her. He'd never suffer from an instinctive need to make sure she was warm and safe at night, that the fire in her cabin was lit, and that everything functioned as it should. And he'd never crave that smile he'd glimpsed earlier, when she had paused to look up from the dock.

But Jade?

Jade was a lovely woman. And this deeply bothered Connor.

Why did she resent being called Mrs. Beck, anyway? Without any conscious summoning on his part, Connor went immediately to defensive mode for her. What had her ex-husband done? Already he'd wondered why a man would let such an attractive woman go. Now he was creating a backstory for her, one that would explain why Jade Beck seemed unsteady and yet determined to stand on her own.

Connor drew up a character who was domineering, condescending, and ungrateful and named him Mr. Beck. A man who took a good woman for granted. Undermined her, underestimated her, and used her for his convenience. At the end of the day, he took her open and trusting heart and crushed it.

Anger burned against the man. Which was insane. Connor had no knowledge of Jade Beck's story, and he shouldn't want to discover it. No matter how endearing those brown eyes were.

God, what am I thinking?

He just needed sleep. This whole situation had been thrown at him without warning. He'd been blindsided, and the jarring blow was still messing with his head. That was all.

It had to be all. He didn't want it to be anything else.

Jade would be Mrs. Beck in his mind. That way, the lines would remain in place and Connor would be safe until he recovered from this blow.

Connor Murphy was a man of his word. And prompt, apparently.

Jade stood in the open doorway looking up at the tall man while a wave of crimson heated her face. It was barely eight o'clock, she only had one cup of coffee in her system, and she was still dressed in her worn-out flannel jammie pants and oversized K-State sweatshirt.

"Mr. Murphy."

"Good morning, M . . . uh—" He looked toward his booted feet. "Good morning, Jade. Did you sleep well?"

Did he wince at the end of that? Was it really so hard to be civil?

That's not fair, Jade, she reprimanded herself. *After all, the man apologized. And he's here to help. At an annoyingly early hour.*

Jade fixed a smile and willed away the color she knew was on her face. "Good morning. We did sleep well. Maybe too well. I wasn't expecting you so early."

"No . . . I mean, I'm just checking in with you. I get going early. For work. I try to get a good hour in before I run Reid into school. I mean, when school is in session. You know, in a few weeks." He paused to clear his throat. "I . . . I wanted to let you know that the coffee is always ready by six." He gestured toward the mug in her hand. "But I see you have your own. I mean, of course you would. That is, if you're a coffee drinker—which clearly you are. I think. Is that coffee?" He pinned his lips shut, as if to stop the outburst he couldn't control.

"It is." An urge to laugh bubbled in Jade's chest as she watched Connor Murphy stutter and stumble his way through that chaotic speech. Was he a shy man? She wouldn't have pinned him as shy, with the way he'd glared at her at their first meeting. Perhaps he was simply a truly awkward man. Jade didn't know why, but that struck her as amusing. Connor Murphy had a commanding build. A disconcerting presence. It seemed funny for such a good-looking, imposing man to be, of all things, awkward.

He peeked at her just as her smile widened. The same scowl he'd greeted her with the day before darkened his expression.

Of course it would. Men, no matter how awkward, did *not* like to be laughed at. The arrogant creatures.

Mr. Murphy jammed his hands into his jacket pockets and stepped back. "Just let me know what time you want to get started."

All amusement froze in the chill of his sulky mood change. Jade wrapped her free arm over her middle and lifted her mug to her lips. The pleaser in her wanted to rush with *Oh! I'll get dressed right now and we'll get started. Skip my second cup of coffee. No need for breakfast. I'm so sorry I wasn't ready when you were!*

Nope. Jade pushed that girl into a back closet and locked the door. After a leisurely sip of her coffee, she lowered the mug and took her time inspecting this Murphy conundrum. His eyes darted toward his cabin, then to the shared path that led around to the back firepit, and then to a spot on the doorframe just above Jade's head. Never did he meet her gaze. He shuffled his feet and crossed his arms.

Jade pressed a shoulder against the door. "I let the kids sleep in. It's a long drive from Kansas, and to be blunt, it's been a long year leading up to this move."

As if against his will, Connor lifted his chin and met her eyes. Something gentle softened his green gaze, and whatever it was made her heart skip. Which was . . . ridiculous.

He blinked twice and quickly aimed his gaze back at the floor before he nodded. "Of course."

"Will ten work for you?"

"Sure." He pivoted and started away.

"Mr. Murphy." Jade cringed at herself. She should have let him skulk away. Why did she always need to make people feel better? No wonder men were arrogant around her. She was a compulsive ego fueler.

Connor Murphy glanced at her over his shoulder.

Goodness, though, those eyes . . .

Jade straightened and lifted her mug. "Thank you. For telling me about the coffee." Mentally, she face-palmed herself. A compulsive ego fueler *and* a fool.

One corner of his mouth poked up, and he nodded. Then he was clomping down the steps. This time Jade let him go, shutting the door and reprimanding herself for liking that half smile as much as she did.

Clearly, by her lack of self-control on the compulsive front and her stupid response to his outward attractiveness, Jade was better off keeping her distance.

Yes. That was exactly what she would do. She'd keep Connor Murphy at a professional arm's length.

Connor wondered what it would be like to pack up everything he had, stuff it in a rental trailer, and move halfway across the country. By himself.

Pondering it made him sad. Despite the sometimes overwhelming grief he'd waded through, he didn't want to leave. Hadn't his most persistent plea of late been no more change? He liked the stability this consistent life had offered. It had been a shelter, in truth. When the tide of sadness threatened to take him under, he could go about his maintenance chores at the lodge and shift into auto. Body worked, mind went numb.

Starting over, the way Jade Beck was doing, would add a whole new layer of complication to life. And that wasn't even taking into consideration kids.

Arms loaded with a large box and a smaller one on top of it, Connor shifted himself so he could pass through the Becks' front door sideways, and as he did so, he caught a glimpse of Kellen Beck. Man, that kid had some kind of massive chip on his shoulder. From the moment Connor had returned to the Becks' cabin, Kellen had been disrespectful and difficult to his mom.

"Kellen, finish your waffles and get dressed. We've got work to do."

"It's Saturday, Mom. Why do we have to do it today?"

Connor had stared at the kid with a frown. When Kellen glanced Connor's way, the boy pinned an exaggerated glare on him. With one lifted eyebrow, Connor very nearly stepped into the cabin to tell the kid to quit acting like a spoiled child.

But that wasn't his place. And Connor was keeping his distance.

Using the practice of discipline he'd learned in his years as an airman, he had forced himself to look at Jade rather than taking the disrespectful punk to task. "Reid and I will get started, if you'll get me the keys to the trailer?"

From that unpromising beginning, things hadn't improved. By the looks of the episode playing out by the trailer right then, it was only going to get worse. Connor could overhear the tense exchange between mother and son as he carried the boxes into the cabin.

"I don't see why I have to carry in stuff that isn't mine."

Kellen's defiance put Connor on edge.

"We're unloading right now, Kellen." By her tone, Jade's patience was wearing thin. "Working together. Just grab a box and stop complaining."

"I don't even want to be here!"

Connor stood from lowering the boxes in time to see Kellen raise his hand . . .

At first look, from his angle looking through the window, it looked like Kellen had slapped his mother. Every muscle in Connor's body coiled tight, and he stormed toward the door, ready to take the kid by his shoulders and explain to him, in his old drill-sergeant tone, how real men don't hit women. Ever. When he reached the top step of the deck, however, his angle changed and he could see Kellen's palm on the trailer.

Had he hit his mother though? Marching forward, Connor knew he wore a dark expression. He also saw Jade inhale sharply when she caught sight of him coming toward them. Her eyes widened, and maybe her head shook slightly? Connor wasn't sure, but it didn't matter to him. He was on a mission.

"Kellen." Years in the air force surged from his voice. "Did you just slap your mother?"

"Mr. Murphy—"

Connor cut a glance back at Jade but quickly refocused on the kid who had turned his head to glare at him.

"You're not my dad, so butt out," Kellen said.

"I don't care who your dad is. If you just hit your mother, you're dealing with me."

"Mr. Murphy, please." Jade stepped forward, positioning herself between Kellen and Connor. "I've got this." She turned to Kellen. "Get another box and take it inside. Now." She sounded cold and dead serious.

Apparently Kellen understood that at least one of the two adults wasn't putting up with his nonsense anymore. Connor knew that was true for him. He hoped, for Jade's sake, that it was true for her. How on earth was a nine-year-old this much of a brat? Had he never been disciplined in his life? Seemed off, especially since all he'd seen of Lily was pleasant and respectful.

Kellen took the smallest box he could find and stomped his way toward the cabin, up the steps, and through the door.

"I can handle my own kid."

Jade's seething whisper pulled Connor's attention back to her. He held a silent look on her face, finding her anger at him both reassuring, in that she could possibly handle herself with a belligerent boy, and frustrating. He was standing up for her, and if she thought for one second he was going to turn a blind eye to a young man hitting a woman, she was about to learn a few truths about Connor Murphy. First lesson: not in a million years, lady. He moved forward, and as he did so, Jade stepped back until she was against the side of the trailer again.

"I would never hurt a woman, Jade." Connor spoke in a low tone, alarmed that she seemed to take his approach as predatory. "And I certainly won't ignore a young man who thinks it's okay to do so."

She visibly swallowed. "He's my son. I can—"

Ignoring her weak protest, Connor lifted her chin with the side of his fingers, tilting her face, looking for signs of impact.

"He smacked the trailer. Not me." Her voice quivered.

He examined her skin for a few more breaths anyway, then removed his fingers and nodded.

Stiffening her shoulders, Jade moved away from the trailer. Likely so she no longer felt trapped. Connor told himself to ease up on what he was certain was an intimidating expression, and he stepped back to allow her space.

"You're a stranger to us, Mr. Murphy." Jade folded her arms over her middle. "And to be blunt, you didn't make the best first impression."

Heat crept up his neck, and he slid another step backward. "I get that, and again, I apologize."

The fire in her gaze cooled. But not entirely. "And the fact is, Kellen's right. You're not his dad. He doesn't know you, has no reason to trust you. You don't really have a place interfering."

With a lifted brow, Connor dipped a single nod. "You're right—but only to a point. Jade Beck, I spent years defending this country as an enlisted airman. Before that I grew up in a home where respect was the standard, and among my six brothers and me, we never knew a single instance when it was okay to behave threateningly, let alone violently, toward our mother. Or any woman, for that matter. Or to play the bully. I meant what I said to your son. I don't care who his dad is or what the man tolerated while you were married. If I see Kellen being violent to you or to Lily, I *will* intervene. I don't care how much that offends you—that's the way it's going to be."

A bright flush bled on Jade's cheeks. "He's only nine."

"And he's only going to get bigger. Stronger."

"He'll grow out of it."

"Think that's how that works? We just naturally grow out of our bad habits?"

Jade shifted her jaw and looked toward the cabin. "I don't appreciate your interference, Connor."

"I didn't ask you to appreciate it."

"And I really resent the insinuation that I'm a bad parent. Just because your son apparently doesn't have angry outbursts doesn't make you an expert."

"I claimed neither, Jade." Connor sidestepped around her and leaned into the trailer to pull out two more boxes. "And I never would." Hefting the stack, he started back to the house, but paused when he reached her side again. "For the record, I'm on your side. And Kellen's. Just so you know."

Feeling her glare like a laser in his back, Connor made his way toward the cabin. Part of him wished he hadn't interfered. But even with that, he knew he'd do it again, no question.

Because, as usual, he was that guy. The one who compulsively did what he believed was right. No matter what other people thought. No matter how much it cost him.

There were times, though, that he wished he wasn't.

CHAPTER SIX

(in which Jade will simply stick to the plan)

JADE WAS ONLY ABLE to push the incident out of her mind by working—and there was plenty of work to be done. She was to start her new position as marketing manager and front-desk supervisor on Monday. That left her the weekend to get their new home in order.

Thankfully, her children put their minds and their bodies to the task alongside her. With Lily that wasn't a surprise. Kellen, however . . .

She'd expected little more than he would unpack his clothes and half his trinkets and that he'd do it with an attitude that would match the disposition of a scorpion. While the attitude thing was as predicted, Kellen's bluster was silent, and he did as Jade asked. Even when it involved doing things that had nothing to do with his stuff.

That fact made it harder to file away what had happened at the trailer between her and Connor Murphy. Jade had little doubt that had Mr. Murphy not stepped into something that didn't belong to him, Kellen would be verbose in his resentment, uncooperative in this getting-the-house-settled endeavor, and flat out unbearable to be around.

Why were a few lines from a man who was a near perfect stranger be what it took to push her son to at least do the work, even if he was clearly not happy about it? Jade could have yelled and screamed, taken away more privileges, threatened worse . . . all to little result. She knew this for a fact from experience.

Kellen's standard response was, "I hate living with you. Dad wouldn't be like this."

And she couldn't argue that point. Peter was never the disciplinarian. If he was around at all, he was either passive (ignore all inconveniences, chief of which were wife and children) or the occasional fun-time guy. Jade had always been the corrector, the let's-be-responsible one, the in-real-life-we-have-to-do-stuff person, the that's-inappropriate parent. More than once Peter had told her, in front of their son, "Boys gotta be boys, Jade. Chillax for once."

If it had been Peter, instead of Connor Murphy, who had thought that Kellen had slapped her out there by the trailer, what would he have done?

Nothing. If he'd even noticed anything going on at all, he'd have done nothing. Worse than nothing, he'd likely have told Kellen, "This is just grunt work. Go on and do something else. Mom and I will take care of this." And then he would promptly disappear, leaving *Mom* to take care of it.

Resentment burned as Jade considered that scenario. Maybe she was being entirely unfair to Peter. Her view of him was skewed, after all. But it seemed like a realistic scene. And the contrast between the man she'd married, and now had divorced, and the interfering guy next door made her feel . . . miserable. Stupid for marrying a man who valued her so little. Insane for hanging on to him for so long.

And strangely, distrusting of Connor Murphy. Maybe not distrusting. Maybe . . . maybe that yucky feeling in her, sidling up to the admiration she didn't want to feel for him, was more like humiliation.

In the two days of knowing him, she'd been belittled by Connor's response to her being there, and then he'd witnessed one of her most embarrassing failures—aside from a dead marriage: when it came to her son, she was an inept mother. And Connor hadn't owned the social curtesy to ignore it.

Even so, Connor's interference had apparently born positive fruit. Kellen did his part, and did so without an angry outburst. Without telling her how much this sucked and how he wished he'd stayed with his dad.

So that was a win. Wasn't it?

Not hers. Connor Murphy's.

She should be grateful. Actually, as she went to bed Sunday night, the bulk of the work of settling in done, she was grateful. But also, still resentful. And leery of the imposing, stern, and undeniably attractive Connor Murphy.

But she'd mapped out a plan earlier. The one where she would keep him at a professional distance. She'd simply stick with the plan.

Two weeks into this new life, and Jade felt herself breathe a bit.

The mountains were glorious. How she'd missed them, living the past fifteen years out on the Great Plains! Not that the wide land of rolling hills and expansive fields didn't have their own sort of loveliness, but Jade reveled in this return to massive upswells of earth and granite, slopes of evergreens, and purple peaks. And her daily view of Lake Tahoe? Simply splendid. It would never get old.

There was also the benefit of having her parents nearby—one she'd taken advantage of the past weekend as she and the kids spent all Saturday at their house. How wonderful it had been to head over midmorning, arrive in time for late cinnamon rolls and coffee, lounge around doing puzzles and puttering in her dad's garden, enjoy his smoked brisket, and then returning to their own home in the evening. No packing up for a two-week stay. No struggling to sleep in the guest bed. No listening to the kids bicker about who had to sleep on the bottom bunk for the duration.

And the best part—the one she'd not banked on—was not having to make up stuff that would leave her parents with the impression that she and Peter had the perfect relationship. Or even a stable, semi-good relationship.

No more pretending. No more covering for Peter, explaining his absence yet again. Telling them that he just worked so hard to make sure they could do the fun stuff. It all had been strangling lies, and the relief to be free of them nearly outweighed the humiliation of Peter's betrayal and their failed marriage.

Maybe not nearly. Maybe it just did outweigh it. Was that wrong for her to feel that way?

As Jade walked the short path from her cabin to the front of the lodge the Monday following that visit, she drew in a breath that tasted like crisp, clean mountain and felt a whole lot like freedom. She paused short of reaching the large double front doors and turned to look at the bay of water shimmering in the morning sunlight. Smiling, she lifted her coffee mug to her lips, shut her eyes, and tipped her face up.

Thank You for this.

Her silent prayer made her smile expand before she opened her eyes to look back at the lake. In her view, at the bottom of the wide steps leading from the small parking lot, stood Connor Murphy, his gaze pinned on her.

The cool kiss of mountain morning air quickly warmed against her heating cheeks. She cleared her throat. "Good morning, Mr. Murphy."

"'Morning." His look swiftly darted toward the doors, and then he climbed the stairs. He opened the main door and held it for her, but he didn't make eye contact. Just rubbed the back of his neck as she passed through the entry in front of him.

This was how it was. Awkward. Stilted conversations, if any were to be had at all. Connor Murphy kept to himself unless their overlapping jobs required him to interact with her. Even then he said only what was necessary and never settled his green eyes on her.

Which worked nicely into her plan of keeping a professional distance between them. Jade should have appreciated that.

But she didn't.

Perhaps it was because she had grown so utterly tired of feeling like the misfit at work, as she had been during her final few months at her old advertising firm. After it had come out that Macey was having an affair with Jade's husband, things in the office had grown uncomfortable, to say the least. It'd been so bad that Jade had quit without another career option on the table. For the interim months it'd taken her to find this job at Lake Shore Lodge, she'd worked as a minimum-wage grocery store clerk. It'd been infinitely better than remaining at the firm.

But that was back when the mortgage was still being paid by Peter. Before Jade had filed for divorce.

Anyway, none of that mattered now. And it shouldn't matter that Connor Murphy seemed as determined to keep Jade at arm's length as she would him.

But it mattered. It bothered.

"Was Reid ready to go back to school today?" Jade set her mug on the desk near the keyboard and raised her eyes to his face, daring him to look at her.

Halfway across the room, Connor froze, and his head jerked straight. Slowly he turned, and those eyes settled on her. His crumpled brow seemed more fitting for if she'd smacked him on the back of the head with a spitball, not asked him a harmless question. Crossing his arms, he shrugged. "He likes math, so yeah, I guess he was. Not excited, but ready. I guess." He moved to give her his back and then stopped. Cleared his throat. "How about Lily and Kellen?"

Ah. A civil response. Looked painful for him.

Jade lifted her brows. Was she really so beneath the dignity of being noticed? Oh! She was so exhausted with feeling that way!

"Lily likes school. She always has. But she was nervous about starting in a new place. And Kellen—" Oy. What had she done, opening this conversation? She didn't want to talk about how Kellen had slammed the door to his room when she'd told him to get ready to go, or about the frigid silent treatment he'd given her all morning, despite her efforts to be positive and offer encouragement.

Jade sighed. "Kellen doesn't like anything right now." Shoulders slumping, she slipped into the swivel desk chair and retrieved her coffee.

Nice small talk. Totally pleasant. Glad she made the effort. *Stick with the plan, Jade. Why would you crave this man's notice anyway?*

She peeked up at the Murphy bear and was shocked to find him still standing there, his focus locked on her, and ... and was that *compassion* on his face? His brows folded in again, and he dipped a nod. Jade had no idea what that meant.

"I'll be working on the heating units on the north side." Connor pointed upward, toward the second story where the guest rooms were. "If you need anything." Then he turned and made his way toward the storage closet where Jade knew he kept his tools. Then he double-timed it up the stairs, no glancing her way again.

What was he all about?

Jade shouldn't entertain those kinds of questions. They didn't fit in her playbook of keep her distance. Even so she wondered that very thing more than once. With annoyance, when he explained things rather curtly, with as few words as possible and with as much distance away from her as he could muster. With sincere curiosity when she glimpsed him through her bedroom window on the second floor of her cabin, as he sat out at the firepit every morning, and nearly every evening, open Bible on his leg. And with warm admiration—*dang it!*—when she saw him play catch or shoot hoops with Reid.

When it came to being a good dad, Connor Murphy was evidently the real deal. And that made her wonder more about him. Was he truly a kind man once one got past this hardback cover Connor Murphy portrayed? What kept him so standoffish when she could see that with his son, he was a warm human? Was it just with her that he kept the temperature at frigid levels?

Why on earth should she care?

Not in the plan!

Jade steered her attention to the computer, where she had at least fifteen emails she needed to answer, some reservations to update, and a new marketing campaign to touch up so she could present it to Mr. Appleton that afternoon. She'd spent the past two weeks on that presentation, and she wanted Mr. Appleton to be impressed. Which meant she had no time to ponder a man who obviously had no thought toward her—more importantly, a man she'd had no intention of wondering about in the first place.

For the bulk of the morning, Jade was able to stay the course. She answered all the inquiries about available dates for the fall, group rates, and amenities the lodge offered. She updated reservations. She polished that campaign—one she was rather proud of and was looking forward to presenting to Mr. Appleton. In between all that, she'd fielded phone calls, talked to the few guests who were currently lodging with them, and enjoyed a quick text chat with Lily.

Jade: *Why do chemists like nitrates so much?*

Lily: *Why*

Jade: *They're cheaper than day rates!*

Lily: *<laughing face> You're getting good at this!*

Jade grinned at her phone, feeling accomplished.

JADE: *How's school so far?*

Lily: *So far so good. It's not as bad as I was worried about. I mean being the new girl. I have a couple of girls in my biology class who are nice. They play basketball too, so that's pretty good, right?*

Jade: *Glad to hear it! Have a good afternoon.*

Lily: *You too <heart emoji>*

At least she had Lily to carry on a pleasant, personal conversation with. And on staying on the positive side, she and her kids were fed pretty well with this gig. Inhaling the aroma of baked cinnamon apples and something else divine, Jade smiled. Lifting her face, she squeezed her eyes shut and lifted up silent gratitude.

"My brother does that." Connor Murphy's voice startled her, and she jerked her attention to where he was, just coming down the wide stairway, bracing herself against the high front desk for stability.

"I beg your pardon?"

"No, I'm sorry." He landed on the first floor and paused. "I didn't mean to startle you."

"Oh." He looked so guilty, it made her feel bad. "I wasn't reprimanding you. I was just—startled." She chuckled and then cleared her throat. "I mean, what does your brother do?"

"Lifts his face upward with a grateful look." He gestured with his chin. "That's what your face looked like, anyway. I mean, with that little smile. I just assumed . . ." He rubbed the back of his neck.

It was adorable, the way this imposing man morphed into this uncertain guy stumbling over his words.

Jade pushed that thought into a back corner and told it to stay.

It wasn't very obedient.

"I was enjoying the smell of whatever Emma is making in the kitchen, and thinking this was a pretty good gig."

He very nearly grinned. She thought. Or hoped?

"It is a good gig." After a few beats of terribly awkward silence, Connor visibly swallowed and then gestured with a thumb toward the kitchen at the back of the lodge. "Smells like it's done. Lunch, I mean."

"Right." Jade nodded, fully engulfed in the clumsiness of this interchange. "The guests should be showing up in about a half hour."

"Right." Connor rubbed the thick beard covering half his face. The other half—the exposed skin—bloomed red. "Do you . . . I mean, shall we . . . uh."

"Go eat?"

"Yeah." He pointed his face toward the floor but continued to look at her. Like he was . . . was bashful?

Was that even possible?

Jade mentally slapped herself. She was utterly ridiculous, dreaming such things. Starved for attention. That was what she was. And terribly lonely. Not to mention imaginative. Straightening her shoulders, Jade lifted her chin while banishing all such ideas. "Lunch it is, Mr. Murphy."

He held a silent look on her for another beat. If she would let herself, she could have imagined that his gaze grew warm. And then if she'd let herself, she'd have felt a fluttering in her chest that was also pleasantly warm.

Denying both, Jade turned and headed toward the back of the lodge. Lunch with a coworker wasn't anything to lend toward daydreams. And why she would want to daydream about any man at this point in her life, let alone a bear who went by Murphy, was simply inexplicable.

So she wouldn't.

CHAPTER SEVEN

(in which there are answers . . . and more questions)

CONNOR HAD KEPT HIS distance.

It had seemed the best course. Jade Beck had arrived uninvited—at least by him—and mostly disruptive. He didn't want her there.

Huh. He rubbed his hair as he followed the woman who had circulated through his thoughts entirely too much over the past weeks. For a man who didn't want her there, he sure wondered about her. A lot. And watched her. From a careful distance. Except, not that morning. His quickly attained habit of watching her had been found out that morning.

He'd been caught staring. And that had rattled him further.

What was this chaos within? How could the arrival of a divorced woman and her children stir up so much unidentifiable madness in him? *God, my thoughts won't land. I can't make sense of anything!*

Ah. Finally. An honest confession to his heavenly Father. To that point, if Jade Beck had come up in his conversations with God Almighty at all, it'd been with intentional remoteness. *Watch over my new neighbors. Help Kellen to adjust—he's one angry kid. Keep Lily close—she's a really sweet girl.*

That was it. He'd intentionally *not* named Jade. Which meant he could avoid owning that he thought she was lovely, and that made him wildly uncomfortable. He didn't have to say that he wondered why her marriage fell apart or that he suspected by Kellen's behavior that she might have some pretty tough wounds given by a man who would allow his son to behave so disrespectfully.

Thoughts that didn't make sense to him and that he didn't want to have. Jade was just a neighbor. A coworker.

The woman who had been hired to fill Sadie's vacant job.

And there, the thunder rumbled yet again. Connor paused in the entry to the kitchen, thankful that Jade had walked in front of him. For a breath, he squeezed his eyes shut and surrendered the storm in his heart.

Sadie's gone, Lord. With You, healed and whole. I've accepted that, so why is this so hard?

Blowing out a long, silent breath, Connor opened his eyes and let his vision settle on Jade. She stood across the wide counter from Emma, smiling at the woman who had spent half her life as the lodge's cook. As he watched Jade's profile, his raw heart finally surrendered once again. Stillness settled, and then, in that quietness, something soft and yet profound replaced the madness that had stolen his peace.

Behold, I am doing a new thing . . .

Connor knew those words. Over the years since Sadie's second cancer diagnosis and then her death, he had spent a long time pouring over Isaiah 43. Clinging to the tender words of God spoken to His broken people in the middle of their pain. Displaying His faithful love and holding out the promise that He would not forget them. Connor had wept through many readings. Sometimes raged. Sometimes yielded.

In the end, clung.

But to have that particular line fall on his heart now? What did it mean? *What are You asking of me?*

"Connor, are you going to eat?" Emma's question jarred Connor out of his prayer.

"Yes." He pushed his shoulder off the doorframe and summoned a smile. "Of course I'm gonna eat, Emma. It smells delicious."

Emma rewarded him with her motherly smile and held out a full plate for him.

Connor took it with a sincere "Thank you" and sat on one of the barstools next to Jade.

Mr. Appleton, who had already been sitting with his plate in front of him, nodded. "Shall we give thanks?"

Connor peeked at Jade.

She smiled at their boss. "Yes, sir."

Appleton winked at her, then bowed his head. The old man's prayers were always reverent. They always, always began with an offering of praise, usually patterned from a psalm.

"Great God in heaven! How wonderful are Your works! Your ways are perfect, and my soul knows this very well. We thank You for the food Emma so faithfully provides. Thank You for her skills, and thank You for the gift of taste that we can enjoy this meal. Make us ever aware, our King and Lord, of the generous gifts You give. Help us to acknowledge that You are God and all good things come from Your generous hand. Help us to know that You see our hearts—the good and the bad. The joy and the brokenness. By Your gentle enabling, may we surrender to Your will knowing Your ways are good, Your heart is kind, and Your love is faithful. Amen."

Connor felt the answer to his question breathe into his heart as Mr. Appleton ended the prayer.

My ways are good. My heart is kind. My love is faithful.
Surrender.

Fear wanted to thrash against that. But Connor reached for obedience instead. An obedience that was born of faith. Because, though the road he had walked thus far had been painful, Connor knew one thing even in the heartache: God had been faithful to him. To Sadie. To Reid. God would be faithful still.

That didn't mean, however, that Connor understood what God would ask of him concerning Jade Beck. Other than to be kind. To be a better neighbor. Perhaps a friend.

That didn't seem so intimidating, actually. After all, she'd certainly been through some hard things. And he knew, as a single father, the struggle of that solo position. He could be her friend.

Perhaps that was all God had been asking from him this whole time.

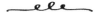

Connor leaned over the small round table in their cabin, one palm pressed onto the surface and the other hand on Reid's shoulder.

"Man, I don't know, Reid. You would think that I would be able to remember seventh grade math, but . . ."

Talk about pressing humility into a man. Sheesh. He'd worked for his dad every summer since he'd been younger than Reid, measuring, cutting—you know, doing math. He'd tested high on all his high school exams, and he had done well with the testing for the military. But with all of that, could he help his son with his prealgebra assignment?

Nope. Apparently not.

Reid tapped his pencil against his book and sighed. "I really should remember this. We went over it last week, and this is actually still review from last year."

Squeezing Reid's shoulder, Connor pulled a chair closer. "Don't be too hard on yourself, buddy. Sometimes we just get a brain block." He reached to the other side of the table for his cell. "I could call Grandpa. He'd likely know. Or your uncle Tyler. Either one would be able to sweep you right through this, I'll bet." Connor's dad and his brother Tyler used math every day in their construction business.

Reid shook his head. "I'd rather have someone who was here, who could *show* me."

"FaceTime?" Connor waved the phone again.

Reid shrugged.

"Okay, buddy. I could look up some online tutorials. Or we could look for another solution. Maybe you could call a classmate? What do you want to do?"

Tapping his eraser against the page, Reid studied the problem all over again. Likely, because he wanted to figure it out. He really wasn't one to ask for help. Sometimes that was admirable. Others . . . well, it might be pride. Which wasn't always a good thing.

For some reason the thought of pride not being a good thing shifted Connor's mind to his neighbor. That thought moved him to her daughter.

"Lily," Connor said.

"What?"

"I'll bet Lily might be able to help you. She's a junior and seems bright. She might know this material."

"I don't know, Dad." Reid dropped the pencil. "She might think I'm stupid."

"Buddy, you're in advanced math. That doesn't say stupid, pal."

Reid pressed his lips closed.

"You even told me Lily seemed nice. Remember?"

"Yeah, but . . ."

Connor watched while Reid turned his face from view. There might have been some color washing those cheeks. Was this a crush they were dealing with here? Lily Beck was a flat out adorable young lady. Dark hair, usually pulled back in a neat ponytail. Ready smile. Big brown eyes, very much like her pretty mother's. Yep. Could definitely have some crushing going on here.

Connor looked away, tucking a grin behind his shoulder. And then he saw himself over the past few weeks, sneaking glances at Jade from a distance. Wondering entirely too much about the woman.

That was not a result of a crush. Grown men didn't have crushes.

Unwilling to step into that argument with himself, Connor opted to let his suspicions alone regarding his son and the new neighbor girl. Even so, the solution of Lily helping was too convenient to let go.

"She's just right next door, buddy. And there's no shame asking for help."

Reid didn't look at his dad, but his face flushed deeper.

Connor cupped the back of Reid's head and then mussed his hair. "Come on. I'll go with you. She can think I'm the dumb one, because

I'm the grown-up and I can't help you." He stood and replaced the chair he'd been sitting on to its proper position. Then he shook Reid's slumping shoulders. "Off we go, buddy. Once this is done, I'll shoot hoops with you, okay?"

Reid eyed him, and then a grin peeked from his face. Used to be, Connor could get Reid to do just about anything with the promise of building Legos with him. The past couple of years, that ploy had shifted to playing catch or shooting basketball. But that had worked less and less of late. More and more, Reid would say "No thanks" and withdraw even more. Sometimes that shot panic through Connor.

He was glad that for at least that night, Reid neither withdrew nor panicked.

At least, that had been his thought right up until they reached the Becks' door. As Connor raised his fist to knock, he felt heat racing through his veins.

So dumb.

He determined to ignore the physical reaction, particularly since there wasn't a good reason for it, and gave that pine door three solid whacks.

Jade answered, and all the sudden that flood of heat that had zipped around his limbs made an expressway path straight to his face. Blast it.

The delicate arch of her brows peaked as she met Connor's stare, and then those brown eyes softened. Smiled. And Connor's middle might have turned a little mushy.

No. It did not.

"Mr. Murphy."

He straightened and let her formality cool the stupid warmth in his veins. "Hi Mrs.—uh, Jade. Good evening. How are you?" He felt Reid's attention wander up to him and wanted to give himself a good facepalm.

A dimple appeared at one corner of her mouth as Jade smiled. "We're good. Thank you. Can I help you?"

"Well, we were hoping so." He glanced at Reid, who was looking at him like he'd tripped in front of all his friends. Wow. He was doing stellar at this. "I mean, we were hoping Lily could help us. Reid is working on some homework—he's in advanced math—and I don't remember how to do the equations. I was hoping your daughter could maybe bail me out?"

"Equations!" A happy squeal leaked from the kitchen. "I *love* equations! Let me see it, Reid." Lily appeared at her mother's side, all bright and cheerful, which Connor had come to think of as typical for her.

"Yeah?" Reid said.

Connor glanced down. *Like father, like son*, he thought, noting the color on Reid's face.

Nope. That would only be true if there was a crush involved here. There wasn't. Not on Connor's part, anyway. Besides, Connor was a grown man in his thirties. He could stand in the presence of an attractive woman and not blush.

Jade stepped back. "Come on in."

Apparently that last silent claim of his was not true. Either that, or Jade Beck kept her home at an unusually high temperature.

Facepalm, facepalm, facepalm.

Connor turned his attention to the kids.

Lily led the way across the cabin, which mirrored the same floor plan as his and Reid's. Once to the kitchen, she pushed aside an open chemistry book and a notebook as she patted the table next to her spot. "Let's see, Reid."

With a breath big enough to move Reid's shoulders, he lowered onto the chair. He opened his math book and pointed to the problem being a problem. "This one. I keep solving it, but when I check it on Canvas, it's wrong."

"Mmm." Lily looked over Reid's shoulder. "Okay. Show me how you solve it."

Nodding, Reid slid off his knee and sat on the chair correctly. "Three plus six times five plus four, divided by three minus seven . . ." His pencil scratched on the paper for a few moments, then he looked up. "See. This is what I keep getting. But the solution bank says it's wrong."

"I see what happened." Lily smiled. "Can I show you?"

"Yeah. Please."

"You just forgot PEMDAS." Lily used the tip of the pencil to point to a section of the problem. "You have parenthesis around the five plus four, so you needed to start there first."

"Oh!" Reid actually did facepalm himself. "Aw, man. That was so dumb."

Lily chuckled. "Nah. It's still the beginning of the year. And lots of people don't even know what PEMDAS even means, let alone how to use it." She gave him back the pencil. "Now solve, and we'll make sure it's correct."

With renewed energy, Reid worked the equation and had a new answer within a minute. "That's right. I remember from Canvas that this is right."

"Nice." Lily leaned back. "Anything else?"

Reid glanced through his assignment. "I don't think so. I've only got eight problems left."

"Well, why don't you just work them here? I have to finish my chemistry." She gestured to the book she'd moved out of the way. "So I'll work on that, and you can finish your math. That way if you have any more questions, I can help."

"You sure?"

"Definitely." Lily grinned first at Reid and then to Connor.

"Thank you, Lily." Connor pushed his hands into his pockets. "Apparently I've become useless when it comes to math."

"I feel the same way." Jade had moved to the kitchen, where she scooped cookie dough onto baking sheets. "Jade outgrew my math skills when she was about Reid's age. Honestly, I don't remember ever even learning PEMDOS."

"PEMDAS. Mom. It's an *A* at the end, for addition."

Jade's complexion shaded to a warm pink. "There you go, Mr. Murphy." She winked. "You're not alone."

Welcomed by her friendliness, Connor edged his way toward the counter where she worked. "What is happening over here?"

"I promised Kellen chocolate chip cookies if he kept his room clean all week."

"Good idea."

"Uh, my mother would call it bribery. I'm not above it, apparently."

Connor chuckled and then looked around the room. "Where is Kellen?"

"He went for a walk. I told him to stick to the road." Jade lifted an alarmed look toward Connor. "That's safe, right?"

"He'll be fine, I'm sure. Reid wanders all over on his own."

Jade nodded. "It's hard to know what freedoms are okay in a new place, you know? I did tell him to be back by seven thirty, so he should be showing up any minute now."

Connor nodded, and then his ability to have a conversation came to an abrupt halt. Squeezing his elbows against his ribs, he rocked back, looked around the room again, and then moved back toward the kids.

Man. Since when was he an awkward kind of guy? Had he been this way before Sadie? He thought back, trying to recall his single self in his early twenties. Military trained, purposeful, generally quiet. But not really awkward.

Might have something to do with the fact that unless it had been work related, he had avoided females. Washed in more guilt than he could navigate, the young man Connor had been back then had been terrified that he'd screw up someone else's life if he tiptoed into romantic relationships. So he'd avoided them.

Connor glanced back at Jade, who slid a cookie sheet into the oven. *Romantic relationship?* He shook his head. Be her friend. That was what Connor had discerned from God.

He wasn't sure how to be that either.

How could it be that hard? Connor interacted with his sisters-in-law all the time. No big deal.

They aren't single moms living next door.

Ugh. Connor wanted to bounce his head against a wall a few times. Hadn't this chaotic thought pattern died away at lunch? He should go back home—wasn't really needed anyway.

"Reid, I'm going to head back over and make sure the woodpile is covered. There's rain in the forecast tomorrow, so . . ."

Reid barely glanced up. "Okay." Then he finished solving what he was working on and looked up. "But you're still going to shoot with me tonight, right?"

"Of course. Just come find me when you're done here."

"Shoot?" Lily glanced between the two Murphys, her expression pure expectation. "Like basketball?"

"Yeah. Do you play?" Reid asked.

"I love basketball! I've been dying to shoot out there, but the ball I brought got a hole in the move, and we haven't gone to a store to replace it yet."

"We have like five balls," Reid said. "Just use one of those. Whenever."

"Yeah? That'd be so great." She looked at Connor to make sure that was okay.

Connor smiled. "Anytime, Lily. They're in the storage shed down by the hoop. Help yourself."

Lily flashed a grateful grin and then returned to her studies. Reid was neck deep in his equations. Jade was making the entire cabin smell intoxicating with those cookies. And Connor . . .

Connor wasn't needed.

Ignoring a gut-deep pull that wanted him to stay, he made his way back to the front door.

"You're welcome to stay, Mr. Murphy."

He looked back at Jade. She stood facing him in the kitchen, hands pressed on the counter, and met his eyes. There was a beat, a moment, their gazes held, and Connor's breath caught.

"Thanks. I'm going to go get that wood covered though."

She nodded and turned back to her cookies. Connor left quietly and unsettled all over again.

CHAPTER EIGHT

(in which Jade wonders what God is thinking)

It was her. Had to be. *She* made him terribly uncomfortable, and she had no idea why.

Jade dried the mixing bowl and put it away in the cupboard, then moved to the window. From that spot, she could see the three of them out there playing basketball—Reid, Lily, and Mr. Murphy. The echoes of the ball bouncing, the rim taking impact, as well as shouts and laughter reached her even from this spot on the hill, inside her cabin. There was an easiness between them as they played, and it triggered a sense of isolation within Jade's heart.

Connor Murphy had no problem interacting with Emma or with Mr. Appleton. Perhaps that was because he knew them? He'd grown comfortable with them. But just that evening, she'd watched him converse with Lily. No troubles. None whatsoever. He was kind, easygoing, didn't stumble over his words—of which he had more than one or two for Lily. And now he was down there being fun and natural—the opposite of brooding and taciturn.

So then, it was Jade.

Was it because she was divorced? Perhaps he looked down on her for not sticking out her marriage and that was why his expression was often dark and closed when he glanced her way—if he bothered to look at her at all. The idea simmered anger in her gut. Connor Murphy had no idea what her marriage had been like, and if all indicators were accurate about what his marriage had been like before his wife died, he had no way of knowing the depth of betrayal and humiliation that had come with Peter's unrepentant affair.

She pressed her hot forehead against the cool glass pane. "Oh, Jade, why does it matter so much to you?"

It was a longing for attention, for approval. That had to be it. At least part of it. The very thing that had snared her to Peter in the beginning. The same insipid flaw that had her trying desperately to make him happy all the years of their marriage. It wasn't simply because she *wanted* Peter to be happy. Or that she *wanted* him to love her.

She *needed* him to, on both counts. Otherwise, what was she worth?

A heaviness pressed in her chest, and Jade shut her eyes as moisture rimmed the lids. "Oh, God, what is this brokenness in me? Why do I feel hollow and worthless without people's approval?"

It was the first time she'd ever really asked that question. Perhaps the first time she realized it was a question that needed asked.

Jade let the honesty hang between her and God as quiet stole through the house. No answers. But . . . but she didn't have the dreadful sense of being ignored either. It was like a silent *wait* held in that space. And though that didn't make sense, it was also enough.

To be heard—that was enough right now.

Sniffing, Jade opened her eyes and brushed away the gathered pools of tears. As she blew out a cleansing breath, Kellen came into view from around the corner of the lodge. Her son smiled, as if he were back to a pleasant nine-year-old, but while Jade wanted to grasp on to that and rejoice, her heart sank.

Kellen was carrying a dog. A squirming, yelping dog that looked as straggly as it did untrained.

"Oh, Lord, what are You sending me now?" she sighed. "There's only so much a girl can take. You know?"

She crossed from the window to the exit, snatching her hooded sweatshirt as she opened the door. "I can't take a dog. I'm sorry, God, but I can't do it." Pulling the door shut behind her, she crossed the deck and clomped down the stairs.

By the time she reached Kellen and his find, her son was surrounded by the other three. Kellen lowered the animal to the ground, and Lily and Reid showered the stray with attention. Mr. Murphy stood there, and at her approach, he shifted only his eyes to look at her.

She couldn't read his severe gaze. He didn't scowl, exactly, but he wasn't smiling either. Which made two of them.

"Mom!" Kellen beamed, and Jade's heart pinched. "Look what I found! It's a puppy, Mom. A *puppy!* Remember how I've always wanted a dog? Look!"

Jade bit her lip until she came upon the group. "I'm not sure that's a puppy, Kellen."

"I think she is," Mr. Murphy said, brows arched. "She's a large breed, or a mix probably. I would guess six to eight months old."

"A large breed?" Jade looked back to him, silently pleading for his help to get her out of this.

Mr. Murphy's look hadn't changed. He nodded and pointed at the dog. "Her paws are huge, and mountain dogs tend to be on the large size."

"Well." Jade searched her personal bank of expressions for a smile. Whatever she found was likely not one. "She's, uh, cute, Kellen. And I'm sure she's glad you found her. But I'm also sure she belongs to someone."

"She doesn't have a collar, Mom." Kellen's tone lost much of its joy and shifted rapidly toward argumentative.

Lord, a little help here?

"Puppies don't just show up, buddy."

"This one did. It can happen." With a wild, desperate look on his face, Kellen whipped his attention to Mr. Murphy. "Right?"

The man swallowed visibly. Then he ran a hand over his beard and glanced at Jade. Still unreadable.

He shifted his attention back to the kids. "How about the three of you take her to the firepit behind the house. Reid, I think there's some leftover stew in the refrigerator. You can give her some of that, but don't take her in the house."

"She's *my* dog," Kellen said fiercely. "Reid can't have her. I found her, so she's mine!"

"Kellen, she's not any of our dog." Panic swirled through her body. The last thing she needed on top of a stray dog was her son going into full-on rage in front of Connor yet again. "I'm sure someone is out there looking for their lost puppy right now."

"Fine. But if no one claims her, then she's mine." He turned a glare toward Reid. "She's not his!"

"It's okay, Kellen," Reid said quietly. "I know she's yours. We can just give her some of our stew, okay? I'll bet she's hungry."

Kellen glowered at Reid for what seemed like a solid minute. Then, thankfully, he pinned his lips shut and nodded.

Lily laid a hand on her brother's shoulder. "Come on. You carry her to the firepit, and Reid and I will get her something to eat. All right?"

Again, a nod. But he still looked loaded for an explosion.

God, what am I supposed to do?

As the kids walked away in a group, Jade's heart hammered. *It'll be okay. Whoever lost her will come looking for her. Maybe even yet tonight—*

"Jade."

Connor's low voice startled her out of her thoughts. When she looked at him, she found his brows furrowed low and something dark in his eyes. Disapproval?

She *hated* disapproval. And dang it, why should he disapprove of her? She was the one stuck here! And he all but indicated that the mutt was going to stay, with his *go take the puppy up to the house and feed it* business! Anger split wide open in her middle, and Jade rolled her fists.

"Well, that was just great of you," she seethed, turning to face him.

"Excuse me?"

"Now he thinks we'll keep it. Once that dog's owner comes, I'll have an angry, heartbroken little boy."

"Jade." He slid a step nearer, those brows somehow lowering. "I didn't tell him he could keep it. But—"

"But nothing, Connor Murphy. To you it might all be . . . puppies and sunshine . . . but I'm barely holding my life together right now! Do you really think, after losing my marriage of fifteen years, moving my kids halfway across the country, starting a new job—one that, frankly, I wasn't very welcomed to—that I can handle adding a *puppy* to my insane life?"

His gaze widened as he watched her silently.

As soon as her tirade settled in her ears, Jade was mortified. "Oh good grief." She covered her face with both hands and stepped back. "I'm sorry."

For a moment they were statues. Frozen in this terrible humiliation created by her own lack of self-control. *God, I am absolutely losing it here! How far are You going to push?*

Then he moved. She thought to step around her, to leave her in the silent chill of his obvious contempt. When a pair of large, gentle hands warmed her shoulders, she gasped and jerked her hands away from her face.

"I'm sorry." He stepped back and dropped his hands. "I'm sorry for all of that—and that I didn't make this difficult move any easier at the beginning. And no, for the record, I don't think a puppy is a good idea for you right now. Though it might be for Kellen—but that's not my business. I only was going to tell you just now that the dog is likely a dump."

"A . . . a what?"

"A dump. She's not a purebred. She looks like a mix of Saint Bernard and Leonberger, with those webbed paws, and by the curved tail, maybe some Appenzeller. Most people who go to breeders want purebreds. Sometimes there's an accidental litter. The breeders will sell them cheap, but by her age, she would have likely been overlooked by a buyer—because she looks almost full grown. There's a spot not too far from here that is known as a dump site."

"A dump site . . . for unwanted puppies?"

He nodded solemnly. "Sadly, yeah."

"What happens to the puppies?"

"If they survive being abandoned and aren't hit by a car, they usually end up at the humane society."

Jade sighed, pressing her fingers to her temples. "That's kind of awful." More than kind of. She knew keenly what it was like to be unwanted. Rejected.

Dumped.

It was awful.

Don't cry in front of this man! She blinked against tears.

Connor nodded again. "I can help you, if you want me to."

"With the dog?"

"I can call the humane society and deliver her tom—"

"Oh." The word was a breath that escaped from her ragged heart.

"Unless . . ." He studied her, as if desperate to understand what she was thinking. As if he truly wanted to help her. Suddenly she knew what that dark expression in his gaze had been. It hadn't been darkness at all, and certainly not disapproval.

It'd been compassion. Was that so unfamiliar to her that she couldn't recognize it for what it was?

"Unless you don't want that."

"I—" She couldn't keep a dog. Everything she'd just flung at him was true, even if she had no business flinging things in anger at him at all. A fresh blush washed over her face and chest. Jade swallowed.

"If you wanted to keep her—"

"I've never had a dog. I don't know anything about owning one."

His steady gaze didn't waver. "I had a few growing up."

Jade watched him, terrified of the hope that was trying to surface in her heart. Would he—

Connor moved forward. "I could help you—help Kellen—with the dog. If you wanted to keep her."

"You . . . you think it would be good for Kellen?"

His gaze redirected toward their cabins. "I don't know, I guess. But dogs can be therapeutic. And diving into the responsibility for another life can be powerful."

Blowing out a breath, Jade let her eyes slip shut. "I don't . . ." On impulse she looked back at him. "Do you ever wonder what God is thinking, Mr. Murphy?"

The full force of his gaze landed on her again. Definitely compassion there. And she found an understanding that she'd not felt from anyone in that long look.

"I have," he said, soul-deep honesty in his low voice. "I still do, I think, more than I want to admit."

"Do you think that makes God mad, that we question what He does?"

A sheen glazed over his green gaze. Connor shook his head, and Jade felt the brush of his fingers at her elbow. "I think God would rather hear my questions, even if I'm shouting them, than have me retreat into an angry silence."

His light touch fell away, and he stepped up the hill.

Jade spun around. "Connor Murphy."

He looked over his shoulder at her. "Yeah?"

"I'm sorry."

"You don't need to be."

"No, I mean—" Heat saturated her face. Why was she going there? The direction of her thoughts had nothing to do with anything at present. Jade wasn't sure why, but the compulsion to do so pushed her on. "I'm sorry that you lost your wife."

The slightest movement of his mouth, and then a tiny dip of his head was all the acknowledgment he offered. And then he continued on his way.

Jade stared after him, more curious than ever about who exactly Connor Murphy was.

Connor shuffled his feet toward Reid, following Lily's pass. The two of them had been working well together, consequently giving Connor a run for his money. Not sure what he'd been thinking, agreeing to a Tuesday evening two-on-one pickup game. He'd known that Reid was getting better and better, both in shooting and with ball handling, but clearly Connor had underestimated Lily and her ball skills.

Or, he was just getting old.

Nope. Not that. Lily and Reid were both good players, end of story.

"Take it up, Reid!"

Catching the ball three feet from the hoop, Reid jump-stopped, faked up, and—while Connor was helpless in the air—took an easy drop step and laid the ball in. Perfectly executed inside move.

"Nice, kid." Connor grinned at Reid, smacking his shoulder. "Where'd you buy your skills?"

"All work." Reid grinned at Connor and then at Lily. "Nice pass. Where does that put us? Seven-five?"

"Eight." Lily held up a high five, and Reid smacked her palm. "Eight-five." She smiled wide while her brows bounced. "Taking on the big guy . . ."

"Killing him," Connor huffed, bending over to catch his breath. "You're killing this big guy. I am definitely not twenty anymore."

The Becks' Explorer turned into the lodge's parking lot and then crawled up the drive to the cabins. Lily tucked the basketball against her hip and watched while her mom parked. "Wonder how the vet thing went."

Connor straightened, wondering the same thing. He wasn't sure what he should hope for—that the vet had heard of an owner missing their mountain mutt or that Kellen would get to keep the soon-to-be massive dog.

Secretly, he was rooting for Kellen. The boy really wanted that dog, and what Connor had said to Jade three days before had been the truth. Taking care of another life could be profoundly life changing. It could be exactly what Kellen needed to bring him out of this self-centered funk.

Maybe.

It could be a nightmare for Jade though.

With a bark and then a shout, dog and boy tumbled from the passenger side of the car. "She's mine! Rex is all mine!"

Lily and Reid exchanged a look. "Oh boy," Lily exhaled. Then as Connor had come to expect of the girl, Lily fixed a smile and waved at Kellen. "That's great, Kel! We always wanted a dog."

Kellen scowled. "She's. Mine."

Lily stepped back, glancing at her mother. Now standing at the back of the vehicle, Jade shut her eyes and shook her head. "No, Kellen. She's the Beck family dog. And she's a naughty one at that. This is a trial basis. We can't keep her if you don't teach her to be respectful."

"I know, Mom," Kellen grumbled. The dog—Rex?—strained against the thin leash, tugging Kellen toward the cabin. Likely, toward food.

"That leash is a bit small for such a big dog." Connor stepped around Lily and Reid and moved toward Jade, Kellen, and the now-barking animal. "If you take her by the collar, you might have more control at the beginning. Here, I'll sho—"

Kellen hid the leash behind his back and held out a stiff arm toward Connor. "*You're* not my dad, and I *don't* need your help."

Misery etched on Jade's face. "Kellen. Mr. Murphy has had dogs before. I asked him to—"

"I don't care. I'm not listening to your stupid new *boyfriend*."

Connor froze, mouth gaping.

"Kellen!" Bright pink stained Jade's cheeks, the shade darkening toward crimson with every breath.

Dragging the dog, Kellen stormed past Connor, down the driveway, and past the lodge. Connor watched him turn onto the road and then slowly turned back to look at Jade. If Connor could read her thoughts, which he thought in that moment he might be able to, she was begging the gravel beneath her feet to become quicksand and take her down.

Horrified, she stared at him, and then her hands covered her cherry-red face. "Oh my gosh . . ."

"Jade." Connor edged nearer, his voice a low whisper.

"I'm mortified." Her hair brushed her shoulders as she shook her head. "Please, just kill me now."

"It's fine. It's my fault." He stopped two feet away and reached to brush her elbow. "I shouldn't have interfered. I just wanted to help."

Jade groaned, still hiding her face. "I know." She blew out a gusty breath and then forced herself to look at him. "I know. It's just Kellen. I'm sorry."

Connor held her gaze, and then he chuckled. This was . . . so dumb. She shouldn't be mortified. He shouldn't be embarrassed. Kellen was simply an angry kid taking out his confusion and frustration on whoever was convenient. If Connor had been in the same situation as a nine-year-old kid, he might have acted the same way.

So. He'd laugh it off. Maybe Jade would be able to as well. With a shrug, he stepped back.

"Mom," Lily called from the court. "Come round out the numbers."

Connor glanced back to Reid and Lily. Both kids looked mildly uncomfortable and yet determined to move past it. He looked at Jade again. "You play?"

"Used to," Jade squeaked, clearly not quite past the humiliation.

"Oh come on, Mom. Tell the truth." Lily marched up the hill and sent a solid pass toward her mother. One which Jade caught, no problem. Lily's eyes lit proudly. "She's good, Mr. Murphy. Taught me everything I know."

"Really?" Connor said.

Jade shrugged. "No. Not really. Lily is very talented—far more than I ever was."

"But you play?" Connor pressed.

"Yeah."

He stepped back, sweeping his arm toward the court down the drive. "Then let's go."

A ghost of a smile cracked through her expression as Jade tossed the ball back to Lily.

"Let's go!" Reid echoed Connor's words. "Me and you, Ms. Jade. We can take the old guy and this girly girl."

Jogging back to the court, Lily shoved the ball into Reid's gut, causing him to double over with an "oafff!"

"Girly girl," she grumbled. "I'll show you girly girl. Let's go, Big Murphy. It's time for Li'l Murphy to get schooled."

The game was on. And Lily hadn't been exaggerating—Jade had game. The score stayed tight. And man, for a woman who seemed shy, Jade had no problem whatsoever playing a physical game. She could box out like no one's business. Connor and Lily made it to ten first, but not without a whole lot of work and sweat. High fives were slapped all the way around, and every one of them was huffing for breath when it was all said and done. Reid and Lily recovered within minutes, and since they had the young legs of the group, Jade sent them up to the cabin for water.

Connor sat on the cold ground, leaning against the storage shed. Sweat soaked his hairline and pooled beneath his beard. Jade remained standing, arching backward, head tipped toward the sky.

"You were being modest," Connor said.

A wide smile broke on her face, though she remained in the skyward-facing pose for another few beats. Finally, she aimed that joyous grin toward him. "It's been a long time."

Man. She was beautiful. Eyes bright with fun, smile full. Connor's heart slid sideways, and he was thankful he was sitting.

Jade's grin faded, making Connor suddenly aware that he was staring. He ran a hand over his damp face.

"Connor." Her voice had dropped to a low tone.

Not trusting his thoughts about how lovely this woman was, or how much he wanted to see her smile like she just had, Connor peeked up at her for one moment, then shifted his attention toward the lodge.

"I'm sorry about my son. He's . . . the things that happened between me and his dad . . . he doesn't understand. All he knows is that his world had been turned inside out."

"I get it." Connor met her eyes again. In them, ache replaced what had been laughter. Sadness plunged through his chest.

She bit her lip, her posture sagging.

Unable to help himself, Connor stood and stepped nearer. "How can I help?"

Emotion wobbled on her face, and then she shook her head. "It's not your problem." Swallowing, Jade squared her shoulders and put on a mask of determined courage. "Don't worry about us, Connor. We'll figure it out. We *are* figuring it out. It just takes time."

He wanted to argue, but instead he edged backward. Connor then moved to pick up the ball that had been left under the hoop. Reid and Lily burst from the Becks' cabin and jogged down the drive, bottles of cold water in their hands.

Topic closed.

Except it wasn't. Not for Connor. Because he did worry. About Jade. And Lily. And Kellen.

He couldn't help it. He worried about all of them.

CHAPTER NINE

(in which Lily opens up and Jade falls apart)

THEY SETTLED INTO A sort of civil distance. Not because over the following weeks he stopped worrying about Jade and her kids—that seemed impossible. But because he had never been one to know what to do in uncomfortable situations.

Connor had no idea what to say to Jade that wouldn't come off as awkward, so he said not much of anything that didn't have to do with work. He had no idea how to help Kellen without the boy exploding on him, so he kept his distance. The only Beck he felt comfortable spending any amount of time with was Lily.

Lily was easy. Particularly since she loved basketball, and also, she and Reid had formed a friendship.

"Nice shot, Lily." Connor caught the ball after it swished through the net and sent it back to Lily at the free throw line.

"Thanks." She dribbled three times, set her feet, and took another shot.

Drained it. Connor smiled as he passed the ball back to her. "The Trail Blazers are sure gonna be glad to have you on their court this year."

Lily smiled. "I hope so. I'd really like to make varsity."

Up went another free throw, swish went the net. He'd known she was out here every evening working on her shots. Reid was often with her—a fact that had Connor praying double time for his son's tender heart. A crush could be such an innocent thing, and Lily was likely purely ignorant of it. But the last thing Connor wanted for Reid was a broken heart. He'd had enough of that already in his young life.

But that wasn't relevant at the moment, and even if it was, Lily hadn't done anything wrong.

"With your work ethic and these free throws, I'd put my money on you." Connor rebounded the ball and bounce-passed it to her.

Three more times Lily dribbled, set her feet, and nailed another shot. After the third ace, Connor chuckled. "Reid told me you were a baller even before our little game the other day. I guess I didn't really take him seriously."

Another sweet smile lit her face, then was replaced by a rumpled look of mild concern. "Is Reid feeling better yet?"

Such a sweet kid. The contrast between this girl and her younger brother was puzzling. Connor still replayed the humiliating scene from a few days back, and it hadn't escaped his attention that Jade was walking the dog and doing the majority of the puppy work. Which wasn't surprising, but Kellen could stop being such a punk about getting help from Connor, rather than simply shoving all the work onto his mom.

But they were talking about Reid, not Kellen, and Lily certainly didn't need to know Connor's opinion about something that wasn't his business in the first place.

"He's much better today. Just tired. Thanks for asking."

"He and I have been working on free throws."

"Reid mentioned that. Thank you for doing that with him. It's been nice for him to have other kids around."

Lily didn't answer, as she put up another free throw. Unlike the previous nine, this one rolled around the rim and dropped off. Connor lunged to grab the ball. "Nine out of ten is pretty good."

She sighed. "Restart."

"What's the goal?"

"Twenty in a row."

Connor whistled. "Aiming high. I like that."

Lily sent the ball up on a high arc. Perfect swish.

"One." He passed her the ball.

She set herself up and did it again.

"Two."

On they went. She made it to sixteen before the ball chipped the back edge of the rim and bounced out.

"Bummer." And then she set herself up and started over.

Resilience. Likely, Lily learned that by watching her mom. Connor couldn't push away the deep sense of admiration he felt for them both. He reached for a distraction instead.

"Does Kellen ever come out and shoot with you?"

Lily shrugged. "Not lately. He used to." Her shot went right and clipped off the rim. When Connor passed her the ball, she tucked it against her hip rather than resetting herself. "Mr. Murphy?"

"Yeah?" Connor covered half the distance between them.

"Kellen wasn't always the way he is now."

Nodding, Connor just listened.

"He's really mad, and he doesn't know how else to handle it."

"I guessed he was angry. Because of the divorce?"

"Yeah. But it's more than that. He doesn't know all the things, and he blames my mom for the breakup." Lily blinked and looked toward her sneakers. "He thinks Mom just kicked Dad out and then divorced him a year later. He thinks it's all her fault, and he's really mad at her for it."

Connor waited to see if she had more she wanted to say. Then he said, "But that's not what happened."

Connor wanted to take the words back. He didn't need to know what happened. But . . . well, he wanted to know.

Lily shook her head. "No." After a big, courageous breath, she looked up. Tears sheened her eyes. "Dad cheated. He was having an affair, and he had been for a while. And even before that, he wasn't very nice to my mom. He called her stupid and lazy, and . . ." Lily's voice cracked, and she sniffed, shaking her head. "He just wasn't nice."

A fire ignited in his chest, seeming very much like anger. He couldn't imagine ever calling Sadie stupid or lazy, and he'd have left bruises on a man's face for daring to do so. What kind of man would treat his wife that way?

Connor wasn't surprised to hear Jade's ex-husband was a jerk. He'd guessed so that second day while watching Kellen with his mom. Little boys learn these things . . . Even so, the livid response that clenched his chest as Lily confirmed his suspicions took him by surprise.

Had it been worse than what she'd said? How abusive had Jade's marriage been? Had this Beck guy hit his wife?

Before Connor could ask, Lily swallowed and stepped closer. "I knew about him cheating. Before Mom did, I think, and it was awful. I saw my dad with this woman . . . Dad told me she was a friend of his from work, but I knew that wasn't true." She shook her head. "She was the same woman he's dating now. And you know what's worse?"

Heart splitting between hurt for this girl and her mother and building rage at a man Connor had never met, he could only shake his head.

"Macey—the woman—was a friend of my mom's, from *her* work." Lily clamped her jaw, clearly fighting to control her emotions. "Kellen doesn't know any of this. And he doesn't remember that Dad was kind of a jerk to Mom. He thinks that everything is Mom's fault and that Mom is taking us away from Dad."

"That's not true either?" Connor wouldn't blame Jade if it was true. Not if Mr. Beck was an abusive man.

Lily shook her head. "I don't know all the reasons Mom decided to move out here, other than she needed a new job and my grandparents are close, but I know Mom would never try to take us out of Dad's life. Not the way Kellen thinks. She always reminds us to call him. To tell him when we have news or just to say good night or whatever. You know?"

Though Connor puzzled over that, he nodded.

Lily shifted the ball to her other hip. "Mr. Murphy?"

"I'm listening, Lily."

"Sometimes I think I should tell Kellen the truth. So he won't be so ugly to Mom."

Seemed like a good idea. Rubbing his chin, Connor kept his thoughts inside, waiting for Lily to finish.

"The thing is . . ." She drew a shuddering breath. "It really sucks to not like your dad." She blinked hard. "I don't mean like most kids when they say they don't like their parents because they make them do homework or whatever. I mean . . . I mean I really, *really* don't like my dad. I think he's a bad person, and that really, really sucks." A single tear rolled down the side of her face. She swiped it and looked up at him, her look begging him for answers. "I don't want that for Kellen. I mean, he's mad at Mom, but he doesn't think of her the way I think of my dad. And I don't want Kellen to know what that's like."

She was wrecking him. *Kids shouldn't have to deal with this garbage!*

Men were supposed to love their wives. Dads were supposed to be people worthy of respect. Kids were supposed to be able to go shoot a basketball and not have to wonder how to protect their younger siblings from the ugliness of a parent.

God, what am I supposed to tell this broken, wonderful kid?

Connor held out an arm, and Lily tucked herself in at his side. He squeezed her shoulders and let her go. "Lily, I think you are an extraordinary girl."

Sniffing, she shrugged. "I don't know what to do. That doesn't seem extraordinary."

"You love so big. Your mom and your brother. And even though maybe it doesn't feel like it, you're even showing love to your dad."

"But what about Kellen? He's angry because he doesn't know the truth. But if I tell him, then . . ." She shook her head. "What should I do, Mr. Murphy?"

Connor tucked away the kneejerk reaction to advise her to tell her younger brother all that she knew so that Kellen would stop being such a punk to his mom. Truth was, he didn't know for sure that that was the right thing to do.

Lily had a point. And she was protecting her brother from a heartache that Connor had never experienced and couldn't imagine. His dad had always been one of Connor's heroes. A good man, a faithful man. A man worthy of honor.

What would it be like to *know* your dad was none of those things? To *know* that he was abusive and a liar and a cheater?

That would be a unique kind of awful.

The conversation he'd had with Reid a few weeks before—after they'd witnessed another furious outburst from Kellen—floated through his mind.

Though he shouldn't have said it, Connor had muttered, "Man, that kid . . ."

Reid had stared at Connor for a moment, and a wisdom beyond his twelve years passed through his son's expression. "I think everyone needs a tornado room sometimes."

Yes. Yes, they did.

Connor sighed, meeting Lily's expectant gaze again. "I don't know what to say, Lily. Truth is always a good thing. But I see your dilemma, and I don't think you're wrong. I think, in fact, that it's noble to want to protect your brother from the hard things that you know about." He rubbed his hair. "Can I think about it and pray about it for a while?"

Biting her lip, Lily nodded. "I keep praying about it too."

"Yeah? What do you think God has been telling you?"

She looked toward the lodge, where her mom was finishing up for the evening. "I feel like He's telling me to take care of them both."

She was like Jonathan, caught between Saul and David. Such an incredibly hard place.

Connor wanted to wrap this brave girl up tight and keep her safe. He wanted to sit down and cry for her. At the moment, he could do neither. Instead, he squeezed her shoulder. A meager offering. "You are, Lily. You're doing an amazing job of that."

Another tear escaped the corner of her eye. "I feel like I'm not. Like Kellen wouldn't be so mad if I was doing a better job."

"Nope. You're not responsible for how Kellen behaves—or for how your dad is. You need to know that, in here." He tapped his chest. "I'm telling you the truth, Lily. You are extraordinary, and you are a blessing to your mom and your brother."

She nodded and sniffed. Then she blew out a breath, as if to rid herself of gloom. "God is still with my family, isn't He?"

Man, these were deep waters. Connor stored away the growing need to have a long heart dump before God. It might be ugly. Wouldn't be the first time.

Lily pulled herself upright, and a small smile curved her lips. "I mean, Mom needed a new job, and here we are. We needed a new home"—she gestured toward the cabin—"and there it is. And we needed new friends." She looked up at Connor. "And you and Mr. Appleton and Reid have been great. So—"

Yep, Lily Beck was an extraordinary young lady.

Connor chuckled in amazement. "You know, a few years back, when my wife died, my younger brother Tyler had to remind me to do exactly what you're doing now. To look for God's goodness, particularly when things are difficult and you really don't feel like doing it."

Wide brown eyes looked up at him, the stormy clouds that had been present in her expression clearing away and hope breaking through the tears.

"Don't ever lose that, Lily." He brushed her nose with a knuckle. "Don't lose eyes that look for God's grace in the darkness. It's there. Sometimes we have to search hard for it, but it is always there."

Lily stepped toward him again, and he squeezed her with another side hug.

"Thanks, Mr. Murphy."

"Thank you, Lily the extraordinary." He moved back toward the baseline under the hoop. "Now, twenty?"

With a grin, she nodded. "Twenty."

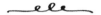

As daylight faded, the sky turning all sorts of oranges and pinks, Jade watched her breath go into the frozen air as puffs of white. This evening, she wasn't out to appreciate the sunset though, and she didn't head toward the dock, as had become her usual practice over the past two months.

She swiped a rogue tear with the back of her glove. Her fast strides took her deeper into the woods, away from the cabin and lodge. Away from the kids and from anyone who could witness her falling apart.

Which she was. Rapidly.

"It's only for a week, Jade. Both of them are bright. They'll catch up on school."

"That isn't the point, Peter," Jade had hissed into the phone. Her heart had hammered, stomach had boiled, and she could not stop the avalanche of her angry thoughts. "The point is they're not ready for this. Kellen isn't ready for this, and for you to ask this of Lily is beyond my understanding."

"Of course I want my kids at my wedding, Jade!" Peter had erupted. "You're being selfish as usual. You can't keep my kids from me."

"You're the one who asked me to move! To take them somewhere so that you and Macey would have a chance to make a clean start. Don't you dare accuse me of keeping them from you!"

"Fine, but I didn't mean across the country, just so we're clear. Now I'm saying I want them to come. Macey wants Lily to stand up with her, and I want Kellen there with me. This isn't that difficult, Jade. Stop making everything all about you for once and just let me have this. Just let me be happy."

Jade's whole body shook as the argument replayed.

Peter was getting married. Fine. Good luck. While the lingering sting of humiliation and rejection remained embedded in her heart, Jade didn't entertain the idea of going back to her marriage. Frankly, now that she had broken free, she saw what had been between Peter and her for what it was: toxic. Perhaps even abusive, though she wasn't quite ready to label it that. Either way, Jade never wanted to live like that again.

Not. Ever.

She wasn't upset about Peter's upcoming marriage, except perhaps to think that Macey had no idea what she was getting into. But Jade wasn't going to address that.

But having the wedding in the middle of the school year and demanding the kids fly across the country *by themselves* and stand up as part of the wedding party? How could Peter be so ignorant? So insensitive?

He never thought of anyone except himself. Not even when it came to his children.

Hands trembling, Jade pressed them to her forehead as her legs buckled beneath her. She landed on a snow-covered log and leaned forward, pressing her elbows to knees as searing pain ripped through her middle.

"Why!" She rocked back and shouted toward the spire of evergreens that pointed heavenward. "Don't you know what this will do to them?"

Energy surged in her veins, and Jade leapt to her feet again, gripping snow in both fists. She flung a tiny snowball toward the scaled bark of a lodgepole and then did it again with the other hand.

No relief.

"How am I supposed to tell my daughter to go be happy for her lying, cheating father?"

Jade knew Lily was aware of more than a girl should be—and that hadn't been Jade's fault. Peter had put their daughter in an awful position, asking her to keep his secrets. He'd also been indiscreet with his insults of her over the years, and Lily hadn't been nearly as oblivious as Peter had assumed.

It was heartbreaking to watch her daughter wrestle with not liking her own father and extremely difficult to encourage Lily to be respectful to her dad when he simply didn't deserve respect at all.

Then, there was her son. Kellen had taken up his father's habit of selfishness. And it seemed no matter what Jade tried, her son had determined that she was evil and he would be like his father. The idea actually made her physically sick. She did not want her baby boy to end up anything like his father.

Jade scooped up another fistful of snow and flung it.

"How am I supposed to raise a decent young man when his father is a lousy human?"

Next to her was a broken branch, and she wielded it like a club against the log she'd sat on.

"How am I supposed to get through to Kellen when he hates me—when he thinks his dad is perfect and everything is my fault?"

She whipped the branch into the air, and it went end over end until it smashed against a rock.

"I can't do this!"

Gripping her head, Jade sank to the ground in a heap and sobbed. "I can't. I can't. I—"

"Jade."

She gasped at the sound of her name—whispered in such a low, tender tone—and jerked her face toward the place from which the voice came. There stood Connor Murphy, brows knitted and with that dark gaze she'd often taken for disapproval. But it wasn't disapproval—she knew that now.

Even so, humiliation crashed over her as she understood he'd witnessed her fit. Her falling apart. Her shouting at God in anger. Covering her head with both hands, she tucked herself into a ball and wept.

A pair of hands warmed her shoulders, the touch tentative at first. And then arms encircled her, the hold initially loose. As her cries became sobs, his hold strengthened.

He said nothing. He simply held her.

And Jade finished falling completely apart in the arms of Connor Murphy.

CHAPTER TEN

(in which there is a time to lament)

HE'D BEEN SENT.

Connor had no other explanation. He never walked back into the forest that way in the evenings. If he didn't land in one of the chairs near the firepit, he was on his front deck or down at the dock. Since the dock had become Jade's place of evening solace, he'd remained at one of the other two. But never out walking the trails that wove up into the hill behind the lodge and cabins. Not during the evening.

After he left the basketball hoop, giving Lily another side hug and telling her to keep up the good work, Connor had gone to the house and checked on Reid. The cough lingered, but Reid said he was feeling better. Well enough to be up and on the couch doing some makeup schoolwork while *Battlebots* played on the TV.

"Homework and television aren't a good mix, buddy." Connor had leaned over the back of the couch to view what Reid was working on.

A purple colored pencil moved between Reid's fingers, and he paused to tip the paper toward Connor so he could see it better. "It's just busywork, Dad. A coloring sheet for the human cell." He shifted it back in front of him and continued shading a part of it purple. "I already know the parts of the cell."

Connor hadn't doubted that. Reid didn't like getting anything below a 96 percent—perfectionism being something that Connor had to address from time to time with his son.

He straightened and mussed Reid's hair. "Have we watched this season already?"

"Yeah." Reid looked up. "I wouldn't move ahead without you."

"Good." Connor smiled, glad Reid was doing better. He nodded toward the TV. "Just this once. Let's not make it a habit."

"'K." Reid went back to the coloring page.

"I'll be back in a little bit."

"Yep."

It'd all been so normal. Connor had grabbed his coat to go back outside, knowing that the air would move from chilly to outright cold this evening. He'd already seen his breath when he'd walked to the house from the basketball court.

He'd assumed that Jade had made her way to the dock—he'd seen her do so nearly every evening over the past two months. Not because he'd watched her . . .

Well.

He had. And had felt compelled to pray for her on more than one occasion. As a commissioned friend might do. Especially as he'd watched her both blossom and struggle over the weeks she and her family had been there. Jade seemed to find new strength—he could see it in her posture, hear it in her voice when she conversed with Appleton and Emma and the guests. He'd heard her laugh more and more often, and the sound of it had a way of tickling a grin to his own lips.

But there were the struggling points that also lingered in his observations. That tirade she'd launched at him the day Kellen had brought Rex home, and her obvious mortification over it. The seeming constant battle her son engaged with her about nearly everything. His homework. The food. Wanting to go back to Kansas. The dog. Truthfully, there were times that Connor struggled to keep his mouth shut because the boy was so unreasonable and terribly disrespectful. Things that wouldn't have been tolerated by Connor's father when he was growing up.

And now, thanks to Lily's confidence in him, Connor knew more of the story. It broke his heart for all of them and made him angry with the man who was responsible for so much chaos and hurt.

That had been what he'd been thinking about as he left the deck and moved toward the firepit. The anger stirring within came with energy, so he wasn't ready to lower onto a chair. Instead, he'd stood, his gaze wandering to the trees that covered the slope.

Go for a walk.

Had he heard that in his head? Now, after the fact, it seemed that the instruction had been there. A silent press into his consciousness to go. And he went.

He'd been sent.

He'd heard Jade's angry cries before he saw her. Snow had flown in loose balls, her hands flinging white streams one direction and then the other. She'd gripped a stick and beat a log. Then collapsed into a broken, crying heap. Connor had no place in that scene.

But he knew it intimately for himself. Had lived it more than once during the wringing of his soul that last year of Sadie's life.

So though it wasn't his place, Connor had softly called her name, and she'd tuned a startled look on him. And then he was undone. She was all brokenness and despair. He couldn't leave her alone in her misery. Didn't want her to stay there cold and shattered.

There were no whys, no reasons. No hesitations and rationales to keep his distance. He'd simply crossed the snowy space that separated them and eased his arms around her. Tucked her in close, pressed against his heart. And she'd wept.

Did she know that she had turned into him, clung to him? Had she realized that he curled around her as if to be her safety and shield?

Hours later, in the quiet of the night, now fully dark and well past sunset, Connor sat where he'd not before—on the chair beside the firepit—and stared at the clear sky above. Diamonds winked white and blue and pink, each star its own version of praise, and Connor wondered how God could know each one by name.

And why, with such great knowledge and power, God would allow the brokenness of everything painful in life to continue.

Do You not see? Have You turned your face away? Connor's honest questions rattled from that raw place in his heart. The spot that still grieved the loss of his wife. And now, it seemed, the same place that had taken in Jade's sorrow and adopted it as his own.

There was a season for everything—including a time to weep. How he had wanted to be past that season and had thought he was. But now . . .

Now he felt it again. Only it wasn't entirely his, and Connor wasn't certain why he'd taken up a burden that he didn't need to.

God, where are You taking me?

Even before his silent inquiry left his heart, Scripture pressed through his thoughts.

Because of the Lord's great love we are not consumed, for his compassions never fail. They are new every morning; great is your faithfulness.

Connor leaned forward, locking his hands together as he bent his head. "What of the nights, Lord? Long, lonely nights full of tears and pain?"

His pain. The great ripping of his heart at losing the woman he'd loved—the very one he had believed, and still did, that God had placed in his life, his heart. That ache didn't throb so much now, but he still remembered how it had. How it had hurt even to breathe.

The Lord is good to those whose hope is in him, to the one who seeks him; it is good to wait quietly for the salvation of the Lord.

And Jade's pain?

"Lord God . . ." Connor breathed. It was too great a thing for such a small woman to carry. And it didn't at all seem fair.

Why were men like Peter Beck even allowed? Men who would demean their wives—even while Christ had called them to *love, as He himself loves His church.*

Why?

Let him sit alone in silence, for the Lord has laid it on him. Let him bury his face in the dust—there may yet be hope.

Hearing at least the partial truth of what Jade's marriage had been had reawaked something in Connor that he'd thought he'd buried with Sadie. The driving need to take Jade in and defend her to the death. And Connor had acted on it that evening, pulling Jade against him. Holding her tight until her tears stopped flowing.

And because of that, normal became anything but. Now Connor had no idea what to do. He'd told God he'd be her friend. In that, there was the implied understanding—at least on Connor's part—that he couldn't offer more than that. There was a line—one that involved his heart—and it would be honored.

It had seemed that God had known it. He would preserve it.

But Connor had been *sent*. That was the only thing that made sense. And the notion was terrifying. Because how could Connor go into that kind of scene and not have it reach straight into his heart, wrecking him as it went?

He wasn't built that way. God knew—Connor *was not* built for indifferent care.

For no one is cast off by the Lord forever. Though he brings grief, he will show compassion, so great is his unfailing love.

As the verse from Lamentations 3 continued to break into his thoughts, Connor could make no sense of it. Or perhaps he was too scared to try. Whatever this was, it was more than Connor had agreed to. More than he could manage.

CHAPTER ELEVEN

(in which stories are shared)

THE SMELLS OF WHITE chocolate and vanilla mingled in the darkness of Jade's kitchen. She stirred the simmering concoction of milk and sugar as the chocolate melted into the rich liquid. But inhaling the delicious aroma brought no pleasure.

She looked over her shoulder toward the window with a view of the backyard. His silhouette remained hunched on the chair. Shoulders rounded like they were weighed by a great burden. Head bent, nose pressed against folded fists.

Guilt and mortification stirred in her chest. And beneath that, longing.

He'd held her while she'd come undone. How he'd known where she was, she had no idea. But suddenly, there he was.

It had been as if . . .

No. That was dumb. God wouldn't send Connor Murphy to be His arms, His provision of refuge. God could do that all on His own. Hadn't Jade's whole life gone sideways because she'd stepped onto the slippery slope of assuming that a man could fill in the place of God?

It was time Jade learned to lean on God Himself, rather than seeking comfort, affirmation, or anything else she so desperately craved, from a man.

She turned back to the sweet concoction, now boiling in the pot. She removed it from the heat and whisked the liquid. She'd made a double batch, a rarity indeed. She seldom even made a single batch—the milk and gourmet chocolate being expensive. But a double batch would allow her kids to enjoy the reheated treat in the morning and give her enough to offer Connor. For some reason, Jade hoped the offering would help her through the conversation ahead.

Though Connor had shown up in the middle of her meltdown unexpected and uninvited, Jade felt deeply she needed to give him an explanation. And hoped, in doing so, that somehow they'd find a new normal that wasn't terribly uncomfortable.

She liked her job. She loved this cabin. With all her heart, she wanted this new life to be happy for her kids and for herself. The past few painful years had taught her that trying to ignore the elephant in the room proved worse than dealing with it. In the end, she would have to address it anyway.

"God, I need You in this," she whispered.

After she poured half the contents of the pot into two steel mugs and capped both, Jade slipped on her coat. Zipped up, gloves applied, she took her warm offering outside and forced herself to face Connor Murphy.

She followed the path around to the back by the light put out by her phone. As she rounded the cabin, she clicked off the artificial light.

"Hey," she murmured as she made the final approach to the firepit.

In the rising moon, nearly full and brilliant white on this night, she could see him lift his head, as if startled, and watch her as she stepped around a rock. Her gut twisted in his typical silence, and Jade fought the urge to pivot on one booted foot and go straight back to where she belonged. Instead, she swallowed, forced her feet to take the final three steps required, and lowered onto the chair next to Connor's.

"Hi." He didn't move, and it seemed the chilled air quivered between them. "I thought all the Becks were tucked in for the night. I mean, your cabin is dark . . ."

Jade thought she heard him swallow, and his voice was tight. Not terribly uncommon for Connor Murphy though.

She reached through the space that separated them, offering him a mug. "White hot chocolate. My specialty."

His glance flicked to her gift, and he hesitated before wordlessly accepting it.

Jade sipped her drink, taking that moment to once again shoot a plea to heaven for courage. "The kids are in bed. I assume Reid is too?" She squeezed both hands around her mug, trying to stop the building trembles that had begun in her core and were shaking their way out.

"Yeah. He's still not one hundred percent, so he headed to bed quite a while ago."

"I'm sorry to hear that."

"He hates missing so much school."

"Lily is like that too." This had been their normal. Stick to the kids, and they could carry a conversation. But that wasn't why she'd forced herself to come out and face him.

Connor nodded, his stare pinned on the empty firepit. Suddenly, his look found her face. "I spent some time with Lily today."

Jade held her breath, sensing more to come. She forced herself not to duck from his gaze.

"She shared some things with me . . ."

Oh dear. A flood of heat took over her face, and she was thankful for the cover of night. "Do I dare ask what?" she squeaked.

Connor sat back, rubbing his neck. "That your ex-husband cheated on you—and she knew about the affair before you did."

Could this day get any more humiliating? Jade shut her eyes as she hung her head.

"She also said that he wasn't very nice to you, even before that."

She swallowed. If she'd been stripped naked and made to walk the dock, she wasn't sure she would be any more mortified. "I'm . . . I'm sorry Lily put that on you, Mist—"

His hand warmed her arm, the pressure of his fingers gentle but firm. "I didn't tell you so that you would feel bad, and I'm not sorry that Lily talked to me. She wanted to know what to do."

"To do?"

"She says that Kellen doesn't know the truth about what happened and that he's angry with you for the divorce. Lily doesn't know what to do, because she doesn't want you to have to deal with any more than you already have, and she knows Kellen's anger isn't right."

Jade's head spun, and she pressed it into one hand. Lily hadn't brought up any of this with her. Poor sweet girl—she carried so much.

"Jade." Connor's grip on her arm tightened, though it remained unthreatening. "Did your ex-husband hurt you? Was he . . ."

"No." She blinked against the hot sting of tears. "Peter wasn't abusive." She felt Connor's steady gaze remain on her, and she forced herself to look back at him.

He shook his head. "Abuse isn't always physical, Jade."

"No." Her voice wavered. "No, it isn't. And Lily was telling you the truth. Peter wasn't a kind man."

Connor eased back into his chair, his touch falling away. He continued to study her even as he pulled back.

This was as good of an entry as any, she supposed. If Connor knew this much about her failed marriage, she might as well tell him what had happened today. She sipped her hot cocoa, drew in a long breath, and began. "Peter called today. He's getting remarried the beginning of November."

Connor nodded. In the darkness, she couldn't read his expression—though even with the aid of light, she doubted she would be able to. And his silence? What was he thinking?

Defensiveness rose up fast. "I'm not upset about him getting remarried," she said in a rush. "Not like you might think. I'm not sure Macey, his fiancée, knows what she's getting into, but to be honest, at this point, that's not my concern. We all make choices . . ."

"But it brought up all the hurt and anger from before?" Connor tried to fill in the gap.

"Some. Maybe. But that's really not why you found me . . . the way you found me." She searched his face in the moonlight, desperately wanting him to understand. To know her heart—though she had no explanation for that desire. Maybe it was just the human need to have at least one sympathetic soul. Someone who would see the weight of her burden and say, *It's so much—let me help.*

There she was again, putting on a man what she should be surrendering to God.

Lord, help me in this.

In the wake of that silent plea, a calm settled in her heart. One that seemed to tell her that *He* was right there. Listening. Caring. And perhaps even providing help right then. In the form of a friend.

Jade looked at Connor again, and that peace expanded. His silence suddenly felt patient and welcoming rather than stiff and condemning.

"Peter wants the kids to fly back for the wedding. He says Macey wants Lily to stand up with her as her maid of honor and that he wants Kellen to stand beside him. He seems oblivious to how that might make the kids feel. Particularly, how Lily might feel about it. When I tried to explain that it might not be the best thing for the kids right now—not only because of how they'll take his new marriage, but also that missing school for a week so close to a holiday is really stressful for them—Peter got mad and called me selfish, and it all went downhill from there."

Jade ended her story on a sigh. "I just lost it, you know? Like I keep trying to keep it all together for Lily and Kellen—and I work really hard to keep my hurt and anger out of their relationship with their dad. But as you already know, Lily knows way more than she should, and it's pretty hard for her. I wish she didn't know—it'd almost be better for her to be mad at me like Kellen is than for—" Jade cut that short and swallowed back emotion. "She always tries to stay upbeat. She's such a people pleaser, and she wants everyone to be happy and comfortable. But the truth is . . ." Jade stopped short again. She didn't want to betray Lily, even if Lily had confided in Connor. She wasn't sure how much more Lily had shared with Connor.

"The truth is that Lily doesn't like her dad," Connor said.

It was both awful and relieving to have it said out loud. "No. She doesn't." Such an unfair and difficult spot for a sixteen-year-old girl to be in. Jade hated that her daughter had been forced there. "She works so hard to stay respectful to him. And I want my kids to behave honorably to their father. But how am I supposed to keep pushing for that when he isn't an honorable man?"

A low grumble came from the man next to her. "That's a tough place."

Feeling more comfortable as Connor simply listened, Jade continued. "And Kellen? One of these days he's going to see who his dad really is. Then what? He's already so angry with me that I don't even recognize my little boy in the kid he is now. What's going to happen when his dad disappoints him too? Am I going to lose him forever?"

After she finished spilling everything, Connor let a quiet space settle between them. In it, Jade sensed a releasing, as well as that presence she'd felt before. Like she'd been heard and her worries valued—and not just by Connor Murphy.

From the far side of the bay, a coyote called into the crystalline air. A beat passed, and then a chorus of yelps answered back. Alone, Jade would have frozen in fear. But there beside Connor, all was safe. The truth of it reached deep inside her. It was such a powerful moment. Her emotions welled up strong, and a handful of tears slipped down the side of her nose. Jade swiped them dry with the thumbs of her gloves.

"I wish I had something wise to offer, Jade." Connor finally broke the stillness between them with his low voice. And then he surprised her yet again as he reached past the void between them and gripped her hand. "I wish I could help."

"You have." She squeezed the strong fingers that held hers. "You have done so much already, just by accepting us. Helping with Rex. Befriending Lily—and trying with Kellen. And this—" She slid her hand from his and motioned between them. "Just listening to my drama. It helps." More than she dared say.

"I don't think it's drama." He returned both elbows to his knees and clasped his hands together. "I think these are hard things, and I know from experience that hard things take time to work through."

Jade clenched her jaw to keep from crying all over again.

"For the record, I think you're doing remarkably well."

Snorting an unladylike laugh, Jade shook her head. "Yeah. That was me doing remarkably well out there in the woods earlier."

"Like my son reminded me not long ago, everyone needs a tornado room."

"A tornado room?"

"When Sadie, my wife, was in hospice, they had one. Specifically for the kids—but I know for a fact some adults use it too. It's padded, completely soundproof. A safe place where you can just lose it."

Jade tried to imagine Connor Murphy just losing it. The image wouldn't quite pull together. Neither did it for his well-behaved, rather reserved son. It was a reminder that she and her children weren't alone in life's struggles. There were so many out there.

"I'm so sorry for your loss, Mr. Murphy."

"At this point, Jade, I think you should just call me Connor." He blew out a long, controlled breath.

His response emboldened her curiosity. "How long were you married?"

"Seven years."

Jade sat up a little. "Seven?" She caught herself after she'd already muttered her response, and wanted to hide all over again.

"Yeah." Connor looked toward his cabin, up to what Jade assumed was Reid's window. "Reid was little when I married Sadie."

"Oh . . ." She wanted to ask all the things. But already she'd put so much on him.

"He and I don't share DNA. But I'm his dad."

"I didn't . . . I'm sorry, Connor. I didn't . . ."

"It's okay. Reid knows. He remembers, and Sadie and I never tried to keep anything about it from him."

Even as he continued to open up about it, Jade was stunned. She wanted to know Connor's story now more than ever. But that still felt too presumptuous. "So you understand the complications of a split family."

"Probably not the way you mean. Reid's biological father knew about him, and he didn't want anything to do with Sadie or his child—which in some ways makes me livid, because I don't understand that. But it mostly makes me grateful. Reid is *my* son. I don't have to share him, and I don't have to battle someone else's idea of how to raise him. I think that probably makes life easier for me."

"I see." Jade didn't know what else to say.

"That probably doesn't help you much."

She gave Connor a half grin. "I wasn't looking for answers."

To her surprise, he mirrored her small smile. "Just like a man, assuming a woman is asking for his advice."

"That wasn't what I was thinking either."

His low chuckle dusted the remaining bits of humiliation that had lingered from the day and from their earlier conversation. Then he rose from his chair, and Jade followed. "Thank you for this." He lifted his mug. "It's delicious."

"You're welcome."

"I'll return your mug in the morning?"

"Sure."

An awkward pause lengthened between them. Finally, he stepped away.

"Connor Murphy."

Pausing, he looked back at her.

"Thank you."

"I didn't do much."

He had no idea how much he'd done. "Thank you just the same."

"You'll tell me if I can help?"

"I will."

"Good night, Jade Beck."

He disappeared into the chilly night, leaving Jade alone to gaze up at the stars. It'd been a long time since she'd been able to do exactly this without the distraction of war in her heart.

As the pack of coyotes yipped in the distance, Jade praised God for the moment of peace.

CHAPTER TWELVE

(in which the past is poison)

REID WOKE UP RESTED and insisting he was ready to go back to school. After checking his temperature twice and watching him during breakfast rather than start on the daily maintenance chores for the lodge, Connor conceded. As had become habit since the second week of school, they met Lily and Kellen at the lodge's large SUV, and Connor took them into town.

After dropping Reid and the Beck kids off at their schools, Connor made his way back to the lodge with the radio off. Though previously he wished for a distraction from thoughts he couldn't untangle, that morning he opted for quiet. He found himself with the lingering need to process.

The previous evening seemed to be a pivot point in his world. Things had changed. *Again.*

Work waited ahead of him, but Connor took a turnoff onto a dirt road that would wind back toward the south point of the bay rather than to the lodge. It'd been a while since he'd found himself there. The spot had been his private sanctuary after Sadie's second cancer diagnosis. He'd landed there often as illness claimed her by bits and pieces, and even more after her battle had ended.

The thick cover of trees thinned as the dirt road neared its dead end. Connor slowed the vehicle and then eased it to a stop at the edge of the overlook. His breath puffed white in the crisp morning air as he stepped out of the SUV and wandered toward a large round boulder. He leaned against it, tugging his stocking cap over his ears, and took in the expansive lake that stretched well past the confines of this bay, and the shimmering waters that lapped against the shore below.

For all the wonder spread before him—plenty enough to lose one's cares in—Jade Beck remained the focus of his thoughts.

How long had her marriage been awful? Had Peter always demeaned her? What about the kids—would they be safe going back to Kansas to their dad's wedding? He couldn't fault Jade one bit for being angry with Peter, and though he really didn't get a say and had no place to have an opinion, he didn't want Lily and Kellen to go either.

Lily had entrusted him with something huge, and as he'd promised he would, he'd spent much of his restless night praying for her. Asking God to place His wisdom in her young, sweet heart. When he wasn't praying for her, he was interceding for Jade. The word *abuse* kept circling his mind, and it summoned the warrior within. It was likely a good thing Peter Beck lived half a country away. Connor would have been mightily tempted to confront the man face to face if he was nearer.

Which was not his place.

Honestly, it would be easier—safer—if he was more indifferent about it all. If he could just pray for them and that was it. No emotional entanglement. No pressing demand within to *do* something.

But there was emotional entanglement—enough to keep him up at night—and frankly, he couldn't figure the why on that.

Natural concern for the kids? Yes. But more. And there his thoughts had landed on Jade yet again.

Given the bits of her story he now knew, Connor wondered at Jade's resilience. She kept going. Kept giving herself to her kids in the midst of the tremendous heartbreak Connor had glimpsed yesterday. She worked hard every day. Treated people with kindness. And though he'd seen her lose it, Connor couldn't say he'd witnessed Jade wallow in self-pity. Instead, she tried to do what was right by everyone involved, including her ex-husband, even when he didn't deserve her consideration.

Connor admired her.

There. He owned it. He admired her.

And he wanted to help her. Felt *commissioned* to help her. Though he still didn't know what that looked like.

But that was where clarity ended.

White gold light danced off the silvery waters as Connor lifted his gaze from the vast lake below to the brilliant morning sun.

"God, what's going on with me?" He jammed both hands into his coat pocket.

He'd named the uncomfortable chaos that continued to tangle his thoughts *loneliness*.

That wasn't quite right, and he knew it.

He'd called the distraction simply *attraction*. Because Jade *was* a pretty woman—he'd thought so from the moment he'd clamped eyes on her.

He'd called the fierceness within *protective instincts*. Because that was a big part of who he was.

And he'd labeled his involvement with the Becks as *doing the right thing*. Because he was, in fact, that guy.

All true. None complete. There was more. Something sweetly inviting and terrifyingly familiar. A thing so vast it could swallow him whole and he'd never be the same. A thing that held the power to wreck him.

Connor didn't want to name *that*.

He stood in the witness of nature, wishing he could lose himself in the symphony of the ages. The trees swaying in the breeze, the brush of their evergreen boughs lending soft percussion to the music. The steady swish of water as it ebbed and flowed to the rhythm of wind and sky. Birds sweetly singing a song of praise to the Creator of all.

It was all captivating, containing the power to draw a man into worship, leaving all else behind. And yet Connor could not.

After the devastation of losing his wife, his life had just rerighted itself, for the most part. It had taken a couple of years, but he and Reid were doing okay—figuring out how to be just them.

Couldn't Connor just *be* where things made sense? Where every day was simply steady and he wasn't subjected to emotional wrestling matches, where life was predictable and safe?

He'd asked for no more change. God had sent Jade Beck instead.

Connor's phone vibrated inside his coat pocket. With a tentative breath of relief—because at last, something to distract him from the turmoil!—he withdrew his cell and allowed the full measure of his cares to roll off his shoulders.

It was Matt. His older brother was sure to tell him about an antic one of his three children had done. They'd share a laugh. Exchange a couple of none-intrusive pleasantries. Matt would ask about Reid and then about Appleton and Emma. Connor would want to know more about the girls.

All safe topics.

"Hey, Matt." Connor settled against the cold granite beneath him as he answered the call.

"Connor, how are you?"

"Good." Had his voice just split on that word? Connor cleared his throat. "We're good these days."

"Yeah?" A hint of skepticism came with Matt's response. Or maybe Connor imagined that. "You sound tired, little brother."

No, he hadn't imagined it. "Maybe a little. Reid's been sick."

"Oh, I'm sorry to hear that. Is it serious?" A question that came with real concern. Things like that happened when one lost someone to cancer.

"No. Not at all. He went back to school today, in fact. He had to stay home for a week though, so . . ." Yeah. That was why Connor apparently sounded tired. He'd been up for nights on end worrying about his mildly ill son. Because that was how he always rolled.

It wasn't. Matt wasn't likely to buy that.

But Connor wasn't going to tell him that he was exhausted because he'd stayed up much of the previous night worrying about his pretty neighbor and her two kids and then wondering why the heck he cared so much that he'd lose sleep over them.

"Well, that might answer my question," Matt said, derailing Connor's worries.

"What question was that?"

"Lauren and I were wondering if you boys would be up for a visit from us this weekend."

"Oh!" Wow, Connor needed to get out of his own head. "Yeah, that would be great."

"Yeah? We'd like to see the lake and the lodge, and of course visit you and Reid, before the busy season takes over our lives. Come November we'll be all go and no stop."

That wasn't hyperbole for Matt and Lauren. They would start digging live trees and packaging them for retail by November 1, and they'd put in twelve- to fifteen-hour days until December 24. Connor didn't envy them the insane holiday schedule that came with their burgeoning Christmas tree farm, but he also knew Matt and Lauren loved it.

"We'd love to have you." Might be exactly what Connor needed to escape this madness twisting within. Matt's three girls would provide plenty of giggling entertainment, and Connor had no doubt Reid would love to see his little cousins again. "Will you come on Friday?"

"That's what we had hoped, if that'll work?"

"You bet."

"I'll plan on helping you with whatever you're working on at the lodge."

"You know you don't need to."

Matt chuckled. "You know I want to. I still miss it there."

Connor snorted. "Yeah. I'm sure you miss the two a.m. calls about clogged toilets and retrieving sunk kayaks from the bottom of the bay."

"Well . . . maybe not those things." Matt paused. "Are you unhappy?"

"No." Connor wiped the side of his beard. He hadn't meant to complain, and he truthfully loved the job Matt had been instrumental in helping him find. What was *wrong* with him? "Not unhappy here at all, Matt. Sorry. I'm just—uh, maybe I'm just a little crabby today. I'll try to get that worked out before you and Lauren get here."

"You're not usually a moody guy. Something going on?"

"No." Had he spit that out too quickly?

Matt didn't respond right away.

"Matt, seriously. Don't worry about me, and please bring your family for the weekend. We'd love to see you."

Another extended break. Then finally Matt said, "We'll do that, then. See you Friday?"

"Absolutely." Connor pinned a grin to his mouth, hoping it would fix whatever was carrying negativity in his voice. "I'll tell Reid when he gets home, and we'll be looking forward to it."

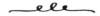

She'd scared him off.

Jade tried to silence the reprimand scrolling through her mind while at the same time she wondered why it would be there in the first place.

Scared him off—off of what? It was a dumb thing to think. They didn't have a *relationship* that Connor would suddenly be skittish about. In truth, they barely had a real friendship. What was between her and Connor Murphy was a semi-comfortable working relationship that had suffered a few brief interruptions of a more personal nature by his interference with her kids. And yesterday with her. None of which amounted to anything that approach *relationship* status, and equally so, none of which was actually her doing.

All that being true, Jade wondered where Connor had hidden himself all morning. He'd not had the fire in the main lodge going by the time she arrived at her desk. Nor was the coffee made. Not normal.

And also not normal, Connor hadn't yet returned from taking the kids to school. It was nearly ten, and he was still gone.

Connor Murphy seemed an immutable character—one unlikely to deviate from a plan or a schedule. He was a man who ran like clockwork.

Predictable and dependable. Which led Jade to believe that she'd scared him off.

The hot cocoa had been too much. Or maybe the fact that she'd sought him out after their kids were in bed. That had been a rather intimate move, hadn't it?

No it wasn't. They had just needed to have an adult conversation, uninterrupted and honest, so she wouldn't feel like a simpering little girl around him after her total meltdown in his arms. That was just being a grown-up.

Why wasn't Connor Murphy being a grown-up? He didn't have to go avoiding her at all costs because her life made him uncomfortable. Were all men incapable of handling awkward situations? Did they all simply believe that life should be as they prefer, no inconveniences, thank you very much?

Peter certainly had. He would have absolutely gone off and sulked, like apparently Connor was.

Ugh!

Well. She'd asked nothing of Connor Murphy. She expected nothing from him. He didn't need to be—

The front french door swung open before Jade's thought ran its course, and Connor stepped inside the lodge. When Jade expected him to avoid looking anywhere near her direction—rather, that he'd stomp off toward the maintenance closet that she suspected he used just as much as a hideout as a workspace—Connor angled his face directly toward her as he pushed the door shut.

"Morning," he said.

She had no business blushing at the low rumble of his voice. While internally she demanded such reactions cease, she molded a stiff smile. "You're late this morning. Everything go okay at school?"

He blinked. "Yeah. The kids are fine."

Turning back to her computer screen, Jade nodded and kept a cool, professional tone. "Coffee's made. Rooms seven and twelve are checking out within the hour. And room five mentioned that the heater is rattling." She tugged the sticky note off the pad and held it out to him.

Connor's approach bled caution. For some reason, that ramped up Jade's ire. He didn't have to make *everything* between them so incredibly clumsy! Couldn't he just smile, say good morning, and stroll on his way? Maybe even whistle while he went so that she knew all was well despite what had happened yesterday?

He tugged off his stocking cap. His hair stuck up in a sexy mess that seemed fresh out of bed and entirely too intimate. And the fact that Jade's thoughts included the word *sexy* made her even madder.

"Everything okay?" he asked quietly.

Fire crept over her face, and she really believed in that instance he could read her mind and it would make him act even more stupid about this whole situation. "*I'm* fine," she snapped.

He drew back, brows folding. "You are?"

"Of course I am. I'm not the one avoiding work because of . . . things."

His mouth hung open, and he stared at her. "Avoiding work?"

Jade turned her attention to the computer and opened the day's schedule for check-ins. Not because she needed to—she already knew that a couple from Idaho were due in later that afternoon, and a group of four would be checking in before supper that evening. She'd known these things since eight this morning.

"What *things*?"

She was certain Connor had just growled. With a huff, she pushed her chair back and spun it to face him. "I make you uncomfortable. Isn't that so? Well, I'm sorry, Mr. Murphy. I'm sorry you saw me fall apart yesterday—but in all fairness, you followed me. I never asked you to get involved. And I'm sorry that I came out last night and apparently made everything worse."

She was so sorry-not-sorry that she didn't bend over backward to make her presence in this man's world just so. Ha! Nope. She wasn't gonna be that woman anymore. Not for Peter. Certainly not for Connor Murphy.

Utter bewilderment scrawled on his face. "We . . . but . . . I . . ." His gaze lifted from her face, and it appeared he was mentally going over previous events. Then he came back to her, looking more confused. "Last night everything was fine." He motioned between them. "I thought *things* between us were fine."

Jade searched his eyes, and he didn't duck away from her inspection. Nor did his look darken into something angry and intimidating. Or sulky. He truly looked blindsided. "You . . . you weren't avoiding me?"

Connor kept staring.

"You weren't giving me the cold shoulder?" *Punishing me for making your world rumpled?*

At that he shook his head. "I overslept this morning. Then after I dropped the kids off, I went to the south lookout." He angled just enough to point in the general direction. "It's a stunning view, and it's quiet there. I . . . I just needed some time to . . . to pray."

It was as if Jade suddenly woke up. Her eyes opened, and she saw how utterly childish she'd been acting. Good grief, why had she done that? It was like she'd taken years of frustration and hurt feelings and spewed them at Connor for no reason at all—other than *she* felt uncertain about *things*.

"I'm sorry." She forced herself to look at him. "I don't know what came over me." *Insecurity.* That was what had come over her. "Please, Mr. Murphy. Forgive me."

"Connor," he said softly. "It's just Connor, Jade."

She silently repeated his name, intentionally putting it over another. *Connor. Not Peter.*

"I . . . uh." Connor rubbed his chin, his attention at last drifting away. "I was praying for you. And for Lily and Kellen."

Ashes on her head. While *she'd* been fuming about shortcomings and attitudes Connor hadn't owned, *he'd* been praying for her and her children. Jade swallowed hard. "Thank you."

Rolling his fists, he laid the sides of his hands on the counter that separated them and dropped his tone to a whisper. "Also, I was wondering, uh—I don't know if it's okay to ask, but . . ."

After that scene, he could ask her just about anything—including to start looking for a new job. She deserved it. "I just railroaded you, so . . ."

His look intensified into a frown. "Will Lily and Kellen be okay? I mean with their dad, when they go back? He . . . he won't—"

Jade's heart split at his obvious concern for her kids, especially since she'd just been so foolishly ugly. "They'll be okay. I don't love the idea of putting them on a plane by themselves, but Peter won't hurt them. Not physically."

Connor nodded, and then he studied her as if she was someone he wanted to understand, even if she was nuts.

Jade held her breath. Had she ever acted so foolishly in front of anyone as she had—yet again!—in front of Connor Murphy? Whatever was the matter with her? Was she *that* needy, *that* broken, that the idea of a man blowing her off—hurting her feelings—made her a complete idiot?

She wanted to weep at yet more proof that she was so incredibly cynical about men and their intentions. For years she had wondered, even as she bent over backward to stick it out with Peter, how she had been so blind to the bad when it came to the man she chose to be with. Now she wondered how she could not see good when he was right there in front of her.

Her past was poison, and once again she faced this reminder that the way forward was shaky at best.

Lord, I keep messing up . . .

"Jade."

There was something tender in the way he said her name, and Jade fought hard against the longing to latch on to that. To make it something it wasn't, something that Connor didn't intend. She was really good at that—taking the things he did and said and twisting them out of shape.

With a hair's grip on her emotions, she forced herself to meet his eyes.

"I want to be your friend," he said. "Honest, I do. I'm just not very good at—"

"You're doing just fine." Wincing, she wrapped her arms tight around her middle. "I'm the one who—" *Who is a total mess. Mind so warped I don't know good from bad.* She shook her head. "I'm sorry, Connor. I don't know what set me off this morning—maybe I'm just so embarrassed about yesterday. I don't know. But that was undeserved, and I'm sorry."

"As I told you last night, you don't need to be embarrassed."

She lifted a helpless shrug. "But I am. About that. About blowing up at you about the dog. Now this. I want to say that I'm not crazy, but . . ."

"You're not crazy." Connor reached across the counter and cupped her shoulder and squeezed.

"Thanks," she whispered.

"Friends?"

She nodded. "I would appreciate that."

His fingers drifted down the side of her arm and fell away when they brushed her elbow. "Me too."

CHAPTER THIRTEEN

(in which there is a spark)

MATT AND LAUREN ARRIVED an hour after supper on Friday evening, six-year-old Fiona letting anyone within a three-hundred-yard radius know of her delight.

"Reid!" she squealed, her short legs pumping from Matt and Lauren's minivan toward the basketball court. "Reid, I'm here! Let's go explore!"

At the sound of his brother's vehicle parking on the gravel, Connor had left the quiet solitude of his kitchen and stepped onto the front deck in time to watch Fiona fly toward Reid. From that vantage point, Connor saw Reid's mildly embarrassed head duck and shy peek at Lily, who had rebounded a shot Reid had missed.

"You must be Fi." Lily grinned at Reid and then aimed a full-blown smile at Fiona.

Fiona stopped just short of flinging herself at Reid—something she'd done every time she saw her older cousin until that moment—and looked from Lily to Reid and back again. "How do you know my name?"

"Reid told me. You're Fiona, the oldest sister, right?" Lily winked. "Then there's Helene, and after her, Ainsley, the baby. Right?"

Connor watched the interactions down at the court even while Matt and Lauren met him as he came off the deck.

"Hey, little brother." Matt shot him a grin, always loving that he could call Connor little brother even though Connor had a good two inches of height on him.

Connor met Matt's outstretched hand and tugged him into a hug. "Hi, old man." He pulled away and reached to hug Lauren next. "Hey, Laurs. How are you?"

Lauren bounced little Ainsley on her hip. "Hoping this one's ear will pop soon so you don't think she cries all the time. She doesn't." Lauren shot him a grin.

"Of course she doesn't. My little angel Ainsley wouldn't." Connor held out his hands to Ainsley.

The two-year-old immediately grunted, pulled away from Connor, and pressed her little body tight against her mother.

Ah, the rejection of a two-year old. Though Connor didn't have first-hand experience of his own kid at that age, he had enough nieces and nephews to know how it went and didn't take it too personal. Ainsley popped her thumb into her mouth and glared up at him. He winked, and she turned her face into her mom's shoulder.

"You won't win with that one." Matt clapped his shoulder. "Even famous Unca Ty doesn't win too many smiles from your angel-Ains, no matter how many of his praises Fi and Helene sing."

"Huh." Connor crossed his arms. "Sounds like a challenge to me."

"You and me both," Matt said as he redirected his attention toward the older kids. Four-year-old Helene had joined the group and was now happily climbing up Reid's torso as he held both of her hands. She turned a flip, readjusted her grip, and went for another go.

Standing to the side, between Reid and Lily, Fiona looked directly up at Reid with a very serious expression. "Who is this?"

Amusement cracked through Reid's rather embarrassed expression. "This is Lily Beck."

"Is she your girlfriend?"

Connor held his breath, certain his son was likely mortified right then. Reid laughed, surprising Connor clean through. It was an honest laugh—not one that seemed like a cover-up for total humiliation—and he looked straight at Lily, who also smiled.

"No, Fi. Lily and I are friends. She's my new neighbor—and she helps me with math and basketball." He pointed to the Becks' cabin. "She and her brother and her mom moved in there."

"She can't help you with basketball, Reid. You're the best at it." Fiona fixed an interrogating look on Lily. "Are you a good neighbor?"

To her credit, Lily met Fiona's serious question with an equally serious nod. "I'm trying to be, Miss Fiona."

"Do you *really* help Reid with math and basketball?"

Lily shrugged. "I think we help each other. You're right about Reid being good at basketball." She winked. "He is. *A* team for sure, I'd say."

Unimpressed, Fi rolled a pair of fists and planted them on her skinny hips. "That sounds kissy-face. What are your intentions with my cousin?"

Connor snorted a laugh and looked at his brother. "What are you teaching your daughter?"

Matt groaned and then grinned. "Fi is her own best self. We never know what's going to happen next with her."

"Yeah." Lauren looked less amused with her daughter as she shook her head. "She's all Murphy, that's for sure. Untamable." She shot a poor impression of irritation at Matt, and a laugh threatened to break through her facade.

"You love me." Matt dropped an arm around his wife. "And I am housebroken."

"Yes to the first. Debatable on the second." She turned back to the scene at the basketball court. "Poor Reid. And Lily." Rolling her eyes, Lauren passed Ainsley to Matt and set her stride toward her ostentatious daughter.

Matt adjusted his youngest daughter in one arm and angled toward Connor. "Reid's feeling better by now?"

"One hundred percent, he says." Connor ran his palm over Ainsley's soft curls. A pair of light-brown eyes peeked up at him. She didn't smile, but she didn't pull away or scowl either.

Nodding toward the kids, Matt asked, "Is there a little crush going on there?"

"I worry there might be."

"Worry?"

"Lily is sixteen and a sophomore."

Matt shrugged. "These things work themselves out."

"Hope so. Reid's been through the wringer enough for a while. They seem to be pretty good friends, so I'm grateful for that. I kind of wish he'd talk to *me* a little more though."

Matt shot him a look. "I don't remember talking to Dad much about girls at Reid's age."

True enough. At twelve, everything was weird, including parental conversations. But with Reid ... it just seemed different. There weren't six other brothers to bounce things off. They sort of only had each other.

"You're not losing him, Connor," Matt said.

Connor's chest squeezed. Some days it really seemed like he was. But those things were, as Matt was reminding him, and as Dad had told him earlier, normal. Reid was gaining independence, as he should.

And anyway, there were still moments between them. Like just last night, when he and Reid had said good night and Connor was walking the first floor, making sure the lights were out and the doors were locked. He'd thought Reid had wandered off to bed, as he typically did. But when he turned to make his way to the stairs, there stood his boy, waiting for him. Reid looked up the risers and then back at Connor. Then without a word, he'd moved toward Connor rather than heading upstairs. At his side, he'd pressed his head to Connor's shoulder.

Love you, Dad.

It was a moment Connor tucked away for safekeeping.

"He's just growing up," Connor said. "Sometimes that's harder to take in than I'd imagined." He bumped Matt with his elbow. "You'll see soon enough."

Adjusting his ball cap, Connor kept watching as Lauren took Helene's hand, rescuing Reid from being the girl's jungle gym. She then reached forward to shake Lily's hand, all friendliness and joy.

Below them, Jade and Kellen appeared on the driveway leading up to the cabins, coming around from the front of the lodge with Rex on a leash. Kellen tried to hold the dog in check, though the pup bounced around as she pleased, nearly tripping Jade more than once. Connor nearly shook his head. He should probably spend more time helping with the dog, as clearly Kellen wasn't making a lot of progress. But that would more likely than not work out poorly with *he who was not to be bossed.*

That thought immediately shifted to resentment toward Peter Beck. A reaction Connor hadn't a real right to have, so he diverted his attention back to the basketball court.

With her wide, welcoming ways, and Helene's hand tucked in hers, Lauren met Jade at the bend in the drive. She stretched a friendly hand forward, and Jade met it with a shy smile.

"That your new neighbor?" Matt asked.

Connor nodded. "Jade Beck. Lily and Kellen—the boy with the dog—are her kids."

"I'll bet Reid has enjoyed having some people his age around."

"For the most part. Like I said, he and Lily get along really well."

Matt raised a brow at that but didn't comment. "It's been nice for Lauren not to have so much on her plate. She's been glad to have someone to do the job here."

"Yeah, I'm glad for Lauren. I'm sorry I didn't realize it had been too much."

"Are things going well?"

Things . . . The comment brought back Jade's anger with him a few days back. Man, he'd been so lost on that one. But contrary to intuition, the whole scene had made him more curious—and concerned for her than it had made him not like her. It was like there was this piece of her that just seemed so off, so out of place. Connor wanted to understand.

In the lengthened quiet, he became aware that he didn't answer Matt's question. "I think so. Jade seems competent."

Matt glanced at him. "What does her husband do?"

Ex-husband, and from what I can tell, he does a whole lot of nothing good. Connor put a clamp on his thoughts even while wondering why exactly he had such a visceral reaction to the thought of this faceless man he'd did *not* like.

"Jade is divorced." Connor was careful to keep his tone neutral.

"Oh."

What did that response mean? Connor swiveled his head to see Matt's expression, which proved fruitless.

Skip it. Likely Matt's quiet response meant nothing. Just a response. Man, he needed to lose this habit of dissecting everything when it came to anything concerning Jade Beck. It was absurd. And exhausting.

Lauren and Jade turned toward the cabins again and side by side made their way to the brothers. Soon enough both women, and the entourage of children, reached the place Matt and Connor occupied between the cabins.

"This is my husband, Matt," Lauren said, taking Ainsley from Matt's arm as the girl strained toward her. "And our youngest, Ainsley. My little storm cloud." She said the telling nickname with affection and kissed the curls on the top of her child's head.

"Ah." Jade glanced to Kellen, and Connor thought he could read her look—*I have one of those too*, though she didn't say anything that would indicate such a thought. Instead, she turned her attention to Matt. "You're Connor's brother?"

"One of them."

Jade glanced at Connor, curiosity on her face.

"Matt's the oldest of the seven of us," Connor said.

"Seven!" Her eyes widened. "Goodness, your mother must be a saint."

Lauren chuckled. "I take it you've seen the Murphy orneriness first-hand."

A blush tinged Jade's cheeks as she glanced at Connor. "No. I don't think I've seen that particular trait. But I have a son—I'm trying to grapple with him plus six more, and I can't imagine surviving. The smell! The laundry!" She smirked at Kellen.

Kellen glared back at her. "I don't smell."

"That's what you think." Lily made a face and waved a hand beneath her nose. "All boys smell."

Reid tugged at the collar of his shirt and buried his nose into the cotton. After a whiff, he also made a face, pulling his shirt back where it belonged. "Ugh. You're right. Why didn't you say anything?"

The group laughed, and a puff of pride surged in Connor's chest. Reid was growing up—and it wasn't all bad.

Jade touched her son on his shoulder. "Kellen, take Rex to the house."

"She's not being bad."

The dog was bouncing from person to person, jumping up and nosing everyone.

"She's not being good either," Jade countered. "Take her up to the house before she knocks one of these sweet little girls over."

Kellen groaned.

As Connor watched Jade's expression tighten, his muscles stiffened. Why was everything with Kellen a fight? He braced himself for an explosion and could tell by Jade's coloring and hardening jaw that she was doing the same.

Not now, he silently implored. *Spare Jade the embarrassment. She doesn't know that Matt and Lauren won't judge.*

Not like Connor did. Eesh. That was a zinger. Though he'd rather bury the thought deep and forget about it, he knew he'd have to examine it later.

Surprisingly, Kellen tugged on Rex's leash and moved to do as told. Connor's body eased into relief.

"Make sure you make her sit while you take off her leash," Jade said as her son trudged toward their cabin.

Something that Connor had told Kellen and Jade several days back, right before Kellen had insisted he butt out.

"I know!" Kellen snapped.

The crimson on Jade's face deepened, and she looked to the ground. An uncomfortable silence settled, and Connor wanted to step closer to Jade, to let her know it was all right. He and his brothers had been mouthy in their day. They'd also had a father who didn't stand by and let his sons lip off to their mother.

Connor pushed away that argument, knowing it had little to do with this situation, and held his place. If he moved toward Jade, he might make her feel worse. She might take anything he did or said as interference. Or judgment. Or something else he didn't intend.

"I brought stuff for s'mores," Lauren announced, her friendly smile aimed at Jade. "And lots of it. You guys should join us at the firepit tonight."

Ah, Lauren. Always the kind one. The feather smoother. One of the reasons that Connor had championed for her from the first time Matt had brought her to the Murphy home—even before his older brother had gained the sense to move past his old flame and date Lauren instead.

She's definitely the kind of girl you bring home to meet your mother. All these years later, and Connor still remembered saying that to Matt—his undertone clear. *Why the heck are you still stuck on Katrine when God literally had Lauren smack into you? She's amazing. Love her and be happy.*

As that memory played in the back of his mind, Connor wondered what his mom would think of Jade. The thought was jarring. Heat crawled over his face. He rubbed his neck, dropping his look toward his feet.

"I don't want to intrude on your family time," Jade said.

Matt glanced at Connor, as if he thought Connor should intercede. Connor was still too lost in his head to say anything. Why should he wonder what his mother would think of Jade? Even as he claimed he didn't wonder and it wouldn't matter, the long-past memory of Mom's reaction to Connor's news about marrying Sadie imposed itself.

She'd not been thrilled, and that had offended deeply. Though that situation had quickly rectified itself, there was a wee bit of lingering resentment at his mother's initial disapproval. Man, how did his thoughts keep getting so mixed up?

Matt stepped forward. "You're invited, Jade, so it's not an intrusion. The Murphys are a large, loud bunch, so be warned on that. But we'd love to have you guys."

"Yeah, you should come," Reid added.

Connor felt Jade's watch land on him. He also felt her keen discomfort. He didn't know what that meant exactly. Lifting his gaze to meet hers, he hoped he could figure out how to read her expression so he wouldn't mess up this time.

Is it okay? There was no doubting the message he read in those soft brown eyes, and his own discomfort eased.

His lips quirked up, and he dipped a subtle nod. "We'd like to have you."

Biting her bottom lip, Jade held his gaze for a heartbeat. Something electric stole Connor's breath. He suspected she felt it too, because she quickly shifted her look to Lauren as a mild blush reclaimed her face.

"Okay then." Jade tucked her hands into her pockets and backed away. "I have a few things to see to, so I guess I'll catch up with you all later?"

"Sundown." Matt aimed his demand at Jade. "And don't stiff us. We'll come find you."

Connor felt Matt's look return to him. Felt the questions rolling through his older brother's mind. Why was he being so oddly silent? What was going on that made him so stiff?

Or maybe the string of questions were just in his own head.

Namely one: What had happened just now?

She shouldn't have agreed to go. Surely she could have found some legitimate excuse to decline.

Jade stared at herself in the mirror. Even as she saw her own boring brown eyes and round face, she envisioned instead a pair of deep-green eyes holding her captive. Breathless. Even just the memory of that moment . . .

and it had been but a moment, hadn't it? Goodness, she hoped so—more than that would be so embarrassing with his family standing there.

Her heart raced. Thrilling heat ran through her veins. And it terrified her.

"Jade." She shook her head and leaned in closer as she lowered her whisper to a mere breath. "Jade Tifton Beck, he's not for you."

Connor Murphy was out of bounds. Out of her league. And most importantly, he hadn't stared at her the way she'd imagined. How could he? With her he was all discomfort and confusing silence. He saw her as his divorced neighbor who took his dead wife's job. The woman he was required to befriend because of place and circumstances. A woman who was plainly nuts, as she'd proven just the other day. There were no possibilities in that. And even if there were . . .

Jade touched the fullness of her jawline and examined the wrinkles that had settled in her skin.

It'd be helpful if you took better care of yourself, Jade. Even hundreds of miles away, Peter had a way of bringing reality to mind with the sharp force of an iron blade.

Jade quickly moved her attention from the mirror to the sink. Flicking on the cold water, she watched as the water ran over her fingers.

There were no possibilities. *None.* Fighting against the sudden need to cry, Jade bent to splash the cool water against her heated face. After repeating that several times, she reached for a hand towel and patted her splotchy face dry.

She shouldn't have agreed to go. She didn't want to feel like this—so unworthy and yet with this stupid growing attachment she knew good and well was not reciprocated. Honestly, she didn't even know why she liked him so much.

As though that last thought was a challenge, a list formed in response.

He is kind, even in his quietness.

He works hard and never complains.

He's a good father to Reid.

When he looks at me like I matter, I think that maybe . . .

And there was where the problem lodged. Yet again the need for attention, for approval.

Jade squeezed the towel in her fist and shut her eyes. "God, I can't find my way out of that. Please fill this brokenness in me . . ."

"Mom!" Lily's call reached from somewhere downstairs. "The bonfire's lit."

With a long-drawn breath, Jade looked back at her reflection. "You're a big girl. Don't act like a fool." With another quick pat of the towel against her face, she straightened her posture and left the solitude of her bathroom.

For her kids, she would go. They would enjoy the treat, and Kellen could certainly use the influence of other people. *Lord, please let my son be the nice boy I used to know . . .*

"I see we're all ready, hmm?" She traveled down the stairs, finding Lily with her jacket already on and Kellen hooking the leash on Rex.

"Yep. Reid texted me a few minutes ago. He wanted to make sure we were going to come."

Jade couldn't help but smile at that, though she lifted a brow at her daughter. "You're being careful with that one, right?"

"What do you mean?"

"He's twelve, Lily."

Her sixteen-year-old daughter rolled her eyes. "We're friends, Mom. I promise."

"Twelve-year-old boys are prone to crushes on pretty, nice older girls."

Lily shot her a rare scowl. "It isn't like that. We shoot baskets and talk about things."

"What things?"

"Things, Mom. Nothing that's inappropriate, I promise." Lily tilted her head and then laid a hand on Jade's arm. "He's been through a lot too, you know? Sometimes you just need someone to talk to. And I know he had a crush at first, but he's smart, and he knows what is what. We really are good friends. Please don't make it weird."

Though Jade had to brush away a little offense at having her daughter give her a mild rebuke, she had to admit that Lily probably had a point. Lily was good at boundaries, even with her people-pleasing personality. Much better at them than Jade had ever been. And she also was right about Reid—the boy had been through a lot in his young life.

She slipped an arm around Lily's waist. "All right, Lil. No weirdness from me. I'm glad you are friends, and I trust you."

"Be nice if you trusted me," Kellen grumbled.

Jade looked him dead on. "I think that would be nice too. How about we work on that?"

For a moment, Kellen held her look, and then he looked toward the floor. A mix of hurt and anger crossed his face, making Jade's heart squeeze. She slid away from Lily and reached for his shoulder. Surprisingly, he didn't jerk away.

"You'll always be my son, and I always love you," she whispered.

He swallowed. Then stiffened. But when she was certain he was going to rip away from her touch, he merely clenched his jaw.

Oh! What she wouldn't give to take away the war in his heart. *God, I just want my son back!*

Rex had enough of waiting. She popped up from her sitting position and bounced back on her hind legs, placing her huge paws on Kellen's chest.

"Down, Rex." Kellen pushed the dog off.

Rex twirled and yipped.

"Sit, Rex."

She twirled again, then looked at Kellen, head cocked to one side.

"Sit," he repeated.

Miraculously, the dog sat.

A grin burst over Kellen's sullen face. "Good girl! Good girl, Rex!" He leaned to scratch her ears and turned that glorious smile up to Jade. "She did it. Did you see? She did it!"

"I did see, buddy." Such a small thing, but it made Jade's heart burst. Particularly as Kellen looked to her for approval. "Good job, you." She also reached for the pup. "And good girl, Rex."

Kellen grinned at her again as she stood straight, and she reached to rumple his hair. "Let's go have a good time tonight, hmm?"

Though he hesitated, none of what had become his typical defiance entered his eyes as he held her look. "Okay."

Jade squeezed his shoulders as a well of gratitude plunged in her heart. She determined to hang on to such good moments. Surely the gathering of them would ease the hard things still to come.

Together, the three Becks and their foundling pup left their cabin and filed into the graying dusk. The air stirred with the chill of coming winter and the inviting smell of burning pine drifting from the firepit around back. Sounds of conversation and laughter lured them along the path leading to the small gathering of Murphys.

As she rounded the corner, she caught a glimpse of Connor in smiling conversation with Lauren, his four-year-old niece perched on his wide shoulders, intermittently patting his stocking cap and flapping her arms as if she were a bird.

What woman didn't melt at the sight of a man spoiling a child? Jade snatched her gushy heart and put it back on the not-available shelf where it belonged.

"So finally after about fifteen minutes of *not* finding her, Matt thought to call Ty." Lauren pinned a mocking scowl on Fiona as she finished telling a story. "Guess where the little pickle had run off to?"

Shaking his head, Connor also looked at Fiona, who stood beside Reid, a long roasting stick pointed toward the low flames of the fire and a marshmallow at the end of it.

The little girl looked up at her uncle with all the seriousness of a lawyer giving her closing arguments. "Of course I would be at Uncle Ty's. He's my favorite. Where else would I be?"

"What?" Connor grabbed at his left shoulder, as if he'd taken a hit. "I thought I was your favorite. And what ever happened to *Unca*?"

"Unca is for baby girls. *I* am not one of those. I am six years old, thank you very much. And Uncle Ty is my favorite. Everyone knows that."

"Good grief, Fi." Matt shook his head at his oldest daughter. "We can't take you anywhere."

Connor chuckled. "I'll try to go on living. But we both know, Fiona Murphy, that Ty is only your favorite because Becca makes you cupcakes."

Fiona pasted an angelic look on her face and shrugged. "I don't know what you mean."

The adults, including Jade, all laughed. Though Jade wasn't entirely sure what the whole story had been about, it was quite clear that Fiona was a bucket of cute mischief and Matt and Lauren Murphy had their hands full.

Lauren turned to Jade, still shaking her head at her daughter. "I don't suppose Lily was ever this much extra, was she?"

Jade looked at Lily, who stood on the other side of Reid. Reid passed a roasting stick to Lily and then one to Kellen.

Lily took a mallow Reid offered. "I always end up burning mine."

"That's criminal." Reid lifted his roasting stick from the arm of a chair, a puffed mallow at the end of it. "Look. Perfection. This is what you've got to aim for."

"Yeah. Except I'm not very patient, so I end up with flames."

"I like 'em charred," Kellen said.

"Here." Reid passed his roasting stick to Lily and exchanged it for hers. "I can't live with you not having experienced the perfect marshmallow."

Jade watched the exchange and then turned her attention back to Lauren. "Lily was a quiet, compliant kid who always wanted everyone to be happy. So not really the mischievous sort. Kellen, however . . ." She shrugged and grinned.

"Fiona says whatever pops in her head, to whomever is there to hear her."

"She's pretty cute."

"Don't tell her. She hears it enough from Ty."

"Ty is another Murphy boy?"

"He is. He and his wife, Becca, live just down the road from us. Becca runs a little cupcake shop, and Ty works with his dad. Fiona has adored both of them since she was old enough to talk. Sadly, none of the other brothers ever had a chance."

"Are all the Murphys close?"

"As a family? Yeah, they're close. Some brothers are closer to each other than others." Lauren winked. "Between you and me, they're a little overwhelming at first."

"We're an acquired taste," Matt interjected. "Big, loud, all-in-your-business families usually are, I think."

Jade tried to picture Connor in the midst of a big, loud, all-in-your-business family. It didn't work. She peeked at the man in question, finding his expression not unpleasant, but not open either. Why was he always so unreadable? Was he that way with everyone? And what happened to the *friends* agreement they'd come to?

An instant replay of what she'd walked in on—Lauren exchanging an animated story with Connor and Connor bantering easily with both Lauren and Fiona. Once again the answer to that unreadable question was *no*. Connor wasn't that way with everyone.

Just, it was becoming clearer, with Jade.

Her heart shrank at the sharp nick produced by that reality. There wasn't a good reason for Connor's cool demeanor toward her to injure what she couldn't offer anyway. Even so, she instinctively put a sleeve around her already shelved heart and mentally switched tracks.

Turning to Lauren, she asked, "You were doing the job I have, is that right?"

"Correct." Lauren nodded. "I just couldn't manage all of it though, and I hated to think that Mr. Appleton's beautiful lodge wouldn't continue doing well." A wistful smile wreathed her face. "Matt and I fell in love here, you know."

"Did you?" She didn't know that. She'd no idea the Murphys had such strong ties to the lodge. Perhaps, then, it was no wonder that Connor had had such a guarded response to her arrival. Not an excuse, per se, but . . .

"We met at the airport." Lauren's eyes glittered with laughter as she recounted the story. "I threw up on his tux."

"You didn't!"

"I did. Right in the middle of a terminal, and he was an absolute stranger."

"And you both ended up here?"

Lauren aimed a smirk toward her husband, who wasn't listening but was bantering with the kids and Connor. "There was a blizzard, and Matt needed an escape—which was why he was at the airport. But all the flights were grounded, and I couldn't get myself to the lodge, which was where my new job was. He drove me through a whiteout on the back roads and ended up working here himself. The rest"—she nodded toward the baby dozing against her shoulder—"is history."

Comfortable with the woman at her side, Jade reached and stroked the baby girl's soft curls. "A lovely history, apparently."

The soft grin on Lauren's face said everything. She was a woman still in love with her husband. Happy with her life. Jade knew a moment of tight jealousy as she withdrew her hand.

After a lingering silence between them, Lauren asked, "Has the transition gone smoothly since you've come?"

Jade sank into the relief at the change in subject as well as Lauren's easy ability to converse. "Very." Well, the actual working part, anyway. Which was certainly what Lauren meant. "I was going to ask you about some of the social media ads though. Some of the ones that are switched off look like they were doing fairly well. Was there a reason you turned them off?"

"Only that I couldn't monitor them as they should be, and I didn't want them spending money without oversight."

"Would you mind if I used them, then?"

Lauren waved the hand that wasn't holding little Ainsley. "Of course I wouldn't mind. They're for the lodge. Use whatever you think will be of benefit."

"Thank you."

Switching his attention to the women, Matt leaned forward to glance around Connor at Jade. "I hear you're from the Midwest. Do you miss it?"

"I was a transplant to the Midwest. I actually grew up not far from here." Jade paused, tilting her head upward in thought. Above, the stars gleamed all twinkling laughter and beauty. She made up her mind to enjoy this night. "As to missing it—there are some things, yes. Big, rolling fields of wheat rippling in the July sun. Or huge blocks of sunflowers in bloom toward the end of summer. And wide-open sunsets. But to be honest, I'm a mountain girl at heart, and it's good to be back."

Their conversation continued from there. Mostly comfortable, as Matt and Lauren made Jade feel welcome and a part of the little group. And the kids all talked and laughed together with ease—even Kellen, thank goodness.

But even with her determination to take in the loveliness of the night, there was Connor. Quiet, watchful, subdued.

Jade was ever conscious of him, and she didn't want to examine why.

CHAPTER FOURTEEN

(in which the truth is hard)

"You weren't yourself last night." Matt flicked his wrist, casting the line out long and far, past the thin ice near the shore and into the deep steel of the bay.

Connor's breath eased long, billowing a misty white before his face. Rather than look at his brother, he focused on making his cold fingers secure the bait in the meager light of predawn so he could cast his own line.

"How's that?" He tried to make his voice sound nonplussed, though he knew Matt spoke the truth. He'd not felt like himself last night, so it wasn't a stretch to think that he hadn't acted normal.

Jade had been there. As if she belonged in his world. She and Lauren had chatted easily. The kids had gotten along splendidly—so much that Lauren had suggested that Lily come up during the peak season to help with the girls. An idea Lily seemed to latch on to. The whole evening had been smooth and friendly.

And there he'd been, unable to stop himself from snatching glances at Jade. Unable to cease the unending madness going on within.

Matt climbed the scattered rocks on the inclined shore until he reached a large boulder. He leaned back against the granite, the insulation of his waders presumably protecting him from the certain chill of the stone. After a stretch of silence, he chuckled. "To quote my wife, you were all stiff and military. Silent and decidedly *un*friendly."

"Lauren said that?" The traitor. Connor had always been on her side.

"She did—though you know she adores you and it about kills her to see you as anything less than a superhero. And, Connor, she wasn't wrong."

Though the sun was only just cracking open the darkness in the eastern sky, the muted gray light allowed a decent view of the lake. Bait secure, Connor picked a spot on the rippling water and aimed his cast in that direction. Dawn was usually the best time for fishing. Brothers often the best company. Be that as it may, this outing obviously had nothing to do with a lake catch. And Connor was questioning the company.

As he set the bail, Connor felt Matt's unwavering study on his shoulders. With a long inhale, he pulled in a deep breath of the cold mountain air, mildly flavored by frosted earth and nipped by the frigid waters. "Seems out of character for Lauren."

"Seemed out of character for you." Matt adjusted the drag, then slowly turned the reel handle.

"That's not true. I'm not nearly as chatty as you or Jackson."

"True. But you're not usually the intimidating silent type either. That, we left for Brandon."

Connor tuned a folded brow toward Matt. "Brandon is as good as they come, and you know it." More than once over the years, Connor or Tyler had had to defend their younger, much more serious brother. Brandon was exactly as Connor claimed: as good a man as God had ever made. Just ask Meagan, his wife. Through she was precisely Brandon's opposite—all bubbly and a little on the silly side sometimes, she adored her quiet husband. Because he was a good man.

A good-natured grin split Matt's face. "He is that. And you're derailing me. We're talking about you, not our little brother."

"I thought we were fishing."

Matt snorted. "I don't even like trout."

"Huh," Connor grunted.

The sound of rocks scrambling behind Connor had him glancing back at Matt again. He'd reeled in his line and was picking his way closer to shore, ready to toss out another cast. The soft hum of the open reel cut through the air as Matt flicked another perfectly placed cast to the deep. After the click of the bail set, he gave his line one quick tug and then let the bait settle in the deeper waters.

"You're pretty good at this for a guy who doesn't eat fish," Connor said.

Matt shrugged, his easygoing countenance still on his face. "Dad."

Yeah, that explained everything. Their dad liked to fish, and he'd taken his boys out as much as his busy working schedule had allowed. Often, each son on his own. It was their one-on-one guy time with their dad, and Connor suspected that as he and Matt did, all the Murphy boys treasured those moments.

"Talk to me, Connor."

Also something from their dad. A line Dad had opened with when he knew one of his boys was struggling with something. Or when they were in trouble but he wanted them to own up to it themselves.

Part of Connor wanted to tell Matt that he was thirty-two years old and could navigate life on his own. No big brother input required. But that wasn't really the case, was it? Connor was floundering in a sea of things he couldn't name, let alone understand. Maybe it would help to talk with Matt about it.

Connor summoned some courageous honesty and plunged in. Though he wasn't entirely sure how to answer Matt, as he had yet to make sense of the tangle within for himself. "You know last summer, when we had that gathering before Brayden and Audrey moved?"

"Yeah." Matt sounded caught off guard, like that wasn't where he expected Connor to start.

"I visited Sadie's grave, like I always do when we're back home."

"I know."

"And I prayed. I asked God for no more change."

Matt held a listening look on him.

"It's like I'm finally able to breathe again without it hurting so much. I can close my eyes at night, and I don't have to imagine that Sadie is beside me—instead of there being a cold, empty space—so that I can go to sleep.

I've finally stopped reaching for my phone to text her every time I see something that I know she would like."

Matt nodded, deep sympathy carving twin lines between his brows. "I can't imagine, Connor. I'm so sorry."

Connor winced and then glanced back at the cabin. "Reid is growing up, and I don't know how to be a single dad. He's pulling away, and it scares me. Even though Dad assures me that it's all normal and Reid is fine—and he's really a good kid, and I know all of that. I still feel like I'm fumbling around alone in the dark. It's *so* much, Matt."

He swallowed, bracing against the surge of emotions. "So I asked God for no more change. Just for a while. Until I can get my bearings . . ."

Would he ever get his bearings? Life had seemed like a series of unexpected changes since that Christmas all the way back in high school, when his world had flipped upside down. After that, there was the military—something he'd never planned on before that massive upheaval. But it had been, ironically, his respite. His escape.

Then that fateful holiday when he reunited with Sadie, meeting her four-year-old son, Reid, and finding out that she had cancer. Life had pivoted again. He'd married Sadie to take care of her and to make sure that Reid wouldn't be an orphan. Not far into that arrangement, he'd fallen in love with his wife. Months later, after excruciating treatments and clear scans, it had seemed he and Sadie had their happily ever after.

And they did. For a time.

But life kept going. Changes kept coming. Connor had separated from the air force and started a new career. There was a new residence and figuring out how to be a husband and father.

And the cancer came back.

After agonizing months of watching the woman he loved get sicker and sicker, Connor found himself in the middle of grief the depths of which he'd never imagined, as well as being a single father.

He couldn't get a grip on bearings. Not when life continued to rock him off kilter.

With a tight hold on his fishing pole, Connor stared at the lake as a streak of golden light stretched toward them on the waters. "I asked for no more change. God planted Jade Beck in my path instead."

"That upset you?"

A bulge lodged in his throat. That moment when he'd first glimpsed Jade invaded his mind and triggered that visceral reaction all over again. It was nearly as jarring as it had been the first time. Connor swallowed against the rising sensation of something powerful and yet still unnamed as he continued to strain toward honesty.

"Maybe it was the way Appleton told me. 'I found someone for you,' he said." Connor's heart clenched hard at that memory. "I misunderstood and was offended. Angry. And barely able to wrap my mind around what he actually meant—that he'd hired someone to fill Sadie's job—before I met her. And when I did . . ."

"When you met Jade?"

"There she was, in the lodge's kitchen, sitting in Sadie's chair. Ready to take Sadie's job." Connor glanced at Matt, wondering if his brother could handle the truth. Because honestly, Connor still couldn't. "I walked in, looked at her, and thought, *she's beautiful*. And resented her for all of it." There it was. The truth.

Man, he was an unreasonable mess.

Morning birds sang into the dawn as the golden light burned away the lingering gray. Connor stared over the water, the rippling movement making the strengthening sunlight dance against the backdrop of hills and pine in the distance.

God, why am I such a mess?

He couldn't be a mess. Reid needed him. Appleton needed him. Now, it seemed, the Becks needed him. He couldn't be a mess.

"You know it's okay if you're attracted to her, don't you?" Matt's gentle question came after a lengthy silence. "It's okay if you like her."

No. No Connor didn't know that. "It doesn't feel okay to me."

"She seems like a nice woman. Lauren liked her very much. And you're right—she is pretty."

"That's all fine."

"Connor, Sadie wouldn't want you to be alone for the rest of your life."

"I know that. But—" But he didn't know what. Just . . . something. Something that made his very core tremble.

"Is it that she's divorced?"

Connor tested that. It didn't fit quite right. He shook his head. "No, I don't think so. I mean, that would add some complication, but . . ." Actually, there was more than mere complication, as he thought on it. Thought about Jade and about her ex-husband. About all that Lily had shared with him. Fierce emotion surged, and he turned a scowl toward his brother.

"Here's the thing—I've never met Peter Beck. But I've never disliked a man so much." Connor crammed forked fingers through his hair. *Disliked* was putting it mildly. What he felt toward Peter Beck bordered on something ungodly, and he'd never even laid eyes on the man. "What is that?"

"You've always been one to defend and protect. That's who you are."

"But she and I are barely friends, yet when I hear of how he cheated on her and how he treated her before, I have this surge of . . . of near rage. *Rage*, Matt."

Matt watched him, concern in his eyes. "And that scares you?"

"Terrified." The confession was a startling admission. Connor was sure this patchy conversation didn't make a whole lot of sense. "I'm terrified." The obvious question came quickly on the heels of that revelation.

Of what?

That first encounter with Jade hit Connor with physical clarity—how at first glimpse, he'd had a profound, electrified response. He'd been fighting it ever since. Perhaps as a younger, less life-tested man that would have been thrilling. Not now.

"Matt, I've loved a woman with everything I have. Losing her—" Connor's words cut off, raw emotion overwhelming him. Heat pricked the back of his eyes.

Connor searched Matt for understanding, not really thinking that his brother could. What he found was unwavering compassion. It gave just him enough courage to crack open the thing he hadn't wanted to face.

The thing that truly, utterly terrified him.

"What if God asks me to do it again?" Emotion quaked through him. "I can't, Matt. I can't do that again. Even the mere possibility has me cowering."

Matt bent over to secure his pole in a crevasse made by two stones and then reached for Connor, fisting the material of his puffer coat and dragging him in close. With a clenched fist, he wrapped his other arm around Connor's shoulder.

Connor bit his lip, battling back the tide—and losing.

For a long moment, Matt kept him in a firm hold, lending Connor strength.

"Here's what I know, brother." Matt stepped back, looking Connor in the eye. "You have a rare strength most men never imagine, let alone possess." With one cupped hand, Matt gripped Connor's neck. "God built you for hard things."

Not exactly what Connor wanted to hear—though he couldn't say what he did want to hear. "Sadie's death shattered me. Entirely. That's not strength."

Matt stepped back, releasing his hold, but the intensity of his gaze didn't waver. "Would you do it again?"

Connor gave him a quizzical look.

"Would you marry Sadie again, even knowing—"

Connor didn't need Matt to finish. He nodded. Loving Sadie had been the best blessing of his life. Even with the excruciating pain of losing her, he could say without a doubt he'd do it all over again.

"You've had a hard road, Connor. Harder than I can imagine. But I wager there was joy in the journey."

"There was." So much joy. He and Sadie had been happy—precisely why it had been devastating to lose her. He'd married her out of obedience to what he'd believed God had asked of him. But he'd been the one who had been blessed. Love had been an unfathomable gift. And even now, with Reid . . . "There's still joy. I can't imagine life without Reid, and I'm unspeakably grateful to be his dad."

Matt nodded and then clapped his shoulder. "You're still standing, Connor. Still living."

The ferocity of emotion ebbed, and Connor welcomed the relief of it. It was as if the honesty of the conversation had ripped out the shrapnel that had been piercing his heart all this time. The wound still bled, but the blade had been removed.

It had been fear. All this time, he'd been thrashing in fear.

Fear not, for I am with you.

As the birds welcomed the new day, a ray of sunlight fell on Connor's cheek.

Be not dismayed, for I am your God.

Warmth seeped into the chill as Connor turned to face the sun.

I will strengthen you. Yes, I will help you. I will uphold you with My righteous hand.

Connor shut his eyes and soaked in the light and warmth. Proof enough of what Matt had just said: He was still living. And more, God was still with him.

CHAPTER FIFTEEN

(in which there is something new)

JADE PARKED THE VEHICLE as close to the back of the cabin as the sloping ground would allow. Rounding the vehicle, she secured her stocking cap over her ears before she opened the hatchback and began wrestling with the fifty-pound bag of puppy chow.

"Here."

Connor's call startled her. She jolted straight, smacking the back of her head on the lift gate. "Ow."

"Oh, I'm sorry!" Suddenly he was there. Right. There. His tall, muscled frame near enough to lend her his warmth against the chill of late October. More, one of his large, calloused hands cupped the back of her head with surprising gentleness. "I didn't mean to sneak up on you."

Jade looked up at him. And froze.

There was something new in his green gaze. Or, rather, something lacking. The distant chill was not present as he looked down on her with unguarded concern. Jade's breath caught as she took in this new warmth staring down at her. Her heart slipped sideways and did a little roll.

"Are you okay?" His near whisper sent a delightful tremble down her spine.

"Yes," she breathed.

What had happened? Three days ago, as she'd enjoyed the company of his sister-in-law at the bonfire, he'd been all cool indifference. No, worse. He'd seemed to mutely resent her being there. Intruding in his personal life, imposing on his family time. His silence toward her had nicked her heart—though she had confessed to herself that was only the infernal, unrelenting need for attention that she hadn't yet demolished.

The apparent cold shoulder had also irritated her. If he hadn't wanted her to be there, all he'd had to do was tell her so. He did have her cell number—a quick text would have worked just fine.

But now? This?

How could she teach herself not to hunger for the tender care that Connor Murphy was quite capable of showing? And he did so, often, with others. Occasionally, with her.

That evening in the snow, when she'd fallen to pieces in his arms sprang to mind.

Jade blinked, slamming a mental door on the intrusive memory as she eased away from Connor's touch. He'd offered friendship after that. Perhaps he'd just needed time to figure out exactly what that looked like for him. She wouldn't make more of it than what he'd plainly stated it was.

"I'm fine." She flashed a smile and leaned to grip the food bag. "Just a little bump."

"Let me." With one hand on her shoulder, Connor nudged her out of the way and then leaned into the same space she'd barely vacated to snatch up the dog food. He tossed the shifting bulk of it onto one shoulder and then stepped back. "This is quite a bounty for one dog."

"Rex is a bottomless pit."

Connor chuckled. "She is growing—and wasn't exactly small to begin with. Where are we going with this?" He patted the feed sack.

Jade reached up to shut the lift gate and then pointed to the slight incline that would, in three feet, level off to a narrow path that would take them to the back of the house. "I put a metal garbage can in the little ski shed behind the house."

"Good idea." He motioned the same way. "Lead on."

In little time they rounded the stone foundation, and Jade had the rectangular storage intended for ski equipment opened and the garbage can lid off. Connor ripped open the feed bag and dumped all fifty pounds of chow into the can.

"Thank you. That took roughly half the time."

He folded the empty bag, one corner of his mouth poked up in a half grin. "That might be an exaggeration."

"You didn't wait to watch me wrestle that thing out of the car, let alone stumble over the rocks with it. And I won't tell you how long it took me to figure out how to open the bag the last time." She tipped her head, eyeing him. "Or perhaps you've witnessed that circus surreptitiously?"

"I have not." He laughed, shaking his head in denial. Then he held up the neatly folded trash. "There is a trick to these things. You have to start on the right end."

"Hmm. Or resort to fetching your kitchen scissors."

"There is that option."

As if knowing her new batch of food arrived, Rex barked, her loud yelp coming from inside the cabin. Jade shook her head, turning down the side path that ran the length of the house. "She's about as much work as a toddler."

Connor fell into step beside her. From inside the house, Rex's barks grew impatient. When Jade reached the entry, she thought Connor would continue on his way, his random act of kindness done for the day. Instead, he stopped beside her.

What was this?

Internally scrambling to smooth her confusion, as well as the girlish hope that Connor's lingering attention had unleashed, Jade checked her watch. "The kids are staying for the FCA meeting this afternoon."

"Reid is too. I can pick them all up when they're done, if you'd like?"

"Thank you." See, there was that kindness he did extend—and having it aimed at her wasn't as unusual as her sulking had claimed. He took the kids to school on a regular basis and often picked them up as well. He played ball with Lily. Had tried to help Kellen with Rex. And made sure the coffee was ready at the lodge every morning.

Rex let out another string of demanding yelps.

"It'll be getting close to dark before Kellen gets home. I'd better take little miss barking energy for a walk."

Connor nodded, stepping back. But again, when she thought he'd retreat toward his own home, the old coolness falling back into place between them, he paused instead. A quiet space lengthened between them as he rubbed the back of his neck.

What was going on with him?

Those green eyes peered toward her, a little guarded this time. But not chilled. "I could use a walk too. Do you mind if I join you?"

Jade pressed her lips together to keep from gaping at him. He wanted to go for a walk? With her? Just the two of them?

Rex's bark deepened and grew louder at the same time.

Just the two of them and the dog. He'd promised to help with the dog. And he had, but significantly less so after the third time Kellen had rudely demanded he butt out. Rex's behavior at the bonfire the other night—climbing on people, barking, and even knocking over little Helene—had been less than exemplary. Connor wouldn't have been able to *not* notice that. It had likely gained his stern disapproval.

Perhaps that was what this was? Even if so—which was more than likely—why wouldn't he work on it with Kellen? Or at least wait until Kellen was home so that Jade and her son were both present?

Nerves tightened in Jade's gut. Which was dumb. She pasted on a bright smile and forced herself to look at him. "Of course not. You can make sure Rex doesn't drag me down the road." That should definitely earn a disapproving scowl.

Connor captured her gaze and held it. Such a handsome face hiding behind that thick mass of dark beard. And goodness, the intensity of those green eyes—not a hint of disapproval in them. After a moment she maybe wished didn't end quite so quickly, he nodded and widened the gap between them.

Jade blushed, realizing she'd stared at him. The heat in her face increased as she thought about the fact that she was blushing, and he very likely could tell. Goodness, did she always have to be a fool in front of him?

She ducked into the house, leaving him with a lame "I'll get the dog." *And hopefully find my level-headed, non-little-girl-swoony adult self.* No wonder the man had maintained a chilled wall between them, despite offering friendship. She was unendingly ridiculous.

And that wasn't funny. *It's dangerous, Jade. Have you learned nothing these past fifteen years?*

That cooled the heat racing through her veins.

Rex met Jade with a joyful yelp and a pair of paws in her middle.

"Ooof." She pushed the dog back down. "Rex, don't jump."

Rex twirled, her tail bouncing wildly, and then landed another double-pawed blow to Jade's gut.

"No. Down."

As the Connor-inspired butterflies—which had fluttered without her permission—lay down to die in her middle, Jade wrestled with the overgrown mass of fur called Rex, finally clipping the leash onto her collar. Just that effort made her sweat—which meant she hadn't entirely been speaking tongue-in-cheek when she'd told Connor he could make sure this already-too-large pup didn't drag her down the road.

They had to get ahold of this dog. Rex was too big to be disobedient.

With a sharp bark—one that proclaimed an exuberant *Walk! Let's go!*—Rex leapt toward the back door, dragging Jade in her energetic wake. Three times Jade had to push her clawing paws away from the doorknob before she could open it. The dog bounded outside, jerking Jade behind her.

"Whoa." Connor caught Jade by the shoulder as she stumbled out the door. Without permission, he reached for Rex's leash and worked his hands, one over the other, up the length until he had her by the collar. "Sit, Rex."

She barked at him and then grinned a crazy dog smile, her tongue lolling to one side. Then she tried to bound away. Connor had a firm hold on her collar though, which he gently shook to gain the pup's attention. Rex turned her eyes up to him, her brows folded as if to say, *What?*

"Sit."

Her large brown head tilted to the side, that confused look still on her doggy face.

"Sit." This time Connor used the palm of his hand to put a little pressure near Rex's tail.

Understanding lit in the dog's eyes, and she folded herself onto her hind legs.

"That's right. Good girl." Connor gave her head a hearty scratch.

Rex bounced up at him to lick his face.

"No. Sit."

She eyed him and then slowly lowered to a sit again.

"Good girl." He glanced at Jade over his shoulder. "Would you mind if we brought a pocketful of the puppy chow?"

Having stood back and out of the way, Jade was already near the ski shed. "Sure."

A wave of humiliated insecurity washed over her as she scooped a handful from the bin. They'd had Rex for over a month and had made next to zero progress with the dog. No wonder Connor was intervening. Jade fully expected to see tight disapproval in Connor's expression when she stepped out of the tiny space to hand him the food.

She didn't know if that disapproval was there hardening those eyes—she didn't have the heart to look as she poured the contents of her hand into his. He said nothing as he straightened and then passed the leash back to her.

Yikes. This could be a disaster.

Gripping the leash tight, she sent up a plea for miraculous good behavior and started around the house.

No miracle was forthcoming. Rex took off toward the driveway, and Jade could barely keep a hold on the leash.

"Here." Connor passed a single kibble to Jade. "Get her attention. When she looks at you, tell her 'Good girl' and give her the treat."

That should go well. Every time Jade fed Rex, the dog would nearly knock her backward in her overexuberant gratitude. But whatever.

"Rex. Rexy. Rexy, Rexy, Rexy." Yeah. That was effective. The dog strained forward, entirely oblivious to Jade's call.

"Tyrannosaurus Rex!" Jade tugged hard on the leash.

A muffled sound came from the man walking at her side. Had he just snort-laughed? Jade darted him a glare.

"I wondered where Rex had come from."

Okay, so maybe he could laugh at that. As long as it wasn't at her obvious struggle, and when was the man going to take over for her?

"Try again."

Apparently not anytime soon.

"Rex," she said.

The dog glanced at her.

"Show her the treat. But don't let her take it on the run."

"Like anything could stop her." Between two fingers, she held out the kibble anyway.

Rex spun around like she was on a merry-go-round and then lunged toward the food in Jade's hand. Connor reached for the leash, grabbing it near Rex's collar.

"Wait until she sits." The hold he kept on the dog's leash had him leaning into Jade, her shoulder pressed into his chest.

Jade's heart hammered. From the exertion the dog required, obviously. "I don't think she knows any of this."

"She's smart. She'll learn. It'll just take consistency."

Rex's eyes bounced between the two. Then she looked at Connor.

"Sit," he said.

Of course the mutt would do exactly as the man commanded. Sheesh. Jade gave the dog the treat anyway, stuffing away her annoyance.

Straightening again, Connor released the leash. Rex popped back up on all fours.

"Tell her to sit." His hand warmed Jade's shoulder.

"You could just do this, you know."

"Or you could." Connor passed her another kibble. "She's your dog."

How did this man possess the ability to make her grateful for him and irritated at him at half-second intervals? If he wasn't so condescending, she might like him better.

No. Not so.

If he wasn't so steady and quietly kind, she might like him less.

Jade scowled down at the mutt. "Sit."

Rex looked at Connor, ears perked up. He didn't say a thing. Then she looked at Jade.

"Sit."

Those ears twitched. And then . . . Then! She sat!

The hand on her shoulder squeezed. "There you go."

Jade couldn't resist a grin as she gave Rex her reward and added a good scratch on the dog's head to go with it.

"Now, as we go on, tap the leash back every now and again." Connor passed the kibble from his pocket to her palm and then stepped away. "If she looks back at you, reward her."

"Why?" Jade tucked the dog treats into her coat pocket.

"She'll learn to pay attention to you. Where you are, what you're doing, rather than running off like a wild dog."

"Oh." Jade started down the drive again, and Connor fell into step beside her. For several yards they walked along, Rex dragging Jade a little less than before. Jade tugged on the leash and called her name, and shockingly, the dog responded.

"It worked," she said, amazed.

"She'll learn quickly. She's not dumb."

Jade looked up at him, and he exchanged her look. A bit of distance had returned in his countenance. Perhaps this was all he'd intended—a quick *how to handle your dog so she doesn't drag you down the road* lesson, and now he was stuck taking a walk with her. Ensuring she didn't go gravel skiing behind her big, wild dog.

Should she dismiss him? *Thanks, I got it now. Go do whatever it is you do on your own.*

She didn't want to.

They turned left where the drive met the gravel road. That direction would lead them toward the lake rather than the highway, which was a half mile away. This time of year, and with only a handful of guests at the lodge, the lane was likely abandoned.

Lined on one side by a slope patched with boulders and tall sugar pines, the other side of the narrow road sloped downward toward the lake, leaving open views of shimmering water and the opposite side of the bay. The panoramic view was interrupted occasionally by a lone evergreen. The opposite land swell that rose from the waters was a smattering watercolor of deep blue green from the sugar pines and fiery oranges and glowing yellows of the fall-tinged shrubs. The late-afternoon hour had driven away the bite of snow that the mornings possessed, and the air smelled of damp earth, musty leaves, and sharp pine.

Gravel crunched softly beneath their shoes as she and Connor strolled silently. Rex kept a much more manageable pace and had taken to looking back at Jade every few feet—something Jade rewarded. As the walk and the quiet lengthened, Jade felt Connor's tenseness return.

Or perhaps that was her own?

She could just ask him what was going on. They could try another conversation, as friends, couldn't they?

"Did you have a good weekend with your family?" That wasn't lame, right? Wasn't too personal.

"We did. It's always good to see one of my brothers."

"I'm glad. Your sister-in-law seems nice."

"She is."

"Are all your brothers married?"

"They are."

"Do you like all their wives?"

"I do."

Jade glanced at him. Connor had pushed both hands into his pockets, his elbows pressed into his sides. His brows were folded inward, and discomfort bellowed from the tightness of his expression. She stopped in the middle of the road.

"You're upset with me."

Connor halted as well, and with a slight lift of his chin, he moved his attention from the gravel in front of him to her. "What?"

"I shouldn't have gone to the bonfire. Is that why?"

"I'm not mad."

Rex tugged on the leash. Jade tugged back, and when Rex trotted to her and sat at her feet, Jade fished out one of the remaining treats and gave it to her. Then with a long pull of crisp air to fortify her burgeoning courage, she looked up at him. "You're something, Connor. Mad. Uncomfortable. Disapproving. Something. What is it?"

"Jade—" Connor shook his head, a silent denial of everything she'd suggested.

When he didn't finish, she tried to fill in the blanks for him. "Maybe you just don't like me."

Something sparked in his eyes at that, and he stepped closer. "No. That's not it."

"No?"

He glanced at the dog, who had decided she would lay down on the road. When his gaze came back to her, she found the intensity in his eyes had doubled.

"I like you."

Her middle quivered at the words. Or maybe it was the deepness of his tone. Perhaps the way he seemed to hover over her. She stood there staring up at him. Trembling. And wondering what it was that crackled between them.

Did he feel it too?

"You shut me out. Push me away, and I don't know why. What have I done to offend you?"

His brow lowered, as if her words had caused him pain, and he reached to cup her elbow. "You haven't done anything to offend me."

"You said we would be friends." Jade couldn't keep the huskiness of emotion from her voice, which certainly must have exposed how much she'd wanted his friendship.

He visibly swallowed as he nodded and then came a half step nearer. "Be patient with me, Jade."

"But I don't understand. I feel like you're always put off. By *me*." She winced. "But maybe that is my imagination. Me, always needing attention. Affirmation . . ."

"It's not. I'm not . . . not really myself with you." His thumb brushed along her arm. "But that's not because of something you did. There are things I'm wrestling with. They kind of blindsided me, and—"

"Things?"

The palm that wasn't holding her arm spread over the middle of his chest. "In here. Jade, I can't tell you. Not now. I don't know if—" Again, he swallowed. "I don't know how to do this. None of that is your fault. But . . ." He reached to hold her with both hands. "But I like you, Jade."

She blinked, nearly confessing to him—out loud with words—how much she *wanted* him to like her. How much she liked him. But she sensed that wasn't what he needed right then.

Rex stood and shook herself off, then gave the pair of them a sharp bark. An *enough of this—let's go* bark. Jade glanced at the animal and back at Connor, then she squeezed one of his arms. "That's good. I need someone to help me with this mutt, so that's good."

A ghost of a grin poked up one side of his mouth. "I can do that."

Jade moved, intending to resume their walk, but just as she stepped back, his fingers squeezed her arm again.

"Jade."

She looked back at him. Never had she seen such uncertainty in a man's eyes. Nor would she ever have guessed that he would pull her close, folding her in a hug that wasn't quite intimate, but certainly warmer than anything that had been between them lately.

But he did exactly that. Strong, tender arms engulfed her, folding her in a warm hope of things being much different between them.

"Be patient with me." His husky whisper drifted softly in her ear.

Heart trembling, she wrapped an arm around his back. "Okay."

Who was this man, exposing bits of himself that seemed heartbreakingly vulnerable? Why had he reached for her, confided these tiny pieces of himself to her as if he trusted her? As if she mattered? How was she supposed to understand this?

As questions swirled through her heart and drifted through her mind, she refused to allow herself to imagine what he meant. Surely she would get it wrong, and her heart would be crushed all over again.

Lord, guard my heart.

CHAPTER SIXTEEN

(in which there is pizza and a plan)

He liked her.

That simple, plain fact that had struck Connor with such force after his conversation with Matt continued to hit him afresh over the following week. That first realization had been a shattering blow, cracking the hard shell that had—unknown to him—encased his heart. The telling of it to her had driven that spike deeper, flaking away what remained of that tough outer covering and finding the softness within.

Now every encounter with her felt new and quietly thrilling. He lingered inside the lodge in the mornings, seeing to the indoor tasks first so that he wouldn't miss her arrival. He timed his coffee break to match hers. And returned to the old routine of more evening meals at the lodge than taking them, just him and Reid, at their cabin. After, he'd even ventured twice to ask to walk with her and Kellen as they took Rex down the road for her exercise.

Shockingly, Kellen didn't voice his objections, though he obviously felt them. During those twenty minutes in the chilled fall air, Connor was gratified to see Kellen employ the strategies that Connor had given Jade. Though she still had a lot to master, Rex behaved with marked improvement. Better still, the quiet glances Jade sent his way were full of gratitude and warmth.

I like her.

By Friday evening, as he and Reid covered the distance from their cabin to the lodge, the thought had become familiar. More, it shifted from startling and scary to comfortable.

As they passed through the back door that led them straight to the kitchen, the warm, yeasty aroma of homemade bread mixed with the distinct smell of roasted garlic, tomatoes, and basil made his mouth water.

"Homemade pizza night." Connor's fist bumped Reid's.

"Yeah." Reid grinned. "Reason number nine hundred and twelve for why we can never move. Nobody makes it as good."

The smack of the back door sounded, and then Lily jogged up behind them, inhaling. Her eyes shut as she sagged in rapture. "I've been looking forward to this all day." Straightening, she elbowed Reid and smiled. "Hey! I heard you put on quite a show at noon ball."

Connor glanced between them, not missing the coloring of Reid's face. "What's this?"

"Twenty-five in a row." Lily beamed.

Connor narrowed his attention on his son. "Free throws?"

With a shy duck, Reid nodded. "Yeah."

"Heard it would have been more, but the bell rang."

Reid shrugged.

"Nice!" Connor gripped his son's shoulders and gave him a gentle shake. "Looks like all that time at the line with Lily is paying off." He winked at Lily, who grinned every bit as proud as she would if it had been her hitting those shots and not Reid.

Man, he was so grateful for Lily in Reid's life. Even with the worry that his son might have a moon-sized crush on the older girl—a worry that was receding daily as he watched the pair interact with genuine friendship—Connor was enormously glad Lily Beck brought her work ethic, determination, and selfless encouragement into Reid's world.

Which was also motivating.

Connor glanced over his shoulder to see Jade and Kellen wander down the short hall toward the kitchen. Catching Jade's wide brown eyes, he lifted a grin and then shifted his attention to Kellen.

"How'd the walk go today?" Connor had glimpsed the boy with his dog on the driveway on their own earlier. It had appeared that Rex was paying attention to the boy and that Kellen was significantly less irritated with his dog than a week before.

Kellen shrugged, not meeting Connor's gaze. Even so, he didn't deliver cold silence, as Connor had come to expect from him. "She didn't take off on me. That's good, right?"

He was asking him? Wow. Some massive progress there. "Absolutely. Good job staying with it."

Kellen glanced up, and Connor shot him an approving look. A move that earned him a scowl.

Connor punched down a sigh. One step forward . . . He let the rest of the cliché die, choosing to focus on the step-forward part.

"Ah. My gang is all here." Mr. Appleton hobbled into the area from his living quarters. He stopped when he reached the long table and placed an intentional gaze on each face as they gathered around. "God has given me a fine crew."

"He has indeed." Emma swept in from Connor knew not where and beelined her way to the oven. "A fine crew who is likely hungry."

"Starving for that pizza," Jade said. "I can't believe I've gone my whole life without it. Now there's no way I can go back."

"No going backward, dearie." Emma winked as she slid two large deep-dish pies onto the center of the table.

Without being asked, Lily had gone for the large bowl of romaine and spinach salad, dressed in Emma's homemade balsamic concoction that was every bit as addictive as her pizza, and brought it to the table.

Emma nodded her thanks at Lily and then looked at Appleton. "I think we're set."

"Let's thank our Maker." Appleton bowed, and the rest of the crew followed. "Creator of all things. Giver of life, of laughter, and of abundance. What good gifts you give!"

Connor's mind stilled as he listened to Appleton's prayer. Now, as always, he was pressed toward true worship as his friend and employer made it a point to praise God with his whole heart. Such an example the older man was! Especially when Connor considered the hard places Harold Appleton had walked in his own life. The gentleman knew what it was to grieve deeply, having lost his son and daughter-in-law in a car accident and his wife to illness.

Even so, Harold worshiped.

He proclaimed God's goodness. Pressed into God's mercies. Clung to God's love. It made Connor think of C. S. Lewis's words, *Surely what a man does when he is taken off his guard is the best evidence for what sort of man he is.*

Appleton was the godly sort. Deeply rooted, humble, and despite the scars he must certainly wear, utterly convinced of God's unending love. Something Connor felt a deep need to ponder. As Appleton finished his prayer, Connor tucked his thoughts away for safekeeping and joined the gathering around him as they dug into the food provided.

An easy familiarity had taken over the group. One that up until that moment, Connor hadn't seen or felt. Very likely it was the heart softening that he'd undergone over the past week that contributed to this welcome development. It seemed even Kellen was more at ease, more willing to participate and less prone to glaring.

"What's the weekend looking like?" Connor directed his question to Appleton.

The gentleman set his attention on Jade. "I've not checked, as our lovely Ms. Jade has proven herself entirely capable of handling all of that."

A touch of pride lit Jade's eyes. "I'm glad I'm doing the job."

"Quite well."

Connor's chest swelled, as if the compliment had been for him, not Jade.

"I believe we have one check-in, due tomorrow at four. But the room is clean and ready."

Appleton grunted with approval. "A morning off for you both then."

Connor had hoped so. "Excellent. The ice is moving deeper, so I was hoping to get another fish before it closes the deep." He settled his look on Reid and then on Kellen. "I was wondering if you would like to join us?"

"Fishing?" Kellen asked.

"Yes. At dawn." Connor glanced at Reid again, a touch worried that Reid would look withdrawn—a subtle sign he was upset. Other than looking surprised, Reid seemed open.

"I've never been fishing." Kellen folded his brows into a frown that seemed forced. "It sounds boring."

As if to confirm that he was on board, Reid also turned to Kellen. "It's actually fun. And if you haven't seen the sun rise over the lake yet, you're missing out."

"But it's cold out."

"True." Reid persisted. "I could lend you one of my warmer coats."

"I have a coat," Kellen said flatly.

Appreciating Reid's efforts, Connor squeezed his shoulder. "The invitation is open. Whatever you want to do is fine." He swept his gaze to include Lily and Jade. "You could all come, if you wanted."

"I'm definitely in." Lily shot Connor a full grin. "But if I have to put a worm on a hook, you might have to plug your ears."

Reid shook his head. "You're not a sissy."

Jade chuckled. "She's tougher than most girls, but I doubt you've witnessed her with slimy things. My sweet Lily goes from fearless to ridiculous."

"This I must see." Reid grinned.

Lily tipped her head, shooting him a bit of sass. "You don't get to hold it over me though. Don't forget that I stuffed your layup the other day."

The occupants around the table burst out laughing, Reid included. And Kellen. The subject of fishing died away, as did the layup rejection that Connor hadn't heard about until that moment, but the conversation remained friendly.

At the close of the evening, after Connor had read a chapter in Psalms and spent some time in prayer, his thoughts drifted toward the woman who lived next door. And to her children.

He liked her.

He liked them.

___ele___

She'd fished as a little girl a few times. The only bits about the activity that she remembered were that her daddy had baited her hook and that she never caught a thing. Even so, as Jade summoned those distant memories, she found them delightful.

Her and Daddy out in a canoe on some lake. Floating on glittering water, soaking in the golden sun, and simply being together. She couldn't remember conversation—she didn't even know if they'd talked at all. But she'd like being with him.

A sort of memory that she very much doubted her own children possessed. That was a bitter ache. One that, if she chose to indulge it, could easily give way to resentment. After all, so many other painful moments of the past did exactly that. However, that early morning, as she poured the freshly made hot cocoa into travel mugs, Jade chose not to allow that. Instead, she shifted her thoughts toward gratitude.

It had been kind of Connor to include Kellen—and Jade knew he intended this outing specifically for her son. A gesture that she knew Kellen didn't deserve. One that Kellen would more likely than not have rejected, if not for the fact that Connor had wisely opened up the invitation to all of them.

"Morning, Mom." Lily smothered a yawn, and she rounded the counter. "Is this your homemade hot cocoa?"

"Yes, ma'am."

Lily gazed at her with a sleepy smile. "I already love fishing then."

Jade laughed. "Is your brother up?"

Shrugging, Lily claimed a mug and inhaled its vanilla-chocolatey contents. "If he's not, it's his loss."

"I'm up," Kellen barked. "So don't talk about me."

Lily settled a long look on him and then shook her head. "Don't you think a year is long enough for a bad mood?"

"Shut up, Lil. No one asked you."

Jade nudged Lily's back, hoping her intuitive daughter would let it go. As usual, Lily did not disappoint her. She tucked a mug into the crook of her arm and grabbed a third in her available hand. "These are for Connor and Reid, right?"

"Right."

Lily lifted one mug and turned toward the door. Jade followed her, opening the exit for her and then securing it shut when she'd cleared. Then she turned to face Kellen.

"Son, this isn't required of you."

"What does that mean?"

"It means you can go back to bed if you'd prefer."

"You don't want me to go? Is this like a date or something?"

Jade sighed. "It's not a date."

Kellen snorted and rolled his eyes.

Ignoring his implied argument, Jade continued. "And you were obviously invited."

"Only because he thought inviting me would impress you."

"Oh, Kellen."

"What? It's the truth. It's the reason he suddenly started helping with Rex."

"He tried to help from the beginning. You didn't want his help."

"I still don't."

"That, my sour son, you don't get a choice about anymore. Rex is a big dog and will be even bigger when she's full grown. She *has* to learn how to behave, or we can't keep her."

"Great. Now you're going to take away my dog too."

"You know what, Kellen? Your sister is right, even if she shouldn't have said it. A year is quite long enough for a bad mood. Enough of it."

He glowered, anger making his whole body tense. "I didn't ask for any of this, Mom! I wanted to stay with Dad. You're the one who wouldn't let me, so my bad mood is your fault."

"Wrong." Jade let that slip with more volume and sharpness than she should have. She paused, reaching for self-control, and began again. "You're wrong on that Kellen. I'm sorry that what happened between your dad and me has been so upsetting, so hard. I'm not saying that is a small thing, and I understand that you're struggling. But your mood, your attitude? That's all you, buddy. You choose how to respond in life—to the good and the bad. No one else has to take responsibility for that."

"Whatever."

"No, not whatever, Kellen. That is the truth. You get to be as miserable or as happy as you choose. That's the bottom line."

"Then why couldn't you just choose to be happy with Dad?" His glare shot accusation at her like fiery arrows.

Pain clenched her chest, and Jade had to take in a long breath before she could answer. "Your dad made choices that made it impossible for us to stay together."

"But I thought you said that we choose how to respond?"

Kellen's sass and twisting of her words made her tremble with anger. She clenched her fists to hold herself in check. "Yes. I choose how to respond. You're nine years old, Kellen, so I doubt very much that you'll understand. But maybe you can take a lesson for your future. You cannot be with a woman who is not your wife and expect your wife to be okay with it. It wasn't okay, Kellen." She stood a little straighter and waited for Kellen to dare to meet her eye. "The way your dad treated me wasn't okay. And the way *you* treat me isn't okay. I've put up with it too long, and it hasn't helped. You've become a selfish, mean little boy, and that's not the person God wants you to be."

Kellen blinked and then looked down at his feet. "I don't think I believe in God."

Her heart crumbled. At his sniff, she moved toward him. Cautiously, she laid a hand on his shoulder. When he didn't jerk away but instead sniffed again, she folded her arms around him. Kellen pressed his head against her shoulder.

"I just want my family to be together. Like we used to be."

"I know, son."

"It's not fair." His young voice caught, and then those narrow shoulders shook.

"No. No, Kellen, I know this isn't fair."

Her son continued to cry, his head pressed against her. Jade held him tight, closing her eyes as she prayed for Kellen's broken and confused heart. Something, among so many things, that she couldn't fix.

CHAPTER SEVENTEEN

(in which Kellen catches a fish)

UNDER THE LIGHT OF his headlamp, Connor finished attaching the artificial minnow to Lily's line and then passed her the pole.

"I don't know what I'm doing." Lily looked over the pole.

"Just like we talked about." Connor pointed to the reel he'd set her up with. "Press the button, pull back, and about midway through your forward motion, release the button."

"Like this, Lil." Reid stepped in front of them. Usually, Reid didn't use a button release, but he'd swapped reels last night so that he'd be able to show Lily and Kellen how to cast.

Connor stepped back from between the two kids, and Reid demonstrated with his pole. Catching the weak morning light as little bits of glitter in the air, his line flew out over the quiet waters and then plopped into the gentle ripples twenty feet out.

"Looks easy enough," Lily said, clearly unconvinced.

"Easy peasy." Connor stepped out of the way entirely, not wanting to be snagged by a hook.

Lily cocked her arm back and then flung the tip of the pole forward. About three feet of her line released, and the baited hook smacked against the rocks on shore.

"Uh, that did *not* work."

Chuckling, Connor patted her back. "Try again."

"What if I get it caught on something?"

"You might." He shrugged. "We'll get it figured out, and then you'll try again."

Three more times she attempted a cast. Three more times the bait landed somewhere other than in the deep waters. Three more times Connor said, "Try again."

"Connor. Don't take this the wrong way, but you are a stubborn human."

Reid laughed. "You don't know the half of it."

Though his stubbornness was an undeniable fact, Connor shot Reid a mocking scowl. Reid didn't exchange the look, but his subtle grin let Connor know he felt it. He chuckled under his breath and then reached for the nearly empty mug of hot cocoa.

The sun had made its glorious entrance over the distant hills, setting the rippling waters into lapping waves of gold and white. As the warm rays hit the icy fringes of the shore, steam curled upward, giving the morning a sense of beautiful mystery. Connor wished, as he finished the last swallow of cocoa, that Jade had made it out so that she could witness the lake under dawn's magical spell. He glanced over his shoulder, searching up the hillside, and a delicious warmth spread through his chest at the sight of Jade and Kellen making their way toward him.

In the space that separated one heartbeat from the next, something mysterious and miraculous happened. It was like the sealing of a promise, an amen to a request he didn't remember making. This moment, these people . . .

Near enough now to make eye contact, Jade met his gaze. Connor couldn't keep from staring as the morning light caught the copper in her brown hair and shone golden on her face. As he watched her trek nearer, *I like her* suddenly seemed laughably insufficient.

"Good morning." Jade smiled brightly—perhaps too brightly. Likely to cover up whatever had kept her and Kellen from joining them earlier.

That wasn't Connor's business, so he returned her cheerful greeting. "Glad you could make it."

She held up a large thermos. "I brought more cocoa."

"Perfect timing." He lifted his mug. "I just finished."

Kellen kept his face pointed toward the ground. A fissure of compassion moved in Connor's chest. Whatever had kept them hadn't been pleasant, but Kellen wasn't being defiant about it. Instead he seemed broken in this withdrawn silence.

Poor kid. He hadn't asked for his life to be all upheaval and uncertainty. Connor stepped over the rocky shore. "I saved a pole for you, Kellen. Wanna have a go?"

Somber faced, the boy nodded, though he didn't look at Connor. Having known rough days of his own—days when he'd have rather not seen a soul or even pull himself out of bed—Connor knew a keen sympathy. After grabbing the pole, he stepped close enough to pass it to Kellen. "I can show you how to use it, if you'd like," he said quietly. "Or Lily or Reid can. Whatever you prefer."

"Lily hasn't done this before."

Connor nearly pointed out that she'd been out there for an hour and had figured out the mechanics. But he pressed his lips shut instead.

"I'll ask Reid," Kellen mumbled.

"Sounds good." Connor stepped away but didn't go straight to where Jade stood watching. Instead, he lowered onto a large, round boulder fifteen feet up from the shoreline.

Kellen approached Reid like a pup who had taken a beating. Reid set a mild grin on him and gestured for Kellen to join him.

Connor watched while Reid explained the mechanics of a successful cast and then demonstrated with his own pole. Kellen listened, nodding occasionally, and as the brief lesson went on, the deep furrow smoothed away from his brow. By the time Reid was finished, Kellen's visible attitude slid from disgruntled to willing. Maybe even eager.

This outing held promise after all. Crossing his arms as fatherly pride ballooned in his chest, Connor's lips twitched with a small smile.

"Your refill." Jade tapped his arms with his mug as she settled on a flat boulder at his side.

Connor turned his gaze to her as he accepted the steaming cocoa. "You're spoiling us with this."

"Seems I owe you."

"You don't owe me anything."

She flashed him a tight smile. "I am grateful though. Just so you know."

He motioned to the trio of kids now chatting as they stood at the water's edge. Eager energy vibrated between them, even Kellen. "This is no trouble at all. It's my pleasure."

That was 100 percent true. Standing there watching Reid, Lily, and Kellen made him understand on a deeper level why his dad had carved out time to take them fishing when they were boys. It was, in fact, a pleasure and a privilege. Even if the kids weren't all Connor's.

Jade remained quiet at his side, her features still pinched.

"Everything okay?" He knew the likely answer. Her delay in coming out, and both her and Kellen's subdued presence, told him everything was not okay.

"No. Not really." She turned her face toward Kellen. "But maybe we're getting there. Slowly."

Connor held her confidence in sharing what she wished as something sacred. It was as he'd suspected though, and that made him feel bad.

He cupped her elbow and squeezed. "Maybe this idea wasn't helpful."

"No, it was a good idea." Sincerity shone from her brown eyes. "As I said, I'm grateful. Truly, I am. Some things are just hard. But this morning he actually talked to me instead of storming off and slamming the door. That's something."

Connor just listened, and when she finished, he let a pause settle between them. It felt natural. Comfortable. In this moment—one surrounded by the morning chorus of awakening life, spelled by the golden sunlight on shimmering waters, and filled with a hopeful glimpse of better things to come—Connor prayed that Jade would find a place to lay down the burdens of her heart. That she would know God's faithful presence and His new mercies.

He prayed so, even as he surrendered his own burdens and pressed into God's faithfulness for himself. *Morning by morning, new mercies I see.*

"Connor?"

He gave her his full attention again.

"Please don't take this wrong, but—"

An ominous preface. Connor swallowed.

"—but you've been really good for my kids."

"I haven't done anything."

"That's not true, and you know it."

"Kellen resents nearly everything I do. I'm not sure how that's good."

"He might resent you. But he's watching you anyway. He sees your example, and it's not the same one he's witnessed his whole life. It's good for him, and I feel like even though this morning we had words and it wasn't very pleasant, that you are having a positive influence on him."

Connor stared at Kellen, not able to imagine how that could possibly be true, but also praying that somehow God would use his quiet, often stumbling life to make a difference for others. For Kellen.

"I'm not sure how I could take that wrong."

"I'm not implying . . . or, just . . . um." Jade cleared her throat as sweet rose stained her cheeks. She rubbed at her sleeve as if she'd suddenly spotted dirt there. "You're a good man, Connor Murphy. I just thought maybe you needed to know that."

"Jade." He waited until she stopped fidgeting and met his gaze. "Thank you." He turned so that he faced her rather than the lake and reached for her hand. "You don't know what that means to me—how much I want to be that man. Thank you."

Jade couldn't imagine how Connor Murphy didn't know the truth of what she'd said. He had proven himself over the past several weeks to be one of the best men she'd ever known. His quietness was indicative of a thoughtful and more introverted personality, not him being standoffish. He was subtly helpful, but in a way that spoke of wanting to be supportive, not condescending. Loyalty—first to God and then to his son—was a steady, deep current in his life. And he had, as he was right then, shown himself to be a man of great tenderness.

Such a man should be adored. And right then, as that mesmerizing green gaze held her captive . . .

Jade's heart thumped rapidly against her ribs, and the beautiful world that was all morning light and surreal mist faded. There was his hand, warming hers. His presence beckoning. And the warmth in those eyes . . . Could she dare hope that tenderness was for *her*? Vaguely, she was aware that she'd forgotten how to breathe. But who needed to breathe anyway?

Could he look at her like this forever?

"Fish on!"

One jarring shout, and her surroundings rushed back into mind. Lake. Connor. Kids.

Kids! *Dear Lord, did they see me staring at him?*

That was sure to cause problems, particularly with Kellen. With a quick sucking in of breath—because actually, breathing *was* necessary—she jolted her attention back to the shoreline. At the same time, Connor's hand released hers, and he stepped down toward the activity.

Lily and Reid gathered around Kellen.

Lily hopped up and down, patting Kellen's back. "You've got one! Kel! You've caught the first fish!"

"You have to land him, though, buddy." Though also excited, Reid's response was a little tamer. "Set the hook by giving it a firm tug."

Kellen did so, even while he glanced between the water and Reid with near panic.

"That's it!" Reid fist-bumped Kellen's shoulder. "Now, reel 'em in, nice and steady."

"It's heavy!" Kellen worked the reel with stuttering speed. Way too fast. Slow. Faster. Just right. Too slow.

"Steady." Reid covered Kellen's trembling hand and regulated the pace. "There. You've got it."

Ten feet offshore, a fish tail broke the surface of the lake, flagging the people ashore with an irritated splash.

"Oh my." Jade, standing beside Connor, gasped. "It looks big."

Connor's large hand covered her shoulder, and he flashed her a grin. "It's a good-sized one."

"I need help!" Kellen's excited panic notched up a few levels.

"You've got this," Reid said.

Head shaking furiously, Kellen looked first at Reid, and then, shockingly, he turned enough to find Connor. "Help me!"

Stunned, Connor turned an uncertain look to Jade. She reached for the mug he clutched and nodded. Even beneath that thick beard, she caught the twitch of a small grin.

"Connor!"

"I'm coming, buddy. But you're doing great." He relinquished the hot cocoa and clamored over the rocks, down the mild decline to the shore.

Jade's heart nearly burst as she watched the scene play out. Connor stood behind Kellen, one large hand on her son's shoulder, the other covering the hand that worked the reel. Together, they worked the fish to shore.

"Holy cow!" Kellen's shout was all thrilled exuberance, and he turned to Jade with a smile she hadn't seen in she couldn't remember how long. "Mom! Come see! He's *huge!*"

A laugh—joyful and perhaps a bit teary—bubbled from deep in her chest. "I'm coming. Don't let him get away."

"Connor! We can't lose him. Mom has to see this."

Connor glanced at Reid, and without speaking it seemed Reid knew exactly what his father wanted. The boy lowered his pole, securing it in between some rocks, and jogged to the small pile of tack. He retrieved a hand net and hustled it back to shore.

"Do you want to go get him?" Reid held the net toward Kellen.

Kellen shook his head, his steady gaze on the fish splashing in the shallows, its large, strong body flailing through the thin sheet of ice. "I don't have rubber boots like you."

"Okay. Do you want me to do it or my dad?"

"Connor." The answer was decisive, then Kellen looked back at Connor, who was still at his back, worry and hope in his eyes. "Don't lose him, okay?"

"I'll do my best." Connor mussed Kellen's stocking cap and took the net from Reid. He pulled a pair of thick rubber gloves from his waders, applied them, and then stepped onto the glistening icy film. Immediately his weight broke though. Five steps in he was calf deep in frigid water and clearing the remaining unbroken bits of ice from the spot where the fish continued to thrash.

"Get him, Connor!" Lily called. "Oh, this is so exciting! Get him."

Jade made her way to her daughter's side, and they exchanged smiles. "It is exciting."

"He'll be so glad he came out, right?" Lily whispered.

"I think he is already."

Lily looped an arm through Jade's and pressed a side hug into her. "See, we're going to be okay."

Thank You for this. Tipping her head into Lily's, Jade lifted a heart of gratitude toward heaven. "We just might be," she whispered back.

"Got 'em!" Connor stood straight, holding up the net, now weighted with a large, writhing fish. "He's a good one, Kellen. Nice work."

"What kind is it?"

"A rainbow trout—and a good-sized one, buddy." Connor splashed his way back to shore. "About eighteen inches and near two pounds, I'd guess." Once back on the land, he picked his way to Kellen, lowered the net to the rocks, and hooked the fish by a gill. Holding it up, the sunlight caught the shimmering gold of its back, making the bright pink of its middle stand out brilliantly.

"Here." He passed the flopping trout to Kellen.

"What if I drop it?"

"We'll pick it back up." Connor took the pole from Kellen's hand, set it aside, then flicked off one of his rubber gloves and handed it to Kellen. "You definitely need a picture with your first catch."

Kellen put the glove on, then tentatively reached for the fish, which flexed back and forth, though with diminishing energy. Connor talked him through how to finger the gill, and then passed Kellen's catch off.

Once Kellen had it, Connor stepped away. "Got your camera, Mom?" He flashed a big smile at Jade.

Phone already in hand, Jade took position. "All ready. Are you ready, Kellen?"

He nodded, grinning like he'd won first prize in something. Maybe he had.

Jade snapped several shots. "Got it."

"Can you text one to Dad?"

"Sure." Jade kept her smile in place. It was natural for a boy to want his dad to see his first catch, and she didn't resent that. She just hoped Peter would respond with something positive.

With cold fingers, she forwarded the best shot of Kellen and the trout to Peter and then repocketed her phone. Glancing at Connor, she found his easy countenance unchanged. A knot of tension eased in her chest. She didn't have a reason to believe he'd be bothered by Kellen wanting his dad to see his fish, but there was a hint of uneasiness about it anyway. Seeing Connor remaining steady was a relief.

Head bent, he worked on attaching some sort of hook-bait thing to Kellen's line. Within a minute or two, he had that secure and then was beside her son again. "How about we trade?" He passed the pole and took the fish.

"We'll keep the fish, right?"

"You bet. Catch another one or two like that, and we'll have enough for supper tonight." Connor glanced toward Reid. "Trout with garlic lemon butter, couscous, and roasted carrots, right?"

Something meaningful passed between father and son, and Reid nodded, a hint of a sad smile on his face. "Yeah. It's been a long time since we've had that." He glanced toward Lily, who stood near the shoreline watching Connor rebait Kellen's line. "It was my mom's favorite."

Lily's expression softened. "Oh wow. Would you mind if we tried it, or would that be hard for you?"

Shrugging, Reid ducked and then looked back at his dad. "It's time we try it again, don't you think?"

"I do." Connor's response was deep and quiet but saturated with emotion.

An ache moved deep within Jade's chest, alongside something else she wasn't sure how to define. It seemed a sacred privilege that Connor and Reid would share something so meaningful with her and her children. She wasn't sure how to respond and had to blink away the sudden spring of tears that glazed her eyes.

"Can I do something to help?" she asked.

Connor nodded, his look, though more subdued, not at all unpleasant. "After I help Kellen get this line out to that hole he found, I could text you a list. Would you mind making a store run?"

"Not at all." She held his gaze for a moment, wanting him to know that she understood the value of what he and Reid were sharing with them. That it mattered to her.

The corners of his eye crinkled. Just a bit. Not really in a smile—not the excited, happy sort, anyway. But in a way of understanding. Appreciation. And hope.

CHAPTER EIGHTEEN

(in which the student becomes the master)

"HEY, DAD?"

Connor shook the water off his hands and reached for the dish towel. "Yeah, Reid?"

"You want to play a round or two of *Mario Kart*?"

A grin played on his mouth as Connor hung the towel back in place, then reached for a dishwasher pod from under the sink. How long had it been since Reid had asked him to game with him?

Since before. And that was too long.

"You bet, buddy." He tossed the pod into the washer, shut the door, and hit Start. The aroma of garlic lemon trout and roasted carrots still clung to the air, now muted by the clean scent of dish soap and the vinegar spray that Jade had used to wipe the counters down.

He wandered to the couch in the front room and lowered next to Reid. "Fire it up."

Dinner had been a success. The whole day had been a success—from morning fishing to the midday chores the lodge required to the evening spent with the Becks. In the middle of all of that, Reid had hung out with Lily and Kellen. They'd taken Rex on a hike, played basketball, and had their own tournament of *Mario Kart*.

It had felt comfortably natural. New, and yet easy.

Thank You for a good day.

Connor was especially thankful on the part of Jade and her kids. Lily and Kellen were scheduled to board a plane heading back to the Midwest the coming Friday. At least their last weekend together before more turmoil entered their world was a good one.

Reid had the screen ready, and Connor took up his control. "Go easy on me, kid. It's been a while."

"You wish." Reid shot him a smirk.

"Oh boy. It's on now, buddy."

"We'll see."

They'd selected their avatars, Connor sticking with his standard selection: the heavy-weight Mario, and Reid going for his favorite medium-weight character, Yoshi.

"Going light, eh?"

"I raced Donkey Kong earlier." Reid shrugged, as if that was all the explanation required. Yoshi and the Kong had always been Reid's favorites, even before he understood racing strategy.

With a few clicks and a *go!* they were off to the races. Shoulders bent and twisted, grunts sounded here and *aw yeah* yelps there. First round win went to Reid.

Reid waved his hands in victory. "Want to try again, old man?"

"You know it. I haven't had any practice rounds, unlike some mouthy kid next to me."

"I don't need practice to beat you."

Connor laughed. "Listen to you, getting too big for your britches. Just remember who taught you how to play this game so you could beat your uncle Ty."

Reid chuckled under his breath. "The student has now become the master."

Reaching the width of the couch, Connor mussed his son's hair. "Pride goes before the fall."

Reid shot another mischievous grin.

Heart expanding, Connor tucked the moment in for safe keeping. He always treasured the fact that he got to see this side of Reid. It was a sign of their trust, their bond, because Reid only let loose with the people he felt safest with. It was a balm to Connor's heart to know that though they'd been going through some growing pains, and Reid had been gaining some independence lately, they were still this. Still close.

Round two commenced, and this time Connor found his rhythm. The race was tight, but Connor took it at the end.

"How 'bout that? The old man can still drive."

A mild touch of crimson tinged Reid's cheeks. "Tiebreaker?"

"Absolutely."

Reid owned the next round. Connor didn't even know what happened, but he laughed as Reid celebrated his victory.

After he settled back on the cushions, his jumping excitement worn through, Reid looked at Connor, a bright smile still in his eyes. "Think I could beat Mom?"

"Nope." Connor shook his head as he tossed his controller onto the coffee table in front of them. He chuckled. "Not a chance, son. Your mom was the true master at *Mario Kart*. She never got flustered, and she baffled your uncles and loved every minute of beating all of us."

A brief lull, then, "I texted Calvin this week. Did I tell you that?"

"No, you didn't." Hearing that Reid had done so didn't surprise Connor. Calvin had been a godsend to Reid, which was a gift to Connor as well. The fact that the counselor maintained contact with Reid, checking in with him now and then, was also a blessing. "Anything in particular that you wanted to share? Or did you just want me to know?"

Reid shrugged, his exuberance wearing off. "He just asked how I was, and it was sort of like a realization or something."

"What's that?"

"That I'm okay." The much more somber version of Reid resurfaced, and he held a steady look on Connor. "I'm okay, Dad. You and me, we're okay. Right? I mean, we're always going to miss Mom, but the memories are more like a good thing now. Before, they just . . ." He shrugged.

"They just hurt before."

"Yeah." His nod was quiet hope and understanding. "But like today, making the fish and talking about her just now. It's like all the good she left behind is floating up to the top, and I can hold on to that while the hurt is becoming less."

Connor shuffled sideways and then wrapped an arm around Reid's shoulders, pulling him in tight. "I think that is the perfect way to say it, buddy. And I'm glad you're okay."

"That we're both okay, right?"

Man, this bittersweet squeeze was something. Here his son was still wading through grief as a kid and wanting his dad to be okay. That was Sadie in him. So Sadie. Connor put his other arm around Reid and held him tight. "Yeah, Reid. I'm doing okay. Much better than I was. And I'm grateful for you. Every day more so."

Reid pulled back but didn't move away. "Dad? I know you've been worried about me. But I want you to know, you're not going to lose me. Not ever."

Connor cupped the back of Reid's head and shut his eyes. "That's good to know, son." He sought Reid's eyes and held them. "Really good to know."

A fresh pause settled again, one in which Connor could see Reid was processing, still wanting to talk. Connor slid a touch away, giving Reid space.

Reid pushed forked fingers through his hair and then rubbed his neck. A gesture Connor recognized. *So me.* It made his heart twitch.

"You know," Reid began timidly.

"What's that?"

"Kellen isn't so bad."

Interesting switch. Connor resisted the temptation to ask Reid why he went there and opted to let him say what he was thinking in his own time.

"Like today—we had a good time together. All three of us."

"I'm glad to hear that. Maybe Kellen just needs to know that he's accepted here, no matter how he's acted in the past."

Reid nodded and then swallowed. "I've just been thinking about how hard it was when Mom died." He looked up at Connor again, his brows now pinched. "But maybe in some ways it's harder for Kellen? I don't know. At first I was sort of judgmental to him. I thought, *At least your dad is still alive.* You know? But now . . ." Those ever rapidly broadening shoulders moved again. "I just don't know. At least I know you and Mom loved each other. I know that if you could have chosen different, you and Mom would have always been together. And also, I had the center. I had the tornado room. I have Calvin now. Who does Kellen have? He misses his dad and doesn't understand the things that Lily knows. He's mad at his mom. And he's here in a new place with no one else to dump on. That's gotta be really tough, you know?"

Whoa. Just . . . whoa. Connor couldn't blink back his tears. He couldn't speak. All he could do was bear hug his son.

An emotional silence passed as Reid remained tucked against Connor's chest, willing, for the moment, to once again be his little boy. Allowing Connor the time to process. *Lord! This kid!* As he had many times over since he'd adopted Reid, Connor was washed under a tidal wave of soul-quaking gratitude at the reality that he got to claim Reid as his own.

Connor kissed the top of Reid's head and blew out a breath. "You," he managed, though his voice was raw. "Kellen has you."

"And you." Reid pulled back and met Connor's gaze. "He has you, Dad. He needs you, I think. And I'm good with that. That's what I want you to know, okay?"

"You're sure?"

His nod was solemn. "I wrestled against it when they first came. When you first tried to help him with Rex. After he basically told you to get lost, I was secretly relieved. But I've been praying about it, Dad. Really asking God what He wants. And I saw it today, while we were fishing. He wants us to help Kellen. And Lily and Ms. Jade. He brought them here on purpose. I know it now. So don't give up, okay?"

Connor sat there, stunned all over again. "That is enormously generous, Reid."

He shook his head. "I remember Calvin once told me that pain can either make me bitter and self-destructive, or I can let it work something good in me. I want the good. And—" Reid paused, taking a deep breath. A sheen of tears glazed his eyes. "You didn't have to love me, Dad. But you did. You didn't have to be my dad, but you are."

"It's my deepest honor and privilege to be your dad, Reid. You don't owe me anything because I love that I get to call you son."

"I know that. But you still chose it. You chose love." His chin quavered, but he looked determined to finish. "I want to do that too."

CHAPTER NINETEEN

(in which the Beck children return to Kansas)

THE CABIN FELT SO still. Chilly and lonely, and Jade wasn't sure how she would survive a whole five more days of it. Thankfully, her phone rang.

"Lily." Jade exhaled as if she'd been holding her breath for over a day.

Metaphorically, she had been. Actually, longer—since she'd packed her children up, drove them to the airport, and watched them go through security all on their own Friday night. So technically she'd been holding her breath for over forty-eight hours. Other than a quick text sent to her here and there by her daughter, she hadn't spoken to them. It had seemed like an awful eternity.

"Hey, Mom." Lily sounded . . . not like herself at all. Entirely upset and not even trying to cover it.

"Hon . . . what's going on?"

"I slipped away so I could finally call you. I'm sorry I didn't before. Dad says this is *his* time."

Jade could almost hear Lily's eye roll. And she agreed. She'd had the same reaction when Peter texted her after the kids had landed in Kansas City, telling her that he was not allowing them to call her while they were there. *You have them all the time. This week is mine.*

Sheesh, the man was something . . . Peter had always been this *something*. Jade just hadn't realized what a prison he'd kept around her until the past couple of years of being outside of that. So many years of isolation and feeling like so little . . .

Shaking her head, Jade punched down her rising temper. It wouldn't help anything for her to let off steam with her daughter.

"You don't sound like you're having fun, Lily." Jade figured focusing on Lily would be a better tactic. That was a little bit of a surprise. If he was good at anything when it came to his children, Peter was good at short-term good impressions. At being the quick bursts of fun-guy dad.

"I'm not. At all. Mom, Macey wants me to wear *pink*." Now her tone indicated a dramatic vomit sound.

Jade laughed. That was what this was about? "Oh, Lily. Pink won't kill you."

"She said I could pick whatever dress I wanted, and then we got here and my choices were all pink—from *fade out of existence make me look naked* pale pink to *oh my goodness I'm gonna be sick* Pepto pink. I have a pink complexion, Mom! Pink looks terrible on me, and it's the worst color ever, anyway." Lily's tirade continued to build steam. "I don't even want to be in this wedding. Why couldn't they just sneak off and get married somewhere private? They snuck around for everything else. Why should this be any different?"

"Lily." Jade's reprimand was soft.

"Well. It's the truth, and you don't have to try to shield me from it. I already knew."

Jade lowered to the couch as a sigh dragged out from deep within. "I know, Lil. You know way too much, and I know that. I wish you didn't though."

"That's not your fault, Mom."

Cramming her fingers through her hair, Jade searched for a way to have this conversation without dishonoring Peter. Even if he deserved it, her doing so wouldn't help Lily. And right now Lily needed some honest help, because this bitter, angry girl was *not* normal. "Listen, hon. I know this is super hard for you, and I'm not in any way diminishing that. But this is Macey's wedding. It's not about you. So for one day, wear pink."

An extended pause lengthened, then Lily breathed a ragged sigh. "I know, Mom. I just needed to vent a minute. And to talk to you." Her voice broke. "I miss you. And between you and me, I really just want to come home. I hate that Dad says I can't call you. Why is he so controlling?"

A flare of panic lit. "Is he . . . he's not being ugly, is he?"

"No, other than just demanding we adore him. No." Lily lowered her voice. "He's not being like he was to you."

Jade had no idea how to respond to that. While she'd known that Lily knew too much of what went on with Peter and Macey, they hadn't ever discussed it. Nor had they ever talked about the way Peter had been controlling and demeaning toward Jade.

"Mom, he said horrible things to you. Things you never deserved, and he always thought I was too young and ignorant to understand. You don't have to pretend—"

"Lily." Jade swallowed. "Here's the thing, hon. As long as he's not treating *you* like that, I want you to let go of what you know."

"Mom—"

"Sweetheart, it doesn't help me for you to stay angry with your dad. It doesn't help either of us. I'm not saying that you should ignore bad treatment. You shouldn't, and if your dad is being that way to you or to Kellen, you tell me immediately and I will get you out of there. But right now if you're miserable because you're mad at him for my sake, I'm begging you to let that go. It won't help anyone."

"How can I not be mad at him?" Tears salted her whisper.

Jade's arms ached to hold her daughter, and her heart battled against what she was telling her right then. The truth was, Jade hadn't forgiven Peter yet. The truth was, she felt the threat of bitterness taking root in her own heart. She didn't want that. Not for herself, and certainly not for her kids.

She wanted *life*. One of beauty and hope and joy. That wasn't possible if she allowed bitterness to strangle her and her kids.

"Talk to Jesus about it. Give that anger to Him—and ask Him to help you forgive your dad." Jade spoke to her own heart as much as she did to her daughter, and the enormity of that request rocked her very core. There was nothing easy about anything she'd just said. "Don't hold on to it. It will only make you bitter. You're too sweet and wonderful to go that route."

Another ragged breath came from the other end of the line. "I know, Mom. I know it in my head, at least."

"Me too, babe. Me too."

"Mom?"

"Yeah."

"You're kind of my hero."

Emotion shook through Jade's body.

"I just want you to know that."

"Oh, Lily." She swiped at the single tear that had escaped. "I think that's a little crazy—there are much better people in this world who have made much better decisions than I have. But thank you. I'm honored, and I'm proud of the young woman you have become."

"Thanks," Lily whispered. "I'm not doing a very good job at being that person right now though."

Jade wanted to chuckle. That was more like her daughter—holding herself to high expectations. "You can fall apart with me, Lil. It's okay."

"Thanks, Mom." Her voice sounded brighter. More in control and less fractured.

"Is Kellen doing okay?"

"Kellen is taking this week for all it's worth."

"What does that mean?"

"Dad buys us anything we want. Food. Clothes. Gadgets. Whatever. Kellen is living his most spoiled life ever."

Great. Jade was looking forward to the week of their return. Should be super fun. "Well, at least he's not being a bear."

"I didn't say that."

Oh boy. Typical of Peter. And more and more, of Kellen. Jade had to fight against the build up of irritation.

Just last weekend, when they'd gone fishing with the Murphys, it had seemed like Kellen had a breakthrough. He'd stopped being sulky and demanding and way too much for Jade to handle. For a whole day, she'd glimpsed the sweet little boy Kellen had been not that long ago. And even through the week that had followed, Kellen had been softer. Easier. Less self-consumed. Less bitter.

"I gotta go, Mom."

"Yeah. Okay, Lily. Take care of your brother, even if he is being a bear."

"I always do."

"I know, sweetheart."

"Love you, Mom."

"Love you too." Jade barely had the words out before the call went dead. Hopefully, that didn't mean Lily got caught and was in trouble.

Her heart trembled. *God, maybe I shouldn't have let them go.* Could she have stopped it? The court allowed Peter solo time with the kids. If she'd said no, he could have taken legal action, and she might have lost custody. Not that she really believed Peter wanted custody of them. Clearly he hadn't, as Jade's move had basically been Peter's idea. No, he wouldn't want full responsibility of his children—he never had. But he would have gone after her out of spite.

The tap of bitterness sank in a little deeper. *Lord, I don't know what to do with this—help me! And, please hold on to my kids. Keep their hearts safe. Please.*

Heart unsettled, anxiousness pulsed energy through her limbs. With a glance at the back door, she found Rex sprawled out on the wood floor, napping in the early evening sun.

"Rex." Jade stood and clapped her hands. "Rexy, come on, girl."

Rex popped her head up and looked at her.

"You're taking me for a walk, because I need it."

On the word *walk*, Rex scrambled to her feet and barked. Jade went for the leash, snapped it on Rex's collar, slipped on her coat and hat, and took herself and the dog out into the cold fresh air.

Please, Lord. I need help.

He'd thought before that his mind wandered to her entirely too much. That had been nothing. Since their day spent together, Connor's thoughts had been nearly consumed with Jade Beck.

I like her.

That admission had become comfortable. More like a declaration. A claim that looked toward the future . . . One that was still a touch on the scary side but now leaning toward thrilling rather than terrifying. And he thought about it. A lot.

He liked the way she was with the kids. The memory of their first two-on-two pickup game with the older kids surfaced easily and often. Jade was a baller and not one bit timid on the court. She didn't go easy on Reid, and she didn't hold back with Connor. She owned confidence in that realm, and that was flat out attractive. But she also didn't take herself too seriously—a quality that amped up the appeal factor by ten.

That game had been the most fun Connor had had in a handful of years, and so much of that had been because of Jade.

He liked how she texted corny jokes to Lily and Kellen, and sometimes to Reid, which was how Connor knew about it. She sought laughter, even when obviously things in her life were hard. She continued running hard after Kellen, even when he was being the biggest little pain in the backside. Jade loved with all her heart—though likely hers was a broken heart—and she didn't quit.

Persistent. That was what she was, and who wouldn't stand back and admire it?

He liked the fire she possessed. How she could call him out and stand her ground. Jade Beck was no wispy woman. Life circumstances had tossed her to the dirt, yet there she was, on her feet and holding ground. She was as tough as anyone he'd ever known. Man, he liked that. Wanted to drink it in so that her strength could summon more from of his own broken heart.

Resilience was an underrated charm.

Jade inspired him. Made him curious. Made him smile.

He might be a little bit addicted. Because he really couldn't stop thinking about her.

And worrying about her heart, especially that week, because she'd had to put her kids on a plane and send them halfway across the country to the man who had *not* appreciated all the wonderfulness of who she was and had, instead, destroyed her world.

He did *not* like Peter Beck, faceless man that he was. He didn't like that Lily and Kellen were spending an entire week with him. And he really didn't like the idea of Jade wading through that week on her own. Even if Connor knew she possessed the strength to do it, he didn't like the idea of it.

Nope. Didn't like those things at all. Two of them, he could do nothing about. One, however, Connor had the power to change. The glimpse he had of her out his front window confirmed exactly that.

Shoving arms into his coat and snagging his stocking cap as he scrambled for the door, Connor went after her.

"Hey." He jogged down the steps and across the driveway that ran in front of both their cabins.

Jade turned, tugging Rex with the leash. The dog stopped, though her tail conducted the air in presto time, expressing her impatience with this delay.

"Hi." Jade's expression and tone indicated surprise.

"Going for a walk?" The length of a yard separated them, and Connor shoved his hands into his pockets. Maybe he was being too assertive?

"Yeah."

Too late to back out now. "Would you mind if I joined you?"

She smiled. His heart leapt with joy.

"Sure." Jade turned back the way she'd been heading, and Connor fell into step beside her.

They rounded the side of the lodge, walked the length of the front of it, and neared the entrance of the property before either spoke again.

"What's Reid up to?" Jade asked.

"He's still at school. The junior high basketball coach has open gym for the next few weeks, until season officially starts."

"Oh yeah. High school girls too." She glanced at him. "Lily was bummed she was going to miss the first week. She's afraid it's going to leave a bad impression with the coach."

"Lily has game—something I suspect she got from her mom." He winked. "I don't think she needs to worry."

They paced off several more steps, the lonely road narrowing with a stand of pines on both sides. Connor glanced at Jade, sensing tension in her posture. Because of him? Because he was being . . . forward?

Man, he hoped not. That was his way—who he was. He thought long and hard on things, weighing them carefully. But once that was done, he was resolute. Decisions made, he acted. Maybe it was his former military life spilling out. Or decisiveness was just who he was.

Either way, Connor had decided. He plunged forward, though nerves had him balling his hands. "How are the kids?"

Her long sigh told him the answer before she used words. As did the anxiety that filled her brown eyes, turned up to him. "Lily just called, actually." She gestured toward the dog. "That's why I'm out here. Blowing off steam."

"At Lily?" That seemed odd. From everything he'd seen, Jade and Lily rarely came to blows.

"No. At Peter. At this week. This whole situation."

Alarm crept into his chest, and forgetting his nerves, he gripped Jade's elbow. "Are they okay?" One word and he'd find a way to get to Kansas.

He'd figure out how to get them back. Jade only needed to say *no*—to tell him her children were not okay.

"They're okay." She touched his jacket, near his chest. "Lily was just upset. She doesn't usually let things get to her, so that upset me."

Connor studied her, trying to gauge just how troubled Jade was, not yet done with the idea of extreme intervention. "Why is Lily upset?"

"Well, on the surface, because she has to wear pink for the wedding." Jade shook her head. "But that's not really why. Peter told the kids they couldn't call me while they were there, that this is his time with them."

"What?" His grip on her elbow tightened, and anger roiled in his gut. He stepped nearer. "That's not okay, Jade."

She sighed. "She texts me. And found a time to call me when he wasn't around."

"I don't like it."

"I don't either, Connor." Her looked morphed from frustration to pleading and then to strength. "But right now I don't think it's worth fighting him about. Lily promises that they're okay, and she knows to tell me if the situation is otherwise. Peter is . . . controlling. But he's not violent. He's manipulative. But Lily knows that, and she's not likely to be spelled by it."

"Jade." Connor let his touch slide from her elbow to her hand, and he gripped her fingers. "If you need to get them . . . just tell me. *I'll* go if that's what you need."

Gratitude and relief filled her steady gaze on him. She squeezed his hand but shook her head. "No. I really think they're okay. Lily says Kellen is having the time of his life—Peter is spoiling him." Turning, Jade started walking again.

Connor kept her small hand tucked into his. And she let him. Into this churning of anger, once again directed at a man he'd never met, came a flood of absolute elation. Jade held his hand! Thrilling warmth traveled the length of his arm and pooled in his chest. He dared more intimacy, weaving his fingers through hers, eliminating all possibilities that what had been growing in his heart concerning her could remain secret.

The stand of pine thinned as they walked on, and to their left, a panoramic view of the lake opened. The waters seemed dark as the evening shadows crawled toward the opposite shore. The gravel beneath their shoes crunched softly while the rhythm of his heart kept a staccato pace.

"Connor?"

He met her glance again, finding her brows pinched.

"Please don't pity me. I don't want that from you."

"I don't. That's not what this is."

In a patch of weak sunlight that poked through a pair of peaks behind them, Jade stopped.

"What is this then?"

Connor's heart stuttered as he held her gaze. He tugged her hand, and she slid nearer. Gently he cupped the curve of her face, tracing the plane of her cheek with his thumb. Her skin was soft, and he leaned in. Her eyelids slid shut, fanning those dark lashes over creamy skin, and the warmth of her gentle sigh teased his mouth. Connor closed the space between them slowly, allowing her opportunity to pull away before he grazed the fullness of her lips with his own.

"I like you, Jade," he murmured.

She tipped her chin as one hand braced against his chest. "You've said. But . . ."

Connor moved in for a fuller taste. The jogging of his heart turned into a full sprint as her mouth yielded to his. He slid his fingers from her face to the back of her neck, and the hand that had held hers moved to her lower back. With gentle pressure, he tucked her in close and lost himself in the feel of her. Her lips, so soft and sweet, dancing with his. Her warmth seeping into him. Her fingers grazing his shoulders and neck, then burrowing into his hair, combing into his beard.

I like this woman . . .

It was an understatement. The way this kiss rocked him, stole his breath, and gave his heart new life . . . The way she'd captivated his mind. She'd burrowed into his life in a way he'd thought would never happen again. This was more than *like*.

A whine near his knee preceded a sharp bark, summoning him from the fog of warm pleasure.

Jade too, as she broke away from his mouth, though she tipped her forehead into his nose. "Rex doesn't think this qualifies as a walk."

Connor chuckled as he wove the thick softness of her hair between his fingers. "I'm pretty breathless, so . . ."

He felt the movement of her quiet laughter as he continued to hold her. Man, she felt good in his arms.

"When did this happen?" Jade asked.

He nuzzled her nose. "The moment I looked at you."

She pulled back only enough to find his eyes. "That's not true."

"It's true." He moved his hand to cup her cheek. "I walked into that kitchen, saw you, and thought, *She's beautiful*." He kissed her forehead, then the corner of her eye. "You're beautiful, Jade."

"But you—"

He cut off her breathy argument with a kiss. Then pulled back enough to meet her eyes again. "I didn't want to like you."

A sorrow darkened her gaze. "Because of Sadie?"

"Because of me." He snuck one more taste of her top lip. "Because I'm scared."

Her arms circled his neck, and she pressed into him with a strong hug. "Me too, Connor."

Pulling her in close, he held on to her for dear life. The last time he'd felt so much for a woman, his heart got wrecked.

Though not the same story, Jade's experience had been similar.

There was so much to lose, so much pain possible.

But.

But he knew from a love that had been beautiful and blessed, there was so much to be had too. So much joy and laughter. So much good possible.

Maybe they were both brave enough now. Both healed and ready to risk their hearts for that good.

CHAPTER TWENTY

(in which the stakes are raised)

CONNOR MURPHY *LIKED* HER!

As Jade walked from her cabin to the lodge to begin the new work-day, she grinned as that jubilant thought wound through her mind and squeezed delight from her heart.

Could it be true? Could this dream world she'd entered in the evening before prove itself real? It seemed like such a daring risk—one that put so much more at stake than just her own heart. Her own life.

There were Lily and Kellen to think about. And Reid too. The three of them had already been through way more than three kids ought to have faced.

As she passed the space where Connor usually left his Pathfinder parked, Jade made her thoughts focus on those three precious souls. Right now Connor was driving his twelve-year-old son to school. The boy who only two years before had lost his mother to cancer.

She then shifted her mind toward her own children. In three days Lily and Kellen would stand up with their father and Macey as they got married. As if that weren't enough, hours later they'd hop onto a plane by themselves and fly back to her. Their world was one of constant upheaval. Could she really add to that?

Was this responsible? Was it right?

Oh, so much of her wanted to ignore those nagging questions. Because the handsome and honorable Connor Murphy *liked her*! It was too won-derful to push aside. He'd held her hand. Pulled her close. Kissed her.

As she passed through the double french doors at the front of the lodge, the rich aroma of freshly brewed coffee only made her appreciate the man who woke up early every day to make sure it was ready. Connor was a rare man. And he liked her.

She couldn't help it. Delicious shivers trembled down Jade's spine as she recalled those tender, intimate moments with him. First, on the road while Rex impatiently waited for her exercise. Later that evening, under the cover of a moonless night, near the firepit out back, when she couldn't talk herself out of bundling up to seek him out. She hadn't even known for sure he'd be out there. Just hoped. She had felt like a teenager sneaking into the cover of night.

And there he'd been, as if he'd wished for the same. He must have—Connor hadn't hesitated to stand at her approach, to take her hand, and to pull her into the warmth of himself. To seek her mouth with his. Who knew how long they'd stayed out there tangled in each other's arms. Kissing.

Making out like teenagers.

Heat flooded her chest and filled her face.

Jade tapped the Power button on her computer and then strode toward the Bunn commercial coffeemaker. Even as she thrilled at the memory of Connor's kisses, she tried to push them away. Perhaps this was not responsible at all. They had three kids between them—should they really be acting like that?

Oh, but it felt so good to be held. To feel wanted.

Loved?

Goodness, she was hitting the speedway here.

But this was Connor ... Connor Murphy, the reserved deep thinker. The quiet, responsible man next door. The diligent worker who kept this lodge in order. The respectable father who was raising a responsible son on his own.

Certainly he wouldn't act in such a way if he didn't feel something deep for her. Would he?

I like you . . .

With the level of thrill that rushed through her heart every time she replayed his husky words, you would think he'd declared much more.

"He didn't," Jade whispered to herself as she filled her mug with the first cup of her morning coffee. "He didn't." The reminder warranted repeating, as she knew herself to be needy and thus prone to making big mistakes. She couldn't afford this kind of mistake.

Her heart, her kids, this job, the cabin—they all required that she keep her head in front of her tumbling heart. That she do better than she had so many years ago with Peter.

"Good morning."

There it went again. Tumbling. A fresh thrill prickled down her spine at Connor's quiet, deep greeting. His chest brushed her shoulder, and the tips of his fingers trailed lightly down her spine.

Jade sucked in a sharp breath.

"Did I startle you?"

"I didn't hear you come in." She turned her gaze to find his eyes, and warmth filled her face. No doubt she was blushing. And by the quirk at the corners of his mouth, he noticed.

Jade swallowed, willing away the heat. "Did Reid make it to school okay?"

"He did." Connor took a step back and let his touch drift away.

All at once she was thankful and regretful about that.

"Have you heard from Lily or Kellen?" Connor reached for a clean mug and then the coffeepot.

Jade sipped her coffee, scrambling to sort out her thoughts before he focused that mesmerizing green gaze back on her. "Lily texted early this morning. She said they were going to Sea Life and Lego Land today."

"That sounds fun. Are they excited?"

Shrugging, Jade leaned against the counter. "Hard to tell on a text. I imagine Kellen is thrilled. He used to beg to go to Lego Land. And if she'll let herself enjoy it, Lily would like Sea Life. She's such a science nerd."

Connor nodded, and then he stepped closer. "And how are you?"

Her heart leapt at the tenderness in his look. *Too much, too soon.* As much as Jade wanted to ignore the whispered warning, she also clung to it. She needed a level head. Biting her lip, she summoned courage and resolve.

"Connor, we need to talk."

For a man she had thought to be coolly reserved and frustratingly unreadable, the hesitancy and dread filling his eyes were unmistakable. Jade's heart squeezed, and she couldn't look at him. Instead, she lowered her head and turned toward the small storage room off the guest dining area. Connor followed her, flicking on the light and shutting the door behind him.

"I upset you last night," he said, his voice flat.

"No." Yet again flames crawled over her cheeks. *Upset* had been the furthest thing she'd felt with him.

"Jade, it's been a long time since I've kissed a woman." He combed fingers through his hair. "I'm sorry if . . ." Crimson blotched the skin above his beard. "If it was too much. I—"

"Connor, I liked kissing you last night."

He studied her, hovering over her in a way that seemed sweetly possessive even while vulnerability etched in his expression. "Then why does this feel like the beginning of a breakup?"

A breakup? That would imply they were *something*. Something more than a pair of adults who had made out beneath the stars. More than two lonely people reaching out to fill the void. Oh goodness, she wanted that *something*.

Her heart strained toward that, confusing her purpose—which hadn't been well defined in the first place. What was it she wanted to say to him?

I more than like you, Connor. And that terrifies me because I can't trust myself.

How would that go over? She wasn't bold enough to find out.

Jade found his unwavering, penetrating gaze waiting. "I just think we need to be careful. We have kids . . ."

"I would never dishonor you, Jade."

She wasn't sure what that meant exactly. Well, actually, she could guess. And she believed him. Though she'd discovered last night that Connor was a man capable of breathtaking passion, she'd already known that he was also one of deeply rooted self-discipline. She was safe with him—even when behaving like a teenager under the stars.

Reaching for his arm, Jade stepped closer. "Connor, you're one of the most honorable men I've ever met. I'm not worried about that." It was herself she couldn't trust. But that was not what she was talking about right then. "But our kids have already been through so much. Mine are attending their dad's wedding this week, and it's hard for them. I just don't know if they're ready for this."

Connor nodded.

"I mean," Jade continued, "as far as they know, you and I are barely friends."

At that, he winced. "I don't know about that."

How could he not? She let her touch fall away. This would blindside the kids, wouldn't it? It had taken her by surprise. After all, a few walks to work on dog training, a ball game here and there, and one day fishing . . . did that really equal *friends,* let alone *friends who kiss*?

Apparently so. But it wouldn't be obvious to the kids, would it?

Jade bit her bottom lip, letting her attention fall to the mug of coffee in her hands.

"Jade, you have to tell me plainly what you're saying here. What you want. I'm not good at this. I have never been good at this."

She snorted softly. That couldn't be true. "How did you end up married?"

"I married Sadie because she was a single mother who had a cancer diagnosis. I felt a profound call to be a part of her life and to be the father Reid didn't have. Sadie married me despite my clumsiness in love. I miffed everything back then, including the proposal. We were married for several months before there was romance between us. Even then, I promise if you could ask her, she would tell you I'm not good at it."

Jade couldn't help it. Shaking her head, she sought those green eyes and touched his chest. The beat beneath her fingertips leapt, and the pulse at his neck noticeably surged.

"I very much doubt your wife would say that of you." She reached to trace the line of his jaw, the thickness of his beard rough against her fingertips. "I suspect that she would say that you loved deeply, as I can see plainly you did."

He visibly swallowed and nodded while emotion misted his eyes.

How amazing would it be to be loved like that by this man? Jade wanted to know it for herself. So, so much. But from where they were now to there? That span seemed dangerously terrifying. Could she really risk her already damaged heart? She had messed up before. Had blindly—stubbornly—handed her heart to a man who had never treasured it. A man who took and manipulated everything she gave until he decided it was time to move on. She didn't want to live like that again.

She couldn't.

Was that really the issue here?

Jade pushed the intruding question away. Her concern was her children. And his son. That was what they were dealing with.

"I just want to be careful with our kids."

"I understand that. But what does it mean exactly?"

"Can we keep this between us for a while?"

His brows furrowed. "You mean sneak around?"

Jade pulled back. "Don't say it like that. Like there's something to be ashamed of."

"I'm not a fan of secrets, Jade."

His mild rebuke snagged a touch of offense. Secrets had destroyed her world. She blew out a breath. "I'm not much of a fan either. But they're not ready." Though she knew it was a cheap shot, she pulled out the prime example. "Kellen barely likes you. He outright resents you most of the time. This would not sit well with him."

Connor reeled back as if she'd slapped him, and she wished she'd kept that last part unsaid.

Hugging herself, she shrunk back. "I'm sorry. That wasn't necessary."

For a long moment, he kept still, and she felt a chasm expand between them. *Nice work, Jade.*

When she thought he'd reach for the door handle and let himself out, leaving her alone in her miserable failure, Connor instead slid both hands down her arms. "We can try."

She looked up, finding uncertainty in his eyes.

Even so, he bent to kiss her head. "I'm still not a fan, but if that's what you want, we can keep this between us. For now."

Pressing her forehead into his chest, she hugged him. "Thank you."

Her gratitude was only halfhearted. Because, truly, it wasn't what she wanted, and she, like him, didn't love the idea of going behind the kids' back with this. But the alternatives were equally unstable. They could tell them and risk further issues. Issues she wasn't certain this fledgling relationship would survive. Or—

Or they could end this here. Now.

Either one of those options made her want to cry.

CHAPTER TWENTY-ONE

(in which there is love)

SHE HAD TIED HIM into a knot.

Connor put energy into waxing the skis, hoping as the muscles in his shoulders burned that the exercise would burn off his frustration. It wasn't as if Jade didn't have a valid point. Honestly, he'd worried about the kids' reaction to him and Jade as well. He'd had a very different thought about that issue though.

In fact, he'd nearly brought it up with Reid the night before. The only reason he didn't was the amount of homework his son had. Prealgebra and advanced science had kept Reid up, sitting at the counter working diligently well past a decent bedtime.

But Jade had another point about Kellen not liking him. That was a legitimate concern—along with the fact that her kids were currently going through something rather traumatic with their dad.

Man. He had such bad timing.

Maybe he should just walk this whole thing back. Except, no. He didn't want to. Now that he'd quit fighting his attraction to Jade and surrendered to the idea that he could love again, he'd kind of gone all in. Because that was the way he was. Consider carefully. Decide. Act.

Retreat wasn't on that list.

But this wasn't all up to him. Maybe for her sake, he needed to adjust. For Jade and for her kids.

As he came to the last pair of skis, Connor's internal wrestling settled. Enough so that later when he made his way home after the skis were finished and caught Jade getting ready for a walk, he was able to flash her a genuine-though-mild grin and ask if he could join her. She said yes.

Connor pointed at the cabins. "I just need to change quick, if that's okay?"

After nodding, Jade followed him into his home, Rex close to her leg.

"I'll be just a second." Connor bounded up the stairs, sorting through how to begin the conversation he had determined to have. *I don't want to be deceptive to my son. We can put this on hold . . .* Though he thought he'd settled on that course just hours before, a fresh campaign against it began.

For so long he'd shut himself away from even the idea of dating. He'd given Sadie every ounce of his love, and though she'd told him to keep living, to find love again, and he'd promised he would, Connor simply hadn't believed it possible. His heart had been too broken.

But now there was Jade . . . With her, he felt life quickening again. Once he'd gotten past the paralyzing fear that this risk could end in devastation, his emotions had taken a deep plunge, his attachment to her gripped hard.

The arguments replayed over again as he shed off his smelly sweatshirt and replaced it with a clean one. He headed out of his room and back down the stairs as the turmoil continued. But as he turned from the bottom step to see Jade across the room, the debate died.

She stood at the table near the front door, studying the framed picture of Connor and Sadie that had lived in that spot for over two years. Connor's heart squeezed as Jade fingered the edge of the frame, and he wondered what she was thinking. Feeling.

What if it were him, looking at a picture of her? Connor didn't want to imagine Jade with Peter in such a photograph. But, honestly, that had more to do with his anger toward the man than jealousy. Would he feel differently if her situation had been more like his?

He crossed the room, grabbing the coat and hat he'd tossed over the back of the couch as he closed the distance between them.

Jade looked back at him while he was still a few feet away, giving him an uncertain smile. "I've wondered what she looked like."

Connor stopped at her shoulder and peered at the image he studied often. It had been a tender moment that Lauren had captured. One they hadn't posed for. They had been standing at the end of the dock at the close of day, as they had often done. Sadie's gaze was soft on him, and he was brushing her breeze-tossed hair from her face.

That day he remembered with painful clarity. Later that evening, they had shared with his family their devastating news.

Jade turned her attention back to the picture. "She was smaller than I'd imagined, given Reid's height."

"She was sick in that picture. Small and frail. But beautiful." Even to the hard, painful end—which from that point, came unexpectedly fast—Sadie had been beautiful to him.

"I had imagined brown eyes like Reid's."

"No, Sadie's eyes were blue. Reid has her nose, but other than that, he doesn't favor her much. At least, not in looks. But his quiet, contemplative ways, his genuine kindness, those are all his mom."

Jade looked at him again. "She had cancer throughout your marriage?"

"No." He took up the frame. Sadie looked peaceful. Happy, even. So ironic. "Her scans were clean about a year after we were married and stayed that way for a while." He held up the frame. "This was actually taken a few weeks after we found out the cancer had come back."

Jade leaned in to study it again. "Wow," she whispered. "I wouldn't have guessed that. You both look so . . ."

In love. Yeah, they had been. A fresh flow of pain oozed through his chest.

"I think we both knew we wouldn't have much more time. The years that we did have—they'd been a gift. When her second diagnosis came, we knew the odds." Connor swallowed as his words caught in his throat. "We felt our days shortening."

Jade took his hand and squeezed. "You didn't waste them."

Connor nodded. "Sadie—" He couldn't finish. Sadie wouldn't let their time be wasted. She had been intentional with her love, baptizing him in it, pouring out her affection so that he would never doubt her heart.

He still felt it. The flame of her love still burned in his heart, and he treasured it.

There had been a time when he believed that had been it for him. When it came to a woman's love, Sadie's was all he'd have in his life. And it was enough—all he ever wanted. But now . . .

Replacing the frame on the table, Connor turned his eyes toward Jade. As he gazed at her, taking in the soft curve of her face, the milk chocolate of her eyes, and the thickness of her soft hair, he felt his heart expand. There was room for her there. A space only for her.

Jade blinked against the sheen glazing her eyes and ducked from his study. "What did you love about her most?"

"Her steady, deeply rooted faith." Connor didn't have to ponder his answer. "She had a rough story before Reid was born—and I had a hand in that." He felt a touch of shame as he remembered the events from high school that had tormented him for so many years. It'd been a long time since he'd felt that sting. Some of that tale he'd already told Jade. "She helped me understand the miracle of forgiveness—the freedom of receiving it and living in it. She said that if ever she needed to remember the bigness of God's grace, she only needed to look at Reid. He was born into the darkest part of her life, but God used that baby boy to pull her out of it. God turned her failures into blessings. Sadie held on to those moments, let them fuel her faith. She inspired me to reach deeper, to trust God more."

Except, maybe he hadn't been doing that quite so well the past few years. Instead, he'd sheltered his heart from any hint of possible pain. It'd been the exact reason he'd behaved so ugly toward Jade at their first meeting. It'd been as if he'd sensed God was doing something new, and Connor had wanted no part of it. Particularly if it meant risking more pain.

Fingering the smaller frame that had sat in front of the picture, Jade then lifted the treasure it held. "She wrote this, right?"

Beneath the glass there was a white lined 4 x 6 note card, and indeed the beautiful script scrawled in black ink had come from Sadie's hand. "She did. She often wrote out verses and songs. It was something she started doing during her first round of treatments the year we married. This one"—Connor paused, remembering the sweet sound of her quietly singing—"is from one of her favorite hymns."

As Jade read the words, Connor needed little effort to summon them to mind. *Strength for today and bright hope for tomorrow.*

"'Great is Thy Faithfulness,'" Jade said.

He nodded, though Jade continued to study the words Sadie had penned. Her brows knit together, and her jaw tightened.

Connor cupped her elbow, his hold light. "What are you thinking?" he whispered.

"You loved her."

"Yes." He'd loved Sadie with every inch of his heart.

"You still love her."

"I'll always love Sadie." Taking her hand, he tugged Jade so that she would turn to face him. "But she's gone home to Jesus. Whole and healed and not coming back—and I wouldn't want her to come back to that."

Jade's shoulders moved as she filled her lungs. "I don't think I'm anything like she was."

"No. You're not." He pulled her hand to his chest and pressed her palm against his heart. "But I don't want you to be Sadie."

Jade blew out a shaky breath, then slowly lifted her face to him. "I'm not sure I can measure up."

Connor shook his head as he ran his thumb against her cheek. "I'm not measuring you against her." He leaned to press a kiss to one of her dark brows. "I'm not measuring you against anyone. I like *you*, Jade. When I think about you—which is entirely too much—I'm not comparing you to anyone. I think about how boldly you put me in my place when I was a jerk to you. I think about how fun it was to play ball with you that first game. About how awesome it is that you text dumb jokes to your kids—and how

I sort of wish I got those texts too. I think about how brave you are to start over and how well you're doing it. And I think about how I wish I knew how to make things easier for you."

He moved to kiss the other brow. "I think about how I like the feel of your hand in mine." His nose traced the length of hers, and then he found her mouth with his. "And about this." Angling his head, he moved in for a longer taste. "I've been thinking a lot about this."

Connor felt Jade's hesitation melt, and he gathered her close as she pressed into him. A heady fog settled over him, chasing away the decision he'd made earlier.

He didn't want to step back. He wanted this. More of this.

Even if that meant not telling his son.

Jade inhaled the crisp evening air, which helped to clear the delicious but confusing fog in her mind. Kissing Connor Murphy had become her most favorite activity, and it had only taken a day for that to happen. As intoxicating as that was, it was equally alarming.

She had to keep her head about this.

Connor took her hand, weaving his fingers with hers as they bounced down the deck's steps. Rex rumbled down ahead of them, eager to *finally* get this walk going. If her sharp bark that had Jade pull away from Connor's lips hadn't been an impatient prompt, she didn't know what it was.

Intervention.

Possibly that.

She set a brisk pace, and Connor matched it easily. When they came near the front of the lodge, she slipped her hand from his and tucked it into her coat pocket. He did the same with his—but only until they turned down the road and out of spying range. Then he fished for her hand again, and Jade savored the warmth of his large palm against hers.

I think about how I like the feel of your hand in mine.

Her heart shivered. She very much liked the feel of it too. But there was also fear mixed in with that delightful tremor. *I'm not anything like Sadie was—and Connor so clearly adored his wife.* Jade felt both inadequate and yet a growing desperation. One she was unfortunately intimately familiar with.

She was done being that woman though. The one who would do anything, be anything, just to feel accepted. Wanted.

Loved.

She'd given everything to Peter. Been whatever he'd wanted—even when that *whatever* had made her feel uncomfortable and used. It had never been enough. He only ever took, leaving her feeling so much less.

Jade peeked at the man beside her. Connor met her glance, and concern shadowed his eyes.

"You're upset," he said.

Looking toward the lake, Jade toyed with the idea of telling him exactly what was in her thoughts. That he thrilled her, and that made her distrustful of herself. That she'd spent years seeking the approval and heart of a man who never did truly give her either. But saying those things . . . certainly that would make Connor run.

Surely Sadie hadn't been such a self-destructive woman. *I'll never measure up . . .*

Connor tugged her to a gentle stop. "Jade." He waited for her eyes to meet his. "Talk to me."

She bit her lip. "I'm just worried . . ." *that you'll find me lacking.* ". . . about the kids."

Brows pinching, Connor nodded slowly. "They come home Friday?"

"Yes." Jade battled a pinch of guilt that she hadn't been honest with him. She settled her attention on Rex, who tried to lick her hand as Jade pet her head.

"What are you most worried about?"

Jade shrugged.

"Jade."

Swallowing, she forced herself to look at him. He shook his head. "I don't think you're being honest with me right now."

"What?" She straightened. "Why would I lie about the kids?"

"I just don't think that's what you were thinking about. Worrying about."

How could he know that? Jade scowled.

Connor stepped backward, a flicker of hurt passing over his expression. He rubbed the wool at his jawline, his gaze drifting toward the lake behind her. Then his chest moved with a sigh, and he pivoted to move down the road again.

Hand still in his, Jade made herself walk beside him even as her heart faltered. She'd hurt him just then. Shut him out, and he felt it. She thought about how he'd opened up to her just a bit ago, sharing sacred memories with her when she'd asked him about Sadie. He'd been honest and vulnerable with her, letting her see both how much he'd loved his wife and how painful it had been to lose her. And yet, somehow, he'd made *her* feel treasured in the middle of all of that.

How could she close herself off to him only moments later? Goodness, she was such an insecure woman. So afraid that she'd latch on so tight to something bad that she couldn't open herself up to something truly good.

This wasn't who she wanted to be either.

She wanted to love and to be loved. How did someone as turned around and broken as she was figure out how?

"My marriage was bad." The confession tumbled from her lips. An awkward statement. Out of place. Horrifying and embarrassing. But honest.

They'd just passed the clump of trees that shaded the road, keeping the temperature ten degrees colder than elsewhere. Connor paused again, turning to her so that her shoulders soaked in the late-afternoon sun.

"I know," he said. "At least, I know enough to know that it wasn't good."

Jade gulped. "I'm not sure how to do a good relationship. That's what I was thinking."

Nodding, Connor gripped her hand more firmly.

"I'm afraid, Connor. I like you so much, but the thing is, I made really bad decisions the last time I liked a man this much. That scares me."

He worked his jaw for a few moments. "Will you tell me?"

"About Peter and me?"

Though he nodded, a leeriness lingered in his gaze. As though he was unsure he really wanted to hear.

Jade wasn't sure she wanted to tell. Did she really want Connor to know what a flimsy person she'd been? She drew in a quavering breath, nodded despite her misgivings, and began walking again.

"He was in college, and I was in high school when we met. He was handsome and outgoing and sort of every high school girl's dream. So when we started dating, I thought I'd won some kind of prize." She huffed a quiet, derisive laugh. "He went away, back to college, and I imagined he pined after me the way I did him. So when I heard from a friend attending the same school he attended that she'd seen him with a college girl, I doubted her story. She begged me to confront him—and I did. He said they were only friends and that I was being paranoid and jealous and to stop acting like a child. I thought that was fair. The same friend came to me again at Christmas, telling me that he wasn't just *seeing* this other girl. He was sleeping with her, and I should dump him. And she had proof. Heartbroken, I confronted him again. This time he didn't deny it. Instead, he cried. Pleaded for my forgiveness. Swore it was only because he missed me so much—and he needed the physical healing of sex. He needed it from me . . ."

Flames crept up her chest, claimed her neck, and consumed her face. "So like every idiotic girl in love, I believed him."

They came to the end of the road where it spilled into a parking lot. At the far end, near the lake's shore, a concrete picnic table sat. When they reached it, Connor turned and leaned against the tabletop.

Jade felt his steady watch on her as she battled for the strength to look up. When she did, she found a storm in those green eyes—anger. But when he reached to finger her face, there was only gentleness in his touch. "He manipulated you."

"I let myself be manipulated." She swallowed, facing the hard truth of it. "My dad warned me. My mom begged me to break up with him. My friend also told me. Repeatedly. But I decided that love would triumph. That truly, Peter wanted me—I just hadn't given him what he needed." Blowing out a controlled breath, Jade let Connor fill in the gaps as she skipped to the end of the story. "I spent fifteen years trying to be what he needed. Turns out, all that I had wasn't even close to enough."

"Why did you stay with him so long?"

"We were married, you know?" She shook her head, turning to face the ice-crusted shoreline. "I may have done everything wrong when I had dated him, but I was determined that our marriage I would get right. And I prayed. Connor, I prayed my guts out. I begged for God to change Peter's heart toward me. To love me, to *want* our marriage to be good. To be honest, I still don't understand why God didn't act on that. Why wouldn't He want to fix my marriage? Why wouldn't He want Peter's heart to change?" Hugging one arm over her shoulder, Jade felt the lingering ache of devastating disappointment as she glanced back at Connor.

A painful scowl pinched Connor's brows as he shook his head. "I don't know."

"Me either." She faced the lake again, and a frosty breeze stirred the waters, pushing its frigid fingers into her hair. "But then again, why would he let your wife die when you loved her so much?"

"I don't know." Connor's tone was low and broken as he eased his arms around her. For a moment there was only his arms holding her tight against the chill of the lake breeze and the sudden bitter surge in her heart. "Can I tell you what Sadie told me, after her second diagnosis, when I finally let my resentment have an honest breath?"

Chin wobbling and throat too tight for words, Jade nodded.

His chest quivered at her shoulder as he took in a long breath. "Jesus loves me, this I know. For the Bible tells me so."

The simple words, known to her from her earliest memories of child-hood, hit like a tender sledgehammer, breaking away what had been crusted and smothering. It could have been patronizing. Instead, it was the most profound thing she'd ever heard.

As silent sobs quaked her core. Connor's arms held her fast. Even as Jade sank into them, she wondered if the strength and tenderness she felt there wasn't his. Not his alone.

Jesus loves me . . .

Jade let the overwhelming honesty of that saturate her heart.

This I want to know.

Oddly, beautifully, it seemed God answered that simple request with a cold breath of lake-seasoned air into her lungs. In it was life and hope and an undeniable pressing of inaudible words into her heart.

I want you to know. I love you, Jade.

CHAPTER TWENTY-TWO

(in which all bets are off)

"Lily and Kellen come back tonight." Reid bounce-passed the ball back to Connor.

Connor set up for another jump shot. "I know." The ball banked left, and Reid went up for the rebound. "Will you be glad to have your free throw practice partner back?"

"Yeah." Reid dribbled away from the hoop. "And Lily will be relieved to be home."

Connor did not miss the way Reid referred to the lake as home for Lily and didn't have any trouble believing that the reference had come from Lily herself. "You text her?"

"Yeah, we text." He squared to the basket and flipped the ball up in a perfect arc. Nothing but net. "She didn't want to go to Kansas, and I don't think she had a whole lot of fun while she was there. She said she was glad it was time to come home, and she's ready to get into the gym for basketball next week."

So. They apparently texted often. Connor caught the rebound and held the ball. "Son, I like Lily a lot. You know that."

One corner of Reid's mouth poked up—the closest to a smirk his son possessed. "Dad. Lily and I are friends. That's it, I promise. She's easy to talk to, fun to play ball with, and she helps me with my math and science. But she's also way older than me. I know where I stand."

"Yeah?"

"Yeah." Reid held out his hands, ready for a pass.

Connor sent the ball Reid's way while a thread of relief uncoiled in his gut. At least one issue was resolved. One of several—and much of that created by himself over the past few days. The week had been a roller coaster.

Mornings, he could barely wait to see Jade, and it felt like a bit of sweet torture to have the desk between them when he stopped to say good morning when what he wanted was to pull her in close, kiss those addictive lips, and inhale the bright scent of whatever it was that made her smell amazing.

He couldn't help but wonder if she felt the same. Hoped for it.

Through the days, Connor kept himself busy, taking his lunch with him on projects because he couldn't handle the thought of pretending nothing had changed between them if he spent that break with her and Appleton and Emma. He wasn't the acting type, and he was certain he wouldn't be able to pull it off.

The early evenings, while Reid was at open gym, Connor and Jade walked Rex down the road toward the lake. Once out of sight of the lodge, Connor would slip his fingers through Jade's. At the deserted parking lot at the end of that road, he would lean against the cool concrete picnic table and slide a hand around her waist and to the small of her back, and she would step into him.

He had to admit, they kissed more than they talked at that point, and maybe that shouldn't be so. But it had been one of his favorite parts of the day, second only to the much later hours, when she would find him by the firepit long after Reid had gone to bed.

Maybe they were playing with fire. How was he going to act like there wasn't something between them for the long term? It didn't seem possible, not when he already felt like she was a part of him—a part of what he wanted from here to the end.

While Reid dribbled the ball, Connor rubbed the chilly line of his jaw. The lack of a beard felt strange. He'd only shaved it off two days ago.

"Wishing you'd kept it?" Reid chuckled, apparently keen to Connor's internal reaction.

"Nah." Connor dropped his hand and forced a grin. "Still just getting used to it not being there."

"You and me both. I'd forgotten what you looked like without a beard."

It had been an impulsive act. The second evening with Jade, after they'd shared so much from their pasts and the depth of their hearts, he'd come in chilled through, gone to his room to get ready for bed, and in the bathroom had stopped in front of the mirror. Running his hand over the hair covering his face, he had a visceral memory of Jade's fingers scraping the same spot. He'd wanted to feel her fingertips against his skin, and he wondered if she'd rather kiss a man without a face full of wool.

So he'd shaved it. For the first time in two years.

Reid put up a baseline shot and nailed it. Connor caught the ball and tossed it back to his son, his mind still not on basketball. He had worried what Reid would think, what questions his son would ask when he saw his hairless face the next day.

Reid had looked at him, tipped his head to one side, and gave a small grin. "Look at you, not looking like a bear."

Connor had fought down a billow of heat threatening his face. "It was getting pretty scraggly."

Shrugging, Reid had gone back to his breakfast of poached eggs and toast. "Looks good, Dad. Nice to see your whole face again."

And that was that.

Jade's reaction . . . Connor had to turn away from his son as he replayed the sensation of her fingers sliding over his cheekbones, down his jaw, across his mouth.

Man.

She thrilled him. Having her close, her touch, the feel of her breath against his skin. The taste of her. He couldn't go backward now.

"Bank." Reid lined up behind the three-point line Connor had spray-painted onto the concrete pad.

Connor set up for a wide rebound, though he felt confident that wasn't going to be necessary. "Nail it."

Reid put up the shot while Connor continued to mull over Jade.

He didn't want to go backward.

What he wanted was to tell the world. Beginning with the boy swiftly becoming a young man in front of him. Connor hated not being up front with Reid. It felt . . . sneaky. Dishonest. And unfair to his son, because the longer this went on, the deeper Connor was in it. If Reid had an issue with it—which would matter a whole lot—this delay would make everything harder. So much harder.

Would Reid have an issue with Connor dating Jade?

The only way Connor knew to answer that was to ask him. Connor was a direct person. He didn't like subtlety. He didn't like things left in the shadows. And he and Reid had always been forthright. Always.

But he'd promised Jade.

"Dad!" Reid's call jolted Connor, but not before the ball smashed into his chest.

"Oof." He doubled over but managed to wrangle the ball in.

"Sorry." Reid shot him a puzzled look. "I thought you were looking. It's yours. I missed the last shot."

"Not your fault." Connor dribbled, moving toward the top corner of the key.

"Dad?"

Connor took the jump shot. "Yeah."

"You okay?"

"Of course. No big deal."

"No, I mean . . ." Reid recovered the ball on a bounce and sent it back to Connor. "You've been kind of . . . uh . . . gone lately." He tapped the side of his head.

Great. How was Connor supposed to answer that? Yeah, he'd been gone lately. A little too fixated on a certain brown-eyed neighbor, and a lot frustrated that he couldn't be up front about it with his son. It didn't lend to the kind of relationship he wanted with Reid—especially on the heels of a season when he'd felt his son pulling away.

Connor rubbed his jaw again. "Just thinking about Lily and Kellen coming home." Nice. Now he was outright lying. This could lead to nowhere good. "Maybe we should have a bonfire tonight. What do you think?"

Reid smiled. "If Ms. Jade is good with it. You should ask her."

"Yeah, that's a good idea. She might want her kids to herself their first night back."

"Right." Was . . . was that sarcasm in Reid's voice? Reid dribbled hard in for a layup, made it, and then tossed Connor the ball. "They'll want to come. Bet."

Connor stood, baffled. Then he shrugged. "I'll check with Jade. We'll see."

"Sounds good, Dad." Reid fist-bumped Connor and then started toward the cabin. "I'm going to shower. Let me know if I should build a fire."

Confused, Connor watched him jog up the drive. What had that been?

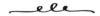

Jade snuggled deep into the plush blanket draped around her shoulders and wrapped both sets of fingers around her steaming mug of coffee. Over the distant eastern hills, muted by a line of wispy clouds, the sun broke the lingering darkness, scattering shadows as day claimed victory over the night. Shutting her eyes, she grinned as a silent prayer of thanksgiving lifted from her heart.

Lily and Kellen slept in their beds, under her roof. Home again, and by all appearances, happy to be there. With Lily, that wasn't surprising. Kellen, however . . .

Even as gratitude rolled in her heart, a touch of pain on his behalf pinched as she thought on her son. When she'd picked them up at the airport, Lily had been all exuberance, all *Let's go home! I can't wait to see the lake! Reid texted that we are having a bonfire. Let's go make hot cocoa to share.* And how delightful that had been. Kellen had been . . .

Quiet.

Not angry-quiet. Just quiet.

Jade had expected a litany of complaints. Everything from *I hate flying and I got sick*—which, by the pallor of his face, he likely had—to *Dad is way better than you. I hate living here and I want to go back to Kansas.*

No complaints had come. When she'd asked him how his trip was, Kellen gave her a subdued, "Fine. We got to go to Lego Land."

"That must have been fun," Jade had said. "You've wanted to do that for years."

"Yeah, it was cool." Kellen had kept his face turned toward the window and had put zero enthusiasm into his answer.

At that point, Jade glanced at Lily, searching for a silent explanation. Lily gave her an expression that said plainly, *He's been through it. Give him time.*

So Jade didn't push it. Not last night—even when she was shocked that Kellen wanted to go to the bonfire with the Murphys. Even when, later, he'd come out of the bathroom after brushing his teeth and mumbled a quiet, "Good night, Mom"—something he hadn't done in over a year. Jade let him have his space and prayed that he'd talk to her when he was ready.

And she did so again, right then as the golden yellow of the sun burned away the peach-white of a cloud.

The sound of scuffling feet against the wood floor drew her attention from the window. Behind her, stumbling from the steps onto the first floor, Jade found the object of her prayer aiming for her direction. Kellen circled the couch and dropped into the space right beside her, and his head dropped heavy against her shoulder.

Not something Kellen had done since she and Peter had separated, though this had been a standard morning tradition when her boy had been young.

Heart growing with an achy yearning, Jade buried her shock and reached across her body to finger the straight brown hair that poked every which way from his head. "Morning, son." She dared to press a kiss to the top of his head.

"Hi, Mom." Kellen snuggled closer.

"It's pretty early for a Saturday, bud."

"It's nine in Kansas."

"That's true." It was two hours later there. "Still kind of early for you."

Kellen shrugged, then pressed his head deeper. He sighed. "The sunrise is pretty."

"It sure is." She risked spoiling this moment by adjusting her position and circling his shoulders with her arm. Goodness, she had missed this!

Kellen leaned against her like he was still her little boy.

Jade had a mighty hard time blinking back tears. She couldn't hold back her curiosity anymore. "Kellen, you okay, bud?"

A shuddering exhale rattled through him. After an excruciating long pause, he sat up and looked at her. "Dad . . ." Tears sheened those dark-brown eyes.

Jade battled the rise of anger even as she reached to cup her little boy's face. "What happened?"

Kellen shrugged. "He doesn't want me."

"What?"

"Before we left, I told him I wanted to live in Kansas. With him. He said no." His head fell forward, then those small shoulders shook. "I thought that you took us from him. I thought if he knew I wanted to live with him, he would be excited. That he would make it happen. I thought we could be like Reid and Connor." A shuddered breath broke his speech. "But Dad doesn't want me."

"Kellen." Jade fisted the back of his T-shirt and reeled him in tight against her. "That's not entirely true. Dad does love you. He's just—" Just what? Too selfish to be an actual father? Too childish to have the responsibility of a child? "He's just trying to reinvent life for himself right now."

A feeble excuse.

"He said if I lived with him it wouldn't be as much fun as it was last week." Kellen sounded every inch a brokenhearted boy. "That he'd have to be the mean one instead of the fun one. He said this way we could have all the fun in the world when we are together. But—" His words cut short as Kellen battled for control.

And that about summed up Peter Beck. Jade blew out a hot breath as anger throbbed through her body. How could a man be that self-involved? How could he destroy his own son like this?

Sniffing, Kellen leaned back and rubbed at a tear that clearly annoyed him. "Why can't he be like Connor? He plays basketball and builds bonfires and hangs out with Reid. Why can't it be like that with me and Dad?"

"I don't know," Jade said.

All bravery fell away, and Kellen broke into a sob. Jade's heart shattered as she reached to pull her little boy in close. "I'm sorry, son," she whispered. "I'm so sorry."

"I hate him," Kellen seethed.

"Oh, Kel." She tightened her already fierce hold. "Kellen, please don't. Forgive your father—even if it takes a long time to get there. Try. Hating him won't fix anything."

"But he made me hate you."

Jade sat backward and gripped Kellen's shoulders. "No. He didn't." She tipped his chin up. "See." Motioning between them, she then tugged him back into her arms. "You don't hate me."

Tears ran like rivers down his face, soaking into her zip-up sweatshirt. "Yes I did. I was so mad at you."

"That's not hate. Anger doesn't have to be hate—and you don't have to let it get that far. You can be angry right now with Dad. I am angry with him right now for making you feel this way. But I am not going to hate him. Not for anything that has happened."

Defiance hardened Kellen's look. "Why? He deserves it. He left you for Macey. He left all of us for her."

Goodness, this was a tough spot. Because Kellen had a point. Peter had crushed them. All of them. He'd been faithless and selfish. He'd been heartless. He'd made her feel unloved and unlovable. Now he was doing the same to her kids.

But that is not who I am.

The thought cut her internal tirade short and summoned that voiceless but undeniable impression back to her heart. *I am loved. Lily is loved. Kellen is loved.*

Jesus loves me . . .

That changed things, didn't it? Peter had acted ungodly. But that didn't change who God was. God was faithful. He was kind and good. And He wanted Jade to look more like Himself, no matter what Peter did. She wanted that too.

In this hard, painful moment, she needed to model it to Kellen. Maybe then her son wouldn't grow up in his earthly father's image. He would choose to look more like his heavenly Father instead.

"Kellen, I can't change your father. I can't fix what he did, and you can't either. We can't change his heart. But God has given me charge over *my* heart. How I respond. He's given you that same responsibility over your heart. He knows—He sees. I'm not excusing your father, and I'm not saying that what he has done doesn't hurt. It does. It hurts deeply. It hurts me to see you with this pain now. But your dad doesn't have the power to make me hateful. I *won't* give him that power."

God, give me strength for that.

Jade fingered Kellen's hair as he watched her. "I get to choose what to do with the pain. I can choose to let it make me sour and ugly. I can let it turn me into a hateful, angry person. Or I can choose to tell Jesus all about the pain and the anger, and then I can give it to Him. I can trust Him with it and ask that He would replace all of that pain and anger with forgiveness and hope."

Please, Jesus.

Pulling him in close again, Jade leaned her head atop Kellen's and prayed with everything she had that what she'd just said would penetrate her own heart. *Take this pain and anger from my heart. Show me how to live the way I want Kellen to live. With forgiveness and hope.*

Help us all to live with forgiveness and hope.

Connor followed Jade toward the back storage room, dread clawing in his chest. The threat of anxiety had awakened the moment she met his eyes that Monday morning and had become a thrashing beast when she murmured, "We need to talk."

Déjà vu.

He did not want to have this talk. Of that he was 100 percent certain. And why should they? He'd been careful over the weekend. Exhaustingly careful throughout their shared bonfire, the late Sunday after both families ate at the lodge with Appleton and Emma. He had promised Jade, though it went against his instincts, to keep their deepening relationship a secret from the kids, and he had behaved in such a way that the three of them could not suspect things had changed.

Could they?

Holding the door open, Connor waited until Jade passed through and flicked the light on, and then he stepped within, closing the door behind him.

Silence swirled tension around them as she met his stare with weariness. Connor wanted to dig right in, to search for answers and draw out a solution. One that would not include what he sensed she had already settled on.

Instead, he waited. Against impulse, he waited.

A tear seeped from a corner of her eye, killing him. With the pad of his thumb, he slowly wiped it away.

"Kellen got up yesterday morning and watched the sunrise with me." Jade's mouth trembled.

Connor understood the deep impact of that simple act, and it shook his core with emotion. Something had happened while Kellen had been with his dad. Something profound—quite possibly heartbreaking—but also, perhaps, hopeful.

With a quick exhale, Jade reset her posture. "I can't do this now. We . . . we just can't." She covered her heart with one hand. "Not because I don't want to, but—"

"You and me?" Connor bent to maintain eye contact. "Is that what you're talking about?"

She nodded. "If Kellen found out I was going behind his back—"

He nodded. "I don't like it either, Jade. We already—"

The hand that covered her heart reached to grasp his arm. "I know. But you and I . . . we can't right now. Kellen's dad broke him this week. He can't take more. He can't handle another massive change in his life right now. And I can't afford to risk the tenuous relationship he and I have. I can't lose my son."

"I don't want you to risk anything when it comes to you and your kids. That was never on the table."

Swallowing, she nodded again and then switched to shaking her head. "Then . . . we need to step back. You agree?"

No, he couldn't say that he did. Well, maybe with his head, he could. She had a point, and he would never want to risk her relationship with her kids—particularly if there was a shot at that relationship healing.

But . . . *step back?*

That had been his conclusion a few days before, when he wasn't reconciled to secrecy. It had been the right way to go, likely. But he hadn't wanted to take that route.

Still, he didn't. What he wanted was this woman's hand in his. For her to stay open to him and to be able to share the depth of his heart with her.

He wanted her heart.

He wanted *them.*

He absolutely didn't want to feel this crumbling pain inside. Hadn't wanted it from the very beginning.

"Connor," Jade whispered into his lack of response. "We can't only think of ourselves. That's just not a luxury either of us have. Kellen leaned against me and cried yesterday. He laid his whole, broken heart in my hands.

He hasn't given me anything more than sass and anger in two years. I simply cannot risk my son."

The splintering inside his chest stung, and in the deep secret places known only between himself and God, Connor felt the fight building. *This! This is why I didn't want to like her. This is exactly what I didn't want to feel. Not ever again!*

But as he studied the beautiful woman in front of him, those lovely brown eyes swimming in tears, he could only nod. "Okay."

Her mouth trembled, and another tear slipped and ran alongside her nose. This time, Connor didn't reach to brush it away.

"Connor, please . . . Please don't let this change how you treat my children."

The breaking ran deeper.

Reaching to grip the front of his shirt, Jade continued. "What I said to you the day you took us fishing, it's still true. Maybe now more than ever. You're good for my kids. Kellen, he needs you. I beg you—please don't let this change things with them."

Connor pushed off the door and slowly closed the gap between them. Even as an earthquake of ache shook his core, he leaned in close, savoring the breath of her. "You don't need to beg, Jade." He pressed a kiss to her temple. "You didn't even need to ask."

After gently squeezing her fingers, Connor turned and let himself out.

In between the painful clutching of his heart, the roiling bubbled up hot. He had tried to trust and to do the right thing. Again.

How much, exactly, did God think he could take?

CHAPTER TWENTY-THREE

(in which things go back to awkward)

CONNOR KEPT HIS PROMISE.

With cello music from her Spotify playlist setting a soft background, Jade curled her fingers around the mug of mocha she'd just fixed and leaned her shoulder against the frame of the window. Outside, in the midst of fluffy white flakes drifting happily toward the wet ground, a noisy basketball match played out.

Two on two. Reid and Lily against Connor and Kellen.

A squeeze of delight and a pinch of ache mixed in Jade's heart as she watched the players below. Reid and Lily worked well together—a product of their daily practices at school with their respective teams.

Connor had the height advantage over all of them—his six-four frame towering above even Reid, who was tall for his age but hadn't yet broken the six-foot mark. Not surprising, Connor didn't use his advantage. Not much, anyway, and when he did, it was usually to snag a wayward shot, which he quickly popped out to Kellen.

Jade's attention settled on her youngest. In the weeks since Kellen had come back from Kansas crushed and angry, she had seen him inch toward light. He still struggled with a quick temper. Still had to battle back the impulse to argue with everything, and his lippy ways had gotten him into trouble more than once. But Kellen's attitude lacked the underlying resentment that had fueled his ugliness before. And Jade could see that he was honestly trying to overcome those negative traits he'd so readily embraced over the last two years.

Habits were hard to break. But Kellen was trying. And Jade was praying.

And Connor was keeping his promise about not letting the awkwardness between them affect how he treated the kids. The game below was just one example among many. Daily efforts. He took the kids to school, just as he had before. When Reid came over for help with his homework, Connor accompanied him. Those evenings, though the time felt terribly uncomfortable to Jade, Connor filled the space by pursuing Kellen.

They talked robots—Reid and Connor had introduced her family to *Battlebots*, and there was no going back. So Connor and Kellen would discuss design and which bot they thought had the most potential to take the Giant Nut. If not that, they played keep away with Rex, and Connor would praise Kellen on the progress made with the now-huge dog, who was, thanks in great part to Connor, becoming a *good* dog. Every now and then, the pair would load a video game and go at it—quickly to be joined by Lily and Reid.

Connor's relationship with the kids was comfortable and growing. But something wedged inside Jade's heart that put up a hard, unyielding resistance against the longing that continued to grow.

Jade knew what it was deep down. But she didn't want to admit it.

Shouts erupted below as Connor stole the ball from Reid. He took the ball hard to the basket, only to jump stop, motion for Kellen to cut in opposite, and fed the kid the ball. When Reid tried to block Kellen's shot, Connor bear hugged his son from behind and picked him up to move him.

"Foul!" Lily shouted, laughing and coming behind to push Connor. "You're such a bully!"

"Bully?" Connor kept a tight wrap on his son. "This guy was trying to block my partner's shot! So rude."

Lily tugged, trying to free her teammate. Connor twisted his arm around and pinned her at his back.

"I got 'em covered, Kellen. Take the shot!"

Grin as wide as the lake, Kellen flipped the ball up toward the hoop, putting exactly the right amount of arc into it, just like Jade had taught him. Up and in . . . nothing but net.

"Yeah!" Kellen shouted, pumping his fists. "That's game!"

"Dad, you're a cheater!" Reid's outrage was barely believable as he, along with Lily, were bent over with laughter—quite possibly because somehow Connor managed to pin both and tickle them at the same time.

Not to be left out, Kellen charged toward the tangled group. "Don't call my teammate a cheater!" He plowed into Reid, and the force of impact unsettled everyone's balance. As a group, the four of them tumbled into a drift of snow at the baseline, all of them laughing.

Jade chuckled as they wrestled. Connor was so good for them. All of them.

Again, her heart squeezed. Truth be told, Jade's fears and doubts about how her kids would respond to Connor becoming more to her than a coworker, a neighbor, and a friend were rapidly vanishing. Lily would undoubtedly be on board. In fact, there had been moments recently when it had seemed that her daughter had even hinted that direction.

"You know, Mom? Mr. Murphy is really nice."

"Have you noticed how much more good looking Connor is without his beard?" She'd tapped her chin, brows arching. "I wonder why he shaved it off?"

Warmth crawled into Jade's face as she thought on that comment, made just two nights before. That had absolutely been a hint. One her daughter didn't even try to veil. So yes, Lily would be fine with the Connor-Jade thing. Lily hadn't ever really been the concern though.

Back at the snowdrift, Connor scrambled to his feet, brushing snow off his sweatshirt. He reached and met Kellen's hand, tugging him free of the pile as well. Smiling down on the boy, Connor said something, and then the pair smacked a high five.

Kellen certainly didn't resent Connor anymore. Perhaps her son would be open to the possibility . . .

A tickle of wings fluttered in Jade's chest as she let her mind wander back to those moments with Connor. She could not forget the secure warmth of his hand holding hers. The thrill that spun in her chest when those green eyes held her captive with such tenderness. Or the way he knocked her breathless with his kisses.

She shut her eyes as delightful shivers raced over her arms. Maybe. Maybe . . .

Her gut twisted as she nearly surrendered to the beautiful possibilities, and the shock of such a powerful, painful response stole her breath.

No, then. Not yet. She wasn't ready. *They* weren't ready.

It was still too big of a risk.

Connor pushed his spade deeper into the cold, black dirt, shoving it with the heel of his boot until it sliced through the last big root so that the small hydraulic spade on Matt's bobcat could finish the lift with a clean root ball. At Connor's nod, Matt moved the joystick, and the tractor lifted the three-foot white fir, transferring the tree to a waiting burlap sack. Ten trees behind them, Lauren helped Reid and Kellen close and secure the burlap around the root balls. Up in the yard, by the house, Lily and Jade were playing with Fiona and Helene, and Rex loped between the group of four, loving every minute of this trip. Baby Ainsley was napping in the house.

"About ready for lunch, guys?" Lauren called. "I've got chili in the Crock-Pot."

Connor's stomach grumbled an amen, and Matt sent his wife a thumbs-up. "Let us get this last one in the row. The boys can head in and help you get lunch on. Connor and I will finish the burlap on these." He gestured toward the trees they'd just dug.

Lauren nodded, turning a grin toward Reid and Kellen. Though they'd worked all morning, both young men matched Lauren's easy smile. The fresh air, sharp scent of Christmas trees, and the group effort had come together for a happy workday.

It had been a good day to dig trees. Though the air was crisp with the bite of heavy frost, the ground was not yet frozen, and the sun shone with brilliant white gold. By 10:00 a.m. it had warmed up enough to shed heavy coats, and Connor was more than comfortable in his long-sleeve flannel and light puffer vest.

Together, Reid and Kellen scrambled toward the house, their jeans and hoodies smudged with black dirt. Kellen tagged Reid with a grin, and then the pair broke into a run. A race, likely—one that Reid held back on, allowing Kellen to take the lead. It was good to see them getting along so well. Good to watch Reid employ the compassion Connor had so deeply loved in his mother. And so very good to see Kellen happy.

This had been a nice thing, bringing Jade and her kids up to the tree farm. Even if the idea of it, proposed by Reid and echoed by Lauren, had twisted Connor's insides. It'd been nearly a two-hour drive to Pleasant Valley. One made all together in one big vehicle. Jade sat up front at Connor's side the whole time, teasing his continual longing to touch her.

How was he supposed to keep pretending like this?

For weeks—all through November, past thanksgiving, and now into December, Connor had to purposefully remind himself multiple times every day that he couldn't reach for her. Couldn't slip his fingers between hers. Wasn't at liberty to run her soft, thick hair through his fingers. He had no right or business leaning in close just to inhale her scent. And he certainly couldn't bend his neck to fit his lips to hers.

Didn't matter how much he wanted to.

Jade was not his.

It had all been such awkward torment. Every day she was there. Wishing him a quiet good morning with a small smile. Discussing lodge business and daily chores, often tapping her chin with her pen—an adorable habit she clearly didn't know she had. Asking this or that about Reid. Always a part of his world, but not the way he wanted her to be.

With him, but not his.

The worst was when their eyes met and held—he could barely breathe for the wringing in his chest.

I like her . . . I more than like her . . . I might—

Such delicious, tortuous thoughts that plagued him entirely too much.

Unsure how to navigate this sweet anguish, Connor had flung himself toward the kids. Maybe that looked like a shameless attempt at winning Jade. Perhaps, deep down, it was. But on the surface, the calculated intent had been his survival. He needed them to distract from the disappointment and frustration that were constant twins to the tenderness and longing. Being with the kids reminded him that life kept on, and he was a part of it. Thus far, whenever the kids were around, it had proven to be a winning strategy.

But a weekend with all of them at his brother's tree farm? That was different.

This felt *very* different. So intimate, like they were a family. Exactly the wish that had rooted in his heart—and the one that seemed stunted and terribly uncertain at the moment. The very thing that had provoked a remnant, simmering anger. Connor wasn't sure how to travel through it.

Matt shut the Cat down, flicked off his leather gloves, and smacked Connor's shoulders, bringing him back to the present. "Moving along nicely. Thanks to all the help." As they walked side by side, Matt shot him a grin. "Thanks for bringing your crew."

"They're not all mine."

"Hmm." Matt knelt at the nearest tree in burlap. "I had sort of hoped that you would have worked on that between now and the last time we talked."

"Yeah." Connor sighed. "I did."

"It's not going well?"

"It was." Connor pushed the frustration out of his tone and tried again. "Jade's worried about how the kids would react though, so we stepped back."

Finished with that tree, Matt sat back and looked toward the house. He then turned furrowed brows toward Connor. "I realize that this might not be simple, but it sort of looks like the kids get along really well."

"They do."

"And it seems like Reid likes Jade just fine."

"He does."

"And her kids?" Matt pressed. "Do you get along?"

"Better now than ever."

Matt's brows lifted. "So why don't you just ask them?"

If it were only that easy. Actually, with Reid, he suspected it would be that simple. Though starting that conversation might be a touch awkward, Connor believed that it would likely go well. Reid would be honest with him about how he felt. Connor also had a strong sense that Reid would be warm to the idea of him and Jade dating. The fact that Reid had suggested that *all* the Becks, rather than only Lily, as had first been planned, come up to the tree farm for the weekend lent a whole lot of weight to that.

Connor shook his head. "Right now it's not my call."

Moving to the next tree needing the burlap tied, Matt narrowed his focus on that for a minute. Connor followed his brother's lead in that and worked on the next tree, which allowed him to process his emotions in the silence.

Matt leapfrogged Connor to keep working. "There's a lot of thinking going on over there."

"Sometimes too much."

"Maybe." Matt shot him a smirk. "Maybe not."

"The thing is . . ." Connor sighed heavily, his shoulders drooping, and he stilled his hands. ". . . I've been mad about it."

"About stepping back?"

Connor stood, made his way to the final tree, and knelt to finish the job. "Yeah."

"But?" Matt read him dead on. There was absolutely a *but* in there.

"But it's like God is holding up a mirror right now. Showing me things I guess I didn't want to admit." Burlap tied, Connor let one arm rest against his knee and looked off into the distance. Rows of cultivated firs lined Matt and Lauren's property, hemmed in by the curve of the river on one side and the rise of the mountain on the other.

Connor couldn't help but recall the day Matt and Lauren had gotten stuck in this valley. Man, that had been some time ago, before they'd been married. Before they had even really started dating. Even then, though, Connor could see what Matt hadn't yet understood: Lauren was exactly what Matt had needed. God's blessing and gift, perfectly chosen for Matt. But at that point, Matt hadn't yet let go of his own plans and ideas for his life. He'd been so wrapped up in wanting his way, and not trusting the goodness of God, that he nearly missed what was right in front of him.

Nearly.

Connor looked at Matt. "Remember when you told me that you weren't trusting God's heart for your good?"

Swiping his stocking cap off his head, Matt nodded and then looked back at the house. He chuckled. "Man, the things I almost missed."

"I think that's where I am. Mad at God all over again. Not trusting that His heart for me is good, because it doesn't feel very good right now. It feels like disappointment and loneliness all over again."

Matt covered the distance between them and offered a hand to Connor. "I don't think anyone could blame you for that, Connor. You've been through some unbelievably hard stuff."

On his feet beside his brother, Connor dusted off the dirt and pine needles from his front. "Maybe so, but I thought I'd worked through it. Honestly, I thought I had. But all it took was Jade saying that we needed to step back—and we'd really only been a thing for less than a week—and there I was. Really mad at God for letting me get hurt again." He looked toward the ground and rubbed his neck. "'Let us test and examine our ways and return to the Lord.'"

"Psalms?" Matt asked.

Connor shook his head. "Lamentations."

A low whistle accompanied Matt's hand on Connor's shoulder. "Tough book."

"Sometimes it's a tough life."

Matt grunted a quiet laugh. "Do you know what Lauren calls you?"

"Not sure I want to . . ."

"Come on, man. I've already told you that she adores you."

"Not any more than the rest of us. And let's be clear here—you're her favorite Murphy."

"Better be." Matt laughed. "But you stepped in the middle of our little crisis all those years ago and took her side. She's never forgotten that, and between you and me, you might be her favorite. *After* me, of course."

"Even ahead of Tyler?" A small, satisfied grin curved Connor's mouth at that. That was a tough feat, considering Ty had married Lauren's best friend. If Connor couldn't be Fiona's favorite uncle, at least he could be Lauren's favorite brother-in-law. "I'll take it."

"She calls you the tender warrior."

Connor rubbed his jaw, brushing at the heat prickling his face. "Didn't she get the memo? I was always Connor the Constant."

"My wife has good judgment. I wouldn't question her." Matt stopped before they passed from the tree field and into the backyard, and his expression switched from jovial to serious again. "Connor, what I'm trying to say is that you're a strong man. One of my heroes, to tell the truth. It takes a strong man to go through what you've been through and still look for the goodness of God. Stronger still, to look at himself, to hear the reprimand of God, and to bend the knee in response."

Clenching his jaw, Connor wasn't sure what to say. Or even if he *could* say anything at all.

"Maybe these weeks of wrestling, they've been a good thing?" Matt said.

As if layers of opacity peeled back, the truth of Matt's simple suggestion became clear. These past weeks, though not what Connor would have chosen, *had* been good. For all of them.

But in particular, for Connor. He wanted to be a godly man. Wanted to walk with his heavenly Father with full trust in His goodness. He so very much *wanted* to be the man Matt and Lauren seemed to see. This revelation—the one that made it clear he still had a whole lot of growing to do—was a good thing, painful and humbling though it had been.

In his mind, he backed up several verses from where he'd just quoted in Lamentations 3.

But this I call to mind, and therefore I have hope; the steadfast love of the Lord never ceases; his mercies never come to an end.

How quickly he'd let that slip out of his heart. But though Connor failed to remain steadfast, God did not.

Praise God, He did not fail.

Jade scanned the small kitchen, looking for something to do. Bowls and plates were already laid out on the counter. Surely there must be some way she could make herself useful.

"I can't tell you how grateful I am that you came." Lauren stirred the contents in the Crock-Pot and shot Jade a quick grin.

Swallowing against the swirl of inadequacy tying up her gut, Jade shook her head. "I've done next to nothing." A fact proven in that moment, as she continued to stand there, useless.

"Are you kidding me?" Lauren tapped chili off her ladle and set the utensil on a plate beside the soup pot. "The girls are having the time of their lives with you and Lily. And the boys? Wow, they're such good workers. Do you know that all of the work we've done this morning would have taken Matt and me two days? Two. Days. That, my friend, is not anything close to *nothing.*"

Lauren tilted her head in the space of her brief pause, as if reading Jade, and then pointed toward a narrow door at the end of the galley kitchen. "There are some canned peaches in there. Would you mind getting out two or three jars? We'll put them in a bowl on the table." She turned to an open shelf and pulled down a medium-sized white ceramic bowl.

Relief sagged through Jade at having something to do. "Sure." She walked the few steps to cross the kitchen and let herself into what proved to be a deep pantry. Lauren was apparently a very busy bee, if the shelves full of canned goods were any indication. Also, she was exceptionally organized. A trait Jade appreciated.

Using the decoratively penned labels as a guide, and quickly recognizing Lauren's mode of organization—fruits, by alphabet, then veggies, then soups—Jade quickly located the peaches. Jars in hand, she stepped back to appreciate the clean order of the space. As she took in the whole of the pantry, her attention zeroed in on the cards that had been attached to the vertical supports of the shelving. Written in the same neat script, though in smaller form as the cards contained sentences, these notes did not proclaim produce and canned stores.

Jade leaned in to read them.

Psalm 34:10 Those who seek the Lord lack no good thing.

She moved to read the next one.

Romans 8:32 He who did not spare his own Son but gave him up for us all, how will he not also with him graciously give us all things?

Thoroughly intrigued, Jade continued from one card to the next.

Philippians 4:19. Psalm 81:10. Ephesians 3:20. Malachi 3:10 . . .

So many cards. So many verses. Lauren not only had stored goods to feed her family, but she had put up stores of God's Word to nourish her soul. As she continued to read, Jade's skin prickled with gooseflesh. One could not enter this pantry for supplies without also taking in spiritual sustenance.

Jade's already strong admiration for Lauren grew.

How would her perspective on life shift if she did such a thing? A thrill buoyed in her heart. Instead of fixating on all of the regrets and hurts in her past, she could set her mind on . . . She moved back to a verse she'd just read.

Psalm 33:20, 22 We put our hope in the Lord. He is our help and our shield. Let your unfailing love surround us, Lord, for our hope is in you alone.

She could set her mind on hope. Hope in God. Hope in his unfailing love.

She could set her mind on *hope.*

Not regret.

Not fear.

Not anger.

On hope. In God.

Jade reread that final sentence one more time, committing it to memory. *Let your unfailing love surround us, Lord, for our hope is in you alone.*

When she stepped out of the pantry and into the kitchen, hands full of canned peaches, her heart had taken a new turn. One for the better. It would start there, now. By putting her hope in God alone. Then it would continue, because she had every intention of mimicking her new friend by writing out her own cards.

"Find them okay?" Lauren looked over her shoulder.

"Yes. I was reading your cards. The ones with the verses."

Pure joy lit Lauren's expression, and a touch of pink colored her face. "When Ainsley was born, I *really* struggled. Actually, make that I *am* struggling. She is such a fussy little storm cloud, and she only wants Mommy. It's kind of exhausting." With a quiet, self-derisive chuckle, Lauren motioned toward the pantry. "That has been my escape."

"The pantry?"

"Yes. I hide in the pantry so I don't lose my mind." Lauren pressed both hands against her cheeks, clearly growing more embarrassed by the moment. "Sort of sad, right?"

Jade chuckled, shaking her head. "When mine were little, I hid in the shower on several occasions, so . . ."

Lauren's hand slipped from her face, and she folded her arms across her middle. "One day Matt came in from spraying, and I was hiding in there. Crying. Mumbling something like *I can't do this . . .*" A tear slipped from the corner of her eye, though a sweet smile was on her face. "He found one of the cards I keep in a box in our room and slipped it beneath the pantry door. It was Philippians 4:19." Her gaze drifted toward the window, and by the softening of her expression, Jade suspected her view had landed on Matt. "Then he said, 'Love you, babe. I've got the girls.' And then just left me alone. Me. In the pantry. With Jesus."

"I love that," Jade whispered. A stirring swept through her heart as she pictured those cards again. It was like her vision for herself, for her life, suddenly grew tenfold. What she'd wanted before—to just find some stability, maybe a hint of happiness—suddenly that seemed too small, all black and white and grainy. Now?

Now she wanted *this.* This immersive joy that defined Lauren Murphy. And she could see exactly where that joy came from. Not from the fact that Lauren's husband was a Murphy and a good man, though that was true and clearly a benefit. Not from this seemingly idyllic life Lauren had.

It was because of what Jade had glimpsed in the pantry.

Lauren had a deep, hopeful, trusting, abiding relationship with Jesus.

Jade suspected the same had been true of Sadie Murphy. Hadn't Connor said that her faith had been one of the things he'd loved most about his wife?

But she didn't want that because of Sadie or Lauren. Not even because of how Connor would perceive it. She wanted a greater faith, a deeper relationship with Jesus, for herself. For the hope and joy of it. For the love of *Him.*

Above all, Him.

CHAPTER TWENTY-FOUR

(in which the kids are up to something)

SOMETHING HAD HAPPENED UP at the tree farm—something that wasn't really about *them*. Connor had sensed it before they had left for home after the weekend of digging was done. He'd desperately wanted to ask Jade what it had been. But once on their way home, he'd gotten no further than simply asking her if she was okay.

"Yes," she'd whispered.

And he'd believed her, though Jade had remained quiet on the ride back to the lodge and over the next few days. There was a settling in her. Somehow a new depth in which she seemed more anchored. It only made him admire her more. And want to know what had been said or done, what had landed in her heart that made her beautiful brown eyes seem happier.

Connor wanted to know it all. He deeply longed for her to share her heart with him. Wished that she'd drop the last barrier remaining between them. But now, after talking with Matt and surrendering once again to God, trusting that He was good and He did good, Connor reached for patience. He added to that patience to the thing that he'd been denying.

Love.

He loved her. And he would love her from this distance until she was ready. Until God let them both know the time had come for all of them.

It was risky. Even just to admit to himself that he loved again was a risk. To admit it not knowing if there was a future for them was like double or nothing—a gamble Connor wasn't prone to make. But one that he prayed about and had been given a surreal peace. So for now, Connor would love her with his deeds. He'd love her by service—whatever she needed, however he could make her life better. He'd love her by loving her kids—not a hard task at all, as they'd already planted themselves in his heart. He'd love her in prayer, asking God for her good.

And he'd love her by waiting, by allowing her space to thrive in this new peace that she'd apparently landed in.

His heart settled in that decision, and the frustration fell away. As it did, Connor was able to go about his work that week with fresh energy and new optimism, even while wishing to know what had happened with Jade at the farm. And it seemed that every day the awkwardness that had lodged between them eroded away. What was left became easy, light conversation. Eye contact that, though still stirring his heart, was no longer painful. Genuine smiles. Renewed friendship. One that somehow felt even deeper than what had existed between them the week her kids had been gone. Like it was no longer all exhilarating emotion and passionate longing—not that those had been bad.

But this . . . this had roots to it. Stability.

Perhaps one day they'd have both. The exhilarating passion and the stability.

Driving toward town to pick the kids up from practice, that hope landed squarely in his heart. In the very place Connor had believed would never beat with such a thing again. It seemed not such a far-off dream, and as it filled his chest, a small grin lifted his mouth.

He parked in between the high school and the junior high, the gyms conveniently located on opposite sides of the lot, so that both kids could exit their respective practices and find him waiting in the middle. Within minutes Lily burst from the high school and jogged his way.

Her cheeks bright from her workout and from the chilly December air, she tugged open the passenger's-side door and hopped into the front seat. "Hi, Connor! Guess what?"

"Hi yourself, Lil. What's up?"

"I'm starting in the varsity game tomorrow!"

"What?" Connor held up his palm for a high five. "That's awesome."

Lily smacked his hand, and then he reached around her shoulder, and she leaned in for a hug. Rather than pulling away quickly, as she usually did, Lily pressed deeper into his shoulder. It was only for a breath longer than normal, but in that moment, Connor's heart squeezed.

Yeah, he loved this kid. He'd claim her. And Kellen. It would be his honor.

How had he thought to resent God for sending him more children who were in apparent need of a dad figure months ago? These moments, the ones where Lily treated him like he was important and special to her, were unimaginable gifts. What an angry, blind man he'd been.

Thanks for knowing better than me and not letting me have my way.

"Proud of you, kid," Connor whispered.

Lily looked up, meeting his eyes. There was a sheen of emotion there, and his chest clenched again. Her sweet look said all that was needed in the moment, and Connor tucked that silent treasure in deep for safekeeping.

He caught sight of Reid running toward them from the other direction. His son flung himself into the seat behind Connor, school and gym bags tumbling onto the floor. "Lily! What's the lineup for Friday?"

Connor suppressed a laugh as he thought *Hi to you too, son.*

"I'm in!" Lily squealed as she rotated in her seat to face Reid.

"Starting?"

"Yes!"

"Yeah!" In the rearview mirror, Connor saw Reid fist-pump the air. "I knew it. I told Jasek Mallard you'd start. He said no way. But I told him he's never seen you play, so he couldn't know." They clapped a high five.

Connor shifted into drive and pulled out of the parking lot. He met Reid's excited gaze in the mirror. "How was your practice?"

Reid shrugged. "My shot was broke today. But Coach says he'd rather it be off today than on Saturday."

"Both are home games, right?"

The kids nodded, their enthusiasm palpable.

"Dad, how about a bonfire after Lily's game tomorrow? We have marsh-mallows. Just need some chocolate . . ." Reid's brows lifted in a wide *please!* look.

"What time do you have to be at the gym Saturday morning?"

"Eight."

"Hmm."

"We don't have to stay up too late. But we *have* to celebrate Lily's first varsity start!"

Connor chuckled. His son did have a point. "We can ask Jade."

Lily looked over her shoulder at Reid, and Connor thought she sent a smirk to the backseat. "We got this," she said.

Connor glanced between the pair, sensing a conspiracy that might or might not entirely encompass s'mores and a bonfire. "What are you two up to?"

"A Friday night bonfire." Lily looked at him with a wide, innocent grin.

"Is that all?"

"Of course, Mr. Murphy."

"Mr. Murphy? Now I'm really suspicious."

From behind him, Reid gripped his shoulders and squeezed. "Dad, Dad, Dad. We're both good kids. You definitely should trust us."

"This is not helping." Connor raised his brow and caught Reid's laughing eyes in the mirror.

His son just smiled, patted his shoulders, and sat back.

Connor glanced at Lily. She sat forward, focus on the windshield and clearly biting back a grin.

Huh.

Now at the curvy part that would take them back to the lodge, Connor had no choice but to keep his eyes on the road. Reid and Lily started a new conversation about the schools' lunches that afternoon—something that looked slimy and unappetizing—and both agreed that Jade's chicken salad sandwiches were lightyears better, and thank goodness for that. Connor thought to press whatever scheme they'd hatched between them when they got to the cabins, but once he parked, both kids were out of the vehicle and gone. When he made his way up the steps and into his home, Reid was already in the shower.

Maybe he was imagining it. Or contriving a hope because of what he wanted. But it sure seemed like those two were up to something. And if he'd had to guess right then, Connor would name it matchmaking.

And though he'd never tell the kids, he was game for it.

Jade zipped up her winter coat all the way to her chin and tugged on her stocking cap, making sure it covered as much of her ears as possible. It was pretty cold to be out roasting marshmallows. But the kids had been so keen on it—and after Lily's varsity start and triple-double game, which the coach had recognized publicly on social media—Jade could hardly say no to the idea of a bonfire celebration. So there she was, shivering among the three kids and Connor, and delighted for all of it.

"Lily, I think they're going to call you the box-out queen." Reid bit into his second s'more, and a trail of gooey, chocolaty marshmallow stretched between his chin and what remained of the dessert. He grinned, wiped his face, and finished chewing. "Twelve rebounds, five put-backs, and ten assists? Not to mention a seventy percent free throw night. Sheesh. No one has ever earned a triple-double in the first game of the season. Bet you go on the record board before the end of the season."

"What's a triple-double?" Kellen looked up from the mallow roasting on a stick in his hand.

"Double figures in at least three statistical categories," Jade explained. "In Lily's case tonight, she had fifteen points, twelve rebounds, and ten assists."

"Oh." Kellen looked up at Lily with a proud smile. "Good job. I knew you had a lot of points, but I didn't know they kept track of the other stuff."

Even in the firelight, Lily's brown eyes danced as she ruffled her little brother's hair. "Thanks, buddy. It was fun. All those games with Connor sure helped." She grinned at the man standing across the firepit.

"Nah. You have a lot of God-given talent, and you work really hard to hone it." Connor winked at Lily. "It was pretty exciting to watch you."

Jade's heart melted at the way Lily blossomed under Connor's praise. It also pooled at the way Kellen and Lily were treating each other. That happened more and more. Though Lily had always been super protective of Kellen, it'd only been in recent weeks that he'd really seemed to appreciate the kindness his sister showed and reciprocated it.

So much good, Father. Like the break of light after a long dark night . . . Gratitude filled her heart.

"Welp." Lily licked her fingers clean and smacked her hands. "I'm done. Reid?"

Next to Lily, Reid also brushed the crumbs off his fingers, and then he took her roasting stick. "Yep. I have a game tomorrow, so that's it for me."

Nodding, Lily turned her face to Kellen. "How about it, buddy? One game of *Among Us*, and then bed?"

Kellen passed his roasting stick to Reid, minus the marshmallow he'd just popped into his mouth, and nodded. "You playing, Reid?"

"Yeah, I'll play from my house. Let me in the game once you're in, okay?"

Holding out knuckles, Kellen nodded. "Later."

"Night." Reid met Kellen's knuckles with his own and then waved toward Lily. "Night, Lil. Awesome game tonight."

"Thanks. Can't wait to watch yours tomorrow. You're gonna kill it." Side by side, Lily and Kellen scurried toward the cabin, and Lily waved. "Night, Mom!"

"Night, Dad!" Reid strode the opposite way.

The sound of feet pounding up steps came from both directions. One door squeaked open, then clicked shut. From the other side, the soft click of another door sounded right after. Suddenly, there she and Connor were.

Just the two of them. Alone.

Turning back to the fire after watching his son go inside, Connor checked his wristwatch. "Huh." Amusement lifted his brows as he turned toward her and closed the four steps between them. "Nine twenty."

"You're kidding."

He turned his watch so she could see, and she leaned in to look. Yep. Nine twenty.

"When was the last time your kids volunteered to go to bed at nine anything on a Friday night?"

Jade shook her head as she felt warm all the way through. "Uh . . ."

His warm, deep chuckle set off a flurry of tiny butterflies in her middle. Suddenly she felt like a young woman left alone with her crush and not sure what to do. She ran her teeth over her bottom lips and nervously peeked at him. "Are they . . . I mean, do you think they're . . ."

Connor reached across the space that was lit with only the dancing firelight and traced the length of her hair that hung beneath her stocking cap and brushed her shoulder. The tenderness of his gaze, narrowed on her, made her heart race.

"I think," he whispered, "that I'm quite fond of those kids."

Her pulse sputtered and then surged. "I think they're quite fond of you." She barely managed to speak as a collision of emotions swelled in her throat.

The lightest touch drifted from her shoulder down to her fingers, and then her cold hand was wrapped by his calloused fingers. Connor leaned in just a bit. Only enough that his warm breath danced across her cheek. "I'm quite fond of you too, Jade."

Now her heart was at a gallop. So much of her wanted to step in closer, to eliminate the sliver of night air between them, to lay her palm against his chest so that she might feel the strong beat of his heart.

But she held back. Or rather, something held her back.

Jade blinked as she forced her chin to tip up, forced herself to meet his steadfast gaze. He watched her with such affection. Such warm patience, as if he knew what tethers and knots were binding her heart.

Could he know? How was that possible?

"Connor . . ." His name was an ache and plea.

He squeezed her hand. "Tell me."

She wasn't sure how, didn't know for sure what it was that held her captive. But he waited, gentleness unwavering. Through a raw and closed throat, Jade made herself try to explain. "I've made such big mistakes before."

For many throbbing heartbeats, he said nothing. Only held her with a thoughtful silence. Then his thumb glided over her knuckles, and he squared to her. "I think that you still see yourself as that teenage girl, ignoring all warnings in pursuit of a happily ever after that was never going to materialize. I think that you haven't forgiven that girl for those mistakes."

Jade blinked against the hot tears as the sting of his words sank in deep. That . . . that was exactly true. She was terrified that she was still that foolish girl.

He pulled her hand up and tucked it close to his heart. "That's not who I see though. The Jade I know is smart and resilient and strong. She's deeply thoughtful. The woman in front of me is surrendered to God and His will."

Her? Resilient and strong? Jade thought of herself as a battered, wind-tossed weed. And surrendered to God? *I am trying on that score . . .* She squeezed her eyes shut, turning her heart upward even as this moment became an ache.

The warmth of Connor's body draped over her as he leaned in close. Then, gentle and warm, he pressed a kiss at the corner of one of her closed eyes. "Take as long as you need, Jade. I'm not going anywhere." He raised her hand to his lips, pressed another kiss to her knuckles, and then released her hand.

Connor walked away, leaving her swimming in a wake of sweet wonder.

Standing there in the fading firelight, Jade watched the flames die as she pondered it all in her heart. What was this?

Love.

The cold December air barely touched her as this extraordinary revelation bloomed in her heart.

Connor loved her. Though he hadn't said it, he was showing her. He had been for weeks—and weren't they all better for it? And wasn't it so much more profound to be shown love than to only have the wispy, fading promise of mere words?

The truth of it enveloped her. Connor Murphy loved her. The question was, would she be brave enough to let herself love again?

CHAPTER TWENTY-FIVE

(in which new mercies are seen)

Reid was apparently not going to be outshone.

He played exceptionally well that morning—though he could not claim a triple-double. It had been, however, the best game Connor had witnessed from his son.

"A sign of good things to come," Connor said as he guided the car in and out of the curves near the lodge. He glanced in the rearview mirror and met Reid's wide grin there.

"You guys are going to come to my games when they start, right?" Kellen asked.

"You know it," Lily said. "You'll have the loudest cheering section in the gym."

From his middle seat, Kellen elbowed Lily. "Maybe we need a little competition between the three of us. Who has the best game streak."

Lily smiled at her brother, but merely shrugged. "I think it's fun to cheer each other on. Like it's more than just about me out there. And more than just Reid, more than just you."

"Yeah," Reid said. "Like we make each other better."

"Good plan," Jade said. "How about you all make each other better about making your beds in the morning, while you're at it?"

Connor laughed. "I can get behind that."

"I made mine!" Kellen's hand shot into the air.

"Kellen's the winner today." Jade looked back at the kids. "Unless Reid made his?"

"That is a negative," Connor said.

"I usually do though," Reid said.

Jade laughed. "Well then, Kellen wins the day."

"Awesome. What do I get?"

"All my love, son."

"Aw, man. That's it?"

"It's not enough?"

More than enough for me...Connor thought. He glanced at the woman in the seat beside him with a smirk. Jade met that look with shy but smiling eyes, making his heart flip.

He could do life like this every day, and it would be a dream come true. Him. The kids. And Jade.

No, edit that. Him and Jade and the kids. He gripped the steering wheel tighter rather than reaching for her hand.

Patience. Lord, help me to be patient.

A strong peace gripped him, just as it had last night when he and Jade had been alone. It was like a silent promise, and Connor believed it with every inch of his heart. He could give Jade time, and as much as she needed. Having gone through the heart-shattering loss of his own wife, he understood that recovering from loss—either by death or divorce—took time. There simply was not a quick and easy way out of it. And for Jade, it was more than just heartbreak. There had been the ugliness of emotional abuse alongside the devastation of infidelity and rejection.

He understood her fears. They went deep and were no small thing.

Connor believed in God's healing power—he knew it intimately. But it wasn't his to command. Only to trust. And he did. After so many months of wrestling in hurt and anger, Connor had come to a place of surrender, and found in that spot, a new strength of faith.

In His time.

"Hey." Lily's enthusiastic voice broke into the song in Connor's mind. "How about after donuts, we go to the shore. Reid said the ice looked solid."

"Not solid enough to walk on." Connor again glanced at Reid in the mirror.

"No, not that," Reid confirmed and then turned his look to Lily. "But we could skip rocks and hear the lake sing. Lily doesn't believe me about that."

Lily shrugged. "I've just never heard of it."

Connor eased against the seatback and grinned. "This you must experience then. I've got some work in the horse stalls this afternoon—you do too, Reid. But we could skip rocks on the ice until lunch."

"Deal." Reid nodded.

Connor parked the car on the back side of the lodge and looked at Jade. "Is that okay?"

"Sounds perfect." She shook the box of donuts they'd picked up in town after Reid's game. "If we eat these at our place, I'll quick make a batch of hot cocoa to take to the dock."

"Yes!" Kellen scrambled out of the vehicle behind Lily. "I call the Jayhawks mug!"

The kids made near-instant work of those sugar-carb confections, and Connor enjoyed a peanut butter twist while Jade picked at an apple fritter. While she stood at the stove whisking cocoa, sugar, and milk, Connor and Reid ran to their house to grab warmer layers. By eleven, the crew was headed down the path that led to the lake shore and the dock.

At the water's icy edge, Reid stooped to sort through the shoreline's litter. "Pick a flat rock and skip it, just like you would in summer." He stood and did exactly what he'd just instructed. The small stone hit the ice with a ping and skipped. Every impact on the ice produced another ping, and each ping resonated against the frozen sheet and echoed in the bowl of the bay. Singing lake ice.

"Whoa!" Lily and Kellen said in unison.

Lily bounced twice. "That's crazy!"

Connor looked down at Jade, who stood beside him as they watched the kids from a slight distance. "That is crazy." Her grin was pure delight. "Do it again, Reid."

After a quick backward glance, revealing his satisfied smile, Reid complied. This time, he got three long skips and a significant trail of shorter ones, producing a longer song.

"Oh man." Kellen searched the shore for the perfect stone. "I wanna try!"

Reid stepped back. "Go for it."

Hot cocoa mugs all but forgotten, all three kids took turns skipping stones, searching for new, perfect ones, and doing it all over again. The singing lake thrilled them every time.

Connor grinned as he and Jade watched them, but when he looked down at Jade, he found a telling shimmer in her eyes. Unable to resist the need for touch, he pressed his hand to the small of her back. "You okay?"

After a shaky inhale and a slow exhale, Jade nodded. "I was just thinking about the hymn Sadie wrote out on that card you keep in a frame. 'Great Is Thy Faithfulness.' You know, 'morning by morning, new mercies I see.'" She swiped at a running tear with her gloved hand and then nodded toward the kids, who were now making their way toward the steep bank that climbed into a patch of forest. "Right there. I am looking at new mercies, and I am astonished."

Her pure emotion, and the fact that he saw exactly the same thing, pricked tears in his own eyes. Connor turned Jade into him, and when she leaned against his chest, he wrapped her close with both arms. For several beautiful heartbeats, they simply remained there in this amazing moment of grace poured out.

"Connor?" Jade sniffed and leaned back to look at him. "I have to tell you something."

He brushed the wind-tossed loose hair that had escaped her stocking cap. "Okay."

Jade inhaled, running her teeth over her bottom lip and looking like she was fighting for courage. Then she settled her brown gaze on his eyes. A peaceful smile took the place of that momentary panic. "I love you," she whispered.

The force of those softly spoken word knocked him breathless. He smiled. Then chuckled. Then tipped his head against hers. "Thank God," he breathed, shutting his eyes. "Thank You, God." He blinked and looked at her. "I've been praying you would. Because I am in love with you, Jade."

"I know that." Her gentle smile was everything beautiful.

"Do you?"

"You show me. You've been loving me in what you do for weeks now, and it's like nothing I've ever known, apart from Jesus."

Not knowing what to say, Connor laughed again. "So I don't have to tell you?"

She joined his teasing with her own smile, then shook her head beneath his. "Tell me, Connor. Tell me I'm not imagining—"

"I love you." He moved to claim her lips. "I love you." He stole another kiss. "I love you, Jade."

She sighed and kissed him back.

"I knew it!" Lily's shout came from directly behind them.

Startled, Connor and Jade broke apart and spun around. At the top of the hill, their three children slapped high fives and whooped.

Reid grinned unrepentantly and blew a whistle. "Took you long enough, Dad!"

"Yeah, yeah." He tucked Jade in snug at his side and then kissed her head before he smirked at his son. "I've got this now."

Reid flashed him a thumbs-up, nudged Kellen, who waved at them, a hint of shyness on his face, and then the three kids turned and ran toward the cabins.

Connor looked back at Jade. "I guess we don't need to worry about them."

"Nope." Her eyes danced. "Did you know this singing-lake thing was a setup?"

Laughing, he shook his head. "No. But they've been at it for weeks. Smart kids. I guess we shouldn't be surprised."

Jade's gaze, held steady on him, turned warm and gooey. "I will ever be surprised, Connor. I never imagined God would take the wreck of my life and rewrite it into this thing of wonder and beauty."

When she tipped her chin toward him, Connor needed no further prompting. He slid his fingers along her jawline as he captured her lips, more hopeful now than ever for a lifetime of such privileges.

Jade was right. This would ever be a surprise. A gift he'd almost spurned. Almost, but for the steadfast grace of God . . .

Thank God, His mercies were ever new.

THE END.

Thank you for spending time with the Murphy family! I hope you enjoyed Connor and Jade's story. Would you please leave an honest review, letting other readers know what you thought? I'd so appreciated it!

Also, be watching for the final Murphy story, due to publish the end of 2022. **A Murphy Gathering** with take us back to the beginning where we'll glimpse snapshots of Kevin and Helen's journey through love, faith, and family. I do hope you'll join me for it!

As always, thank you for joining me on this journey!

Until the Kingdom comes,

Jen

THANK YOU ...

I need to send out a special thank you to Cindy Owen, who reached out to me as I began writing this story. Thank you, sweet friend, for following God's prompting in emailing me. Your insight based on real-life experience helped tremendously in the writing of this story. You have blessed me as, I have no doubt, you have blessed so many others throughout your career. You do a job not many could take on. Heartbreakingly hard, and yet so needed. Thank you for your courage and compassion, for being the quiet superhero that you are.

And now, dear reader, I thank you for risking your time and emotion on this story. Some of you, I know, weren't looking forward to this one. It was hard. Hard to let go of a character we loved. Hard to watch the others struggle through all of the difficult places that were involved in this tale. I hope, though, at the end of it, you have been brought to a place of joy. Perhaps to a moment where you can look back on your own hard places and declare in worship, **"You, oh Lord, have been faithful and good."**

Because He is.

Thank you for joining me through this journey. I pray you've been blessed! Would you take a moment to review Morning by Morning for other readers? They benefit from your opinion!

Printed in Great Britain
by Amazon

63036453R00160